PLAIN PROPOSAL

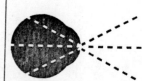

This Large Print Book carries the
Seal of Approval of N.A.V.H.

A DAUGHTERS OF THE PROMISE NOVEL

PLAIN PROPOSAL

BETH WISEMAN

THORNDIKE PRESS
A part of Gale, Cengage Learning

GALE
CENGAGE Learning

Detroit • New York • San Francisco • New Haven, Conn • Waterville, Maine • London

GALE
CENGAGE Learning

LIBRARY OF CONGRESS CATALOGING-IN-PUBLICATION DATA

Wiseman, Beth, 1962–
  Plain proposal : a Daughters of the promise novel / by Beth Wiseman.
    p. cm. — (Thorndike Press large print Christian fiction)
  ISBN-13: 978-1-4104-3682-5 (hardcover)
  ISBN-10: 1-4104-3682-9 (hardcover)
  1. Amish—Fiction. 2. Large type books. I. Title.
PS3623.I83P578 2011b
813'.6—dc22
                                        2011012378

Published in 2011 by arrangement with Thomas Nelson, Inc.

Printed in Mexico
1 2 3 4 5 6 7 15 14 13 12 11

To Eric and Cory

PENNSYLVANIA DUTCH GLOSSARY

aamen — amen
ach — oh
aenti — aunt
bruder — brother
The Budget — a weekly newspaper serving Amish and Mennonite communities everywhere
daadi — grandfather
daed — dad
danki — thanks
dochder — daughter
dumm — dumb
dummkopp — dummy
Englisch — a non-Amish person
fraa — wife
gut — good
guder mariye — good morning
hatt — hard
haus — house
kapp — prayer covering or cap
kinner — children or grandchildren

kumme esse — come eat

lieb — love

maedel — girl

mamm — mom

mammi — grandmother

mei — my

mudder — mother

nee — no

onkel — uncle

Ordnung — the written and unwritten rules of the Amish; the understood behavior by which the Amish are expected to live, passed down from generation to generation. Most Amish know the rules by heart.

***Pennsylvania* Deitsch** — Pennsylvania German, the language most commonly used by the Amish

rumschpringe — running-around period when a teenager turns sixteen years old

schee beh — nice legs

sohn — son

Wie bischt? — How are you?

ya — yes

1

Miriam stepped back and admired the matching quilts lying on the twin beds in her room. Gifts from her grandmother before she died. The pastel circles of yellow, powder blue, and pink were framed by a simple blue border in a traditional double wedding-ring pattern. They were finally making a debut — just in time for company.

"Your room looks nice." *Mamm* walked in carrying a wicker basket filled with towels to be folded. "Your *mammi* would be pleased that you saved her quilts for a special occasion." She glanced at the white vase full of pink roses on the nightstand and smiled. "*Ach,* fresh flowers too."

Her mother unloaded the towels onto Miriam's bed, and they each reached for one as *Mamm's* eyes traveled around the room.

When her mother nodded an approval, Miriam grinned. "When will she be here?"

Mamm placed a folded blue towel on top of Miriam's green one. "Not for a couple of hours. Your *daed* hired a driver, and they went to go pick her up at the airport."

Miriam couldn't wait to hear about her cousin's travels and life in the *Englisch* world. Shelby was eighteen too, and for Miriam, it would be like having a sister for the summer. A nice change from a house full of brothers. Even though Miriam was enjoying her *rumschpringe,* she'd done little more than travel to Lancaster to see a movie. Her *Englisch* cousin was coming all the way from Texas, a small town called Fayetteville.

"I'm excited about Shelby coming, *Mamm.* I can't wait to meet her." Miriam reached for the last towel to be folded as her mother let out a heavy sigh.

"I know you are, and we're glad to have Shelby come stay. But . . ." *Mamm* edged toward the nightstand, repositioned a box of tissue next to a lantern, then turned to Miriam. "We told you — times have been *hatt* for Shelby. Her parents got a divorce, and Shelby got in some kind of trouble."

Miriam couldn't imagine what divorce would be like. It was unheard of in their Old Order Amish district. "What kind of trouble?" Miriam sat down on her bed, crossed her ankles, and leaned back on her palms.

"Her mother said that Shelby was spending time with the wrong young people." *Mamm* sat down on the bed beside her, and Miriam watched her mother's forehead crinkle as her lips tightened into a frown. She knew her mother was concerned about having a young *Englisch* woman come for such a long visit.

"Was she shunned by her family?"

Mamm shook her head. "No. The *Englisch* don't shun the way —" Her mother cocked her head to one side, then met eyes with Miriam. "*Ya.* I guess, in a way, Shelby *is* being shunned. She is being sent away from her family and friends for not following the rules."

Miriam sat taller and folded her hands in her lap. "I'm going to try my best to make her feel welcome here."

"I know you will, Miriam." *Mamm* patted her leg, then cupped Miriam's cheek in her hand. "Please tell me that I don't need to worry about you being taken in by Shelby's worldly ways."

Miriam looked at her mother and said earnestly, "I won't, *Mamm.*"

Her mother gently eased her hand from Miriam's face, then let out another heavy sigh. "I remember when your father's cousin left here. Abner was no more than your age at the time. He chose not to be baptized. We were shocked." *Mamm* leaned back on her hands like Miriam.

"Did he go to Indiana?" Miriam knew that her great grandparents relocated here from Indiana. She'd been asked plenty of times what she was doing in Lancaster County with a name like Raber, an Indiana Amish name.

"No. Your *daed* said Abner went to Texas with three hundred dollars in his pocket and even took rides from strangers to get there. Evidently he had been corresponding with a man there about a job for months before he left. A job building Amish furniture." *Mamm* sat up and folded her arms across her chest.

"Have you seen Abner since he left?"

Mamm nodded. "Only twice, for each of his parents' funerals. It's a shame, too, because your *daed* and Abner were close when they were young."

"But you said he wasn't baptized into the community, so he wasn't shunned, right? He could have come to visit, no?"

"Ya." *Mamm* stood up and smoothed the wrinkles from her black apron. "But Texas is a long way from here, and things between him and his folks weren't *gut*. They never did accept his choices." *Mamm* paused for a moment, then looked down at Miriam. "I remember that Abner met Janet not long after he arrived in Texas, and they were wed two years later. Then along came Shelby." Her mother shook her head. "After that, we heard less and less from your *daed's* cousin. But evidently his furniture was popular with the *Englisch* there, and he went on to own a big fancy store of his own. We got a letter every now and then, but . . ." *Mamm* picked up the stack of folded towels on the bed, then placed them in the laundry basket. "I met Janet, Shelby's mother, when they came here for Sarah Mae's funeral, which is when I met Shelby. But she was only four years old, so I doubt she remembers much."

Miriam tried to think of what she remembered from when she was four years old. Not much.

"I liked Janet a lot, and we exchanged letters for a while after they were here. But I hadn't heard from her in years until last month." *Mamm* bit her lip and was quiet for a few moments. "Anyway, as you know, Shelby doesn't have any brothers or sisters, and the only life she has known has included electricity and all the modern conveniences the *Englisch* have. Things will be different for her here." She picked up the basket, then smiled at Miriam. "But God is sending her here for a reason. I think the *maedel* needs time for healing."

"This is a *gut* place for that, I think." Miriam gave a final glance around her room. She'd dusted her oak rocking chair and chest of drawers and swept the hardwood floors after putting fresh linens on the bed. She'd even slipped a sprig of lavender in the top drawer of the chest, one of two drawers she had cleaned out for Shelby to use.

She was excited for her cousin to arrive, but her thoughts drifted to Pequea Creek where she knew her girlfriends were gathering. On Saturday afternoons during the summer, the older girls in her district met at the creek to watch the young men show off their skills by swinging on a thick rope from the highest ledge and dropping into the cool water below.

Saul Fisher would be there. He was always there. And just the thought of him made Miriam's heart flip in her chest.

"My chores are done, *Mamm*. Can I take the spring buggy to the creek for a while?"

Her mother was heading out the door but turned briefly. "I guess so. But I'd like for you to be home before Shelby arrives."

Miriam nodded. Once her mother was

gone, she opened the drawer to her night-stand, then pulled out the thin silver ankle bracelet she'd bought at the market in Bird-In-Hand. She knew Leah and Hannah would be wearing theirs too, and she liked the way the delicate chain looked dangling from her ankle. She sat down on the bed and fastened the tiny clasp. Her father frowned every time he saw the inexpensive purchase, but Miriam knew her parents wouldn't say anything since she was in her *rumschpringe.*

She stood up and walked to the open window. Through the screen, she could see the cloudless blue sky and the plush grass in the yard where her red begonias were in full bloom in the flower bed. Rays of sunshine warmed her cheeks, and she closed her eyes, feeling the June breeze and breathing in the aroma of freshly cut hay from her brothers' efforts the day before.

She looked down, wiggled her toes, and decided not to wear any shoes today, knowing that the cool blades between her toes would remind her of past summers, playing volleyball with her brothers in the yard or squirting each other with the water hose for relief from the heat. But today going barefoot was more about Saul than her childhood memories. He'd said she had cute toes the last time they were at the creek, and since Saul Fisher wasn't big on conversation, Miriam hoped he might notice her ankle bracelet — maybe comment on it. Or her toes. It didn't matter. Any attention from Saul caused her insides to swirl with hope for the future. Saul didn't know it yet, but Miriam was going to marry him. She'd loved him from afar since they were children, and even though he was often withdrawn and had a reputation as a bit of a troublemaker, Miriam knew — *He is just waiting for the right woman to mold him into all he can be.*

Saul crept closer to the edge of the cliff until his toes hung over the smooth rock, a natural diving board that he had jumped from a hundred times. He tucked the thick rope between his legs and cupped his hands around the knot that met him at eye level.

Then he saw her. Miriam Raber. Sitting with her girlfriends on the bank. Her brilliant blue eyes twinkled in the distance as she watched him, and she was chewing the nail on her first finger — like she always did before he jumped. And his legs grew unsteady beneath him — like they always did when Miriam was watching him.

He pulled his eyes from her and gave his

head a quick shake. He'd always felt confident about whatever he was doing, except when Miriam was around. She had a strange effect on him, always had — since they were kids. He recalled a time when he and Miriam were chosen as leads in the school Christmas pageant, playing Mary and Joseph. They were in the sixth grade, and Saul was still shocked at the amount of detail he remembered from that day. She'd worn a white sheet over her dress and belted it at the waist, and her long brown hair flowed freely past her shoulders instead of bound beneath her prayer covering. Mostly he remembered the way Miriam looked at him when she spoke her lines. And the way he went completely blank and forgot his.

"Jump, Saul!"

He straightened when he heard his buddy Leroy yelling from the bank. Then he took a deep breath and swung out over the water. As he let go of the rope, he didn't have more than a second before he plunged into the creek — but it was Miriam he saw the millisecond before his face submerged. He stayed down there longer than usual, enjoying the refreshing water and thinking about Miriam.

She was a good girl. The best. Every man of marrying age in Paradise had his eye on

Miriam. Everyone except Saul. He'd known for as long as he could remember that one day he would leave Paradise. Leave *her.* So, despite their mutual attraction over the years, Saul had avoided her as best he could. But the older they got, the harder it was for him to keep his eyes from always drifting her way. And she seemed to have the same problem. She was always watching him.

He swam upward until his head popped above the water, and not surprisingly, his eyes found Miriam's right away, as she smiled and clapped from the water's edge. There were others around. But he only saw her.

"I don't know why you like him so much," Hannah said when she and Miriam sat back down on the bank, following Saul's jump. "He never pays you much mind." Hannah stretched her arms behind her and rested on her hands. "He never pays *any* of us much mind."

"He will someday." Miriam smiled. "He's just shy."

Hannah chuckled. "He's not shy, Miriam. He's a loner." Hannah leaned closer and whispered, "Some say that he isn't going to be baptized, that he will leave the community."

Miriam snapped her head to the side to face her friend. "Where did you hear that?"

Hannah lifted one shoulder, then dropped it slowly. "I don't remember. But he doesn't seem to — to fit in."

"I think he fits in just fine." Miriam smiled as she turned her attention back to Saul. She watched him climb out of the creek in a pair of blue swim trunks, then join his friends down the bank.

"He never attends singings, he doesn't gather with the other men after church service, and remember . . ." Hannah gasped. "Remember when he got in a fight on the school yard with that *Englisch* boy who passed by." She shook her head. "Not fit behavior, I say. Not at all."

Miriam swooned with recollection. "*Ya.* I remember. The boy called me a name as I walked across the school yard to get on my scooter."

"So because he stood up for you, he's your hero? That's not our way, Miriam." Hannah sat taller and folded her hands in her lap. "And that's not the only time he's been in trouble. There was that time with John Lapp when the bishop —"

"*Ya,* I know, Hannah." Miriam knew Hannah was referring to the time when Bishop

Ebersol reprimanded Saul and John Lapp for fighting. Saul had refused to shave just after his sixteenth birthday, and John told Saul that only married men could grow a beard — *rumschpringe* or not — and that he'd better shave it off. Their harsh words led to a fistfight. Bishop Ebersol told Saul that the beard was not forbidden during *rumschpringe,* but the fighting was. Miriam couldn't understand why John made such a fuss about Saul having the facial hair, especially since the bishop wasn't very concerned. But John Lapp was married now, and he couldn't seem to grow a beard to save his life. Must have been a sensitive subject for him.

Miriam smiled. At least she'd had a small glimpse as to what her future husband would look like, his face covered with light-brown fuzz and sandy-red highlights.

"He's just a bit of a bad boy, Miriam." They both watched him laughing with his friends for a moment, then Hannah turned to her and grinned. "But he *is* a handsome bad boy."

"It's more than that." Miriam studied his back, the way he stood tall and straight like a towering spruce. His shoulders looked like they were a yard wide and molded bronze. She was glad when he put his shirt on. She took a deep breath. "He's just . . . *mysterious* in a kind sort of way."

Hannah narrowed her brows. "What does that mean?"

Miriam thought for a moment. How could she possibly put into words everything that she loved about Saul? His stunning good looks shouldn't matter, but his face kept her up at night, and the smooth way he spoke in a raspy voice, often barely above a whisper, caused her heart to flutter. He said very little, but Miriam was sure he was filled with goodness, even if his efforts might be misdirected from time to time.

She finally blew out a deep breath. "I don't know how to explain him. I just know that he's a *gut* person."

"How? Have you even been alone with him? You never even talk to him." Hannah's attitude was getting on Miriam's nerves.

"No. But I will."

"When?"

Miriam pulled herself up off the ground, brushed the wrinkles from her dark-blue dress, then put her hands on her hips and stared down at her friend. "I — I don't know for sure, but — but I will." She glanced toward Saul and the other men just in time to see Saul waving bye and leaving. He was nearing his spring buggy, and Mir-

21

iam knew she would have to act fast. "I'm going to go talk to him right now."

Hannah stood up beside her. "Really?" She tipped her head to one side.

"*Ya.* I'm going to go talk to him right now."

"Well." Hannah folded her arms across her chest and grinned. "Go, then. You better hurry. He's leaving."

"I am." Miriam took a step, hesitated, then spun around to face Hannah. "I'm going."

Hannah smiled. "I see that."

"*Ach,* okay." She forced one foot in front of the other until she was close enough to call out his name, and she had no idea what she would say.

Saul recognized the voice and spun around a few feet from his buggy, wondering what Miriam could possibly want. They admired each other from afar. That's the way it had always been. He glanced down at her bare feet, then smiled as he remembered telling her she had cute toes not too long ago. He'd been walking by her at the creek, and she was alone, smiling up at him from her perch on top of a rock near the water's edge. He didn't know why he'd said it, except for the fact that it was true.

"Hi." She hesitated when she got closer, and Saul saw a tiny chain around her ankle.

"Nice ankle bracelet." It was easiest to look at her feet. If he took in the rest of her, he was afraid his mouth would betray him and say something *dumm.*

She kicked her beautiful bare foot forward. "This? *Danki.*" She clutched the sides of her apron with both hands, then twisted the fabric. "Um, where are you going?"

Her face took on a rosy shade of pink, and Saul briefly wondered if his did too. "Home, I guess." He waited, and when she didn't say anything, he asked, "Why?"

She shrugged. "I don't know. It's a pretty day."

"Then let's go do something." His mouth had betrayed him after all. No good could come out of getting to know Miriam better. He already liked what he saw and knew. Why build on that just to leave her in the end? But he had no regrets when her whole face spread into a smile.

"Okay." She stepped closer, and Saul fought the urge to step back. Right now she was close enough to touch, and he wanted nothing more than to brush back a loose tendril of brown hair that had fallen from beneath her *kapp.* Then he locked eyes with her — those brilliant blue eyes.

23

"What do you wanna do?" He towered over her by at least a foot, and he rubbed his chin as he studied her. Her smooth skin glowed in the sunlight, the golden undertones evidence of the hard outdoor work everyone in their community did. Then, just like his mouth, his hand developed a mind of its own. Before his brain had time to realize what was happening, he reached up and pushed the wayward strand of hair off of her cheek. He didn't think he'd ever touched her before, and now he would lose sleep, wondering when he could do it again.

"Danki." She avoided his eyes and lowered her chin as she spoke. When she looked back up at him, her eyes lit with excitement. "Let's go fishing at the old Zook farm. No one lives there, and the pond is full of fish."

Saul folded his arms across his chest. "You fish?"

"Of course. Don't you?"

He pulled his straw hat off and wiped sweat from his forehead. "*Ya.* I just didn't take you for the fishing type."

She giggled. "The fishing *type?* I can handle a fishing pole." The sound of her laughter made him want to hear it for the rest of his life. Then she grabbed at her chest with both hands. "Oh no!"

"What?"

"I can't go." She gazed into his eyes. "I'm sorry." And the way her face folded into a frown, she seemed to mean it. "I forgot that my cousin is coming this afternoon. She's staying with us for the summer."

Saul tried to hide his disappointment but knew it was for the best. "Do I know her?"

"No. She's *Englisch*. A cousin on my father's side." Her eyes brightened as she smiled. "She's coming all the way from Texas. She's our age." She paused. "I'm sure you'll meet her."

Saul nodded as he looped his thumbs beneath his suspenders, then glanced down to see his wet swim shorts had soaked through his black trousers. "I guess I'll see you around, then." He turned to leave, not sure what else to say to her. Spending time alone with her was a bad idea anyway.

"Saul?"

He unwrapped the reins from the tree where he had his horse tethered, not turning around. *"Ya?"* Then he felt a hand tap him on the back. Her simple touch rattled him so much that he dropped the reins. He quickly reached down and picked them up. "What is it?" As he stood, he couldn't look her in the face, so he stared at her toes again.

He watched her wiggle them, and he couldn't help but wonder if it was for his benefit. She looked up, and Saul finally locked eyes with her. When she smiled, Saul knew things were about to get complicated.

"Maybe we could go fishing tomorrow after church?" Her long eyelashes swept down across high cheekbones before she looked back at him.

This was a bad idea. But there wasn't one thing in the world that Saul could think of that he would rather do. So he nodded.

Tomorrow he would spend the afternoon with Miriam Raber. Alone. Something he had dreamed about for years but had put just as much energy into avoiding. His life, his plan, was set. And there was no place in any of it for Miriam.

But as she looked up at him with a smile that threatened to melt his resolve, he knew that he was going to do the unthinkable — date her for the summer. Then leave her in August. *God, forgive me.*

2

Miriam pushed her horse hard on the way home, grateful that the distance was short. She was late, and she feared Shelby would already be there. *Mamm* wouldn't be happy with her for not being home in time to welcome her cousin.

As the buggy neared her house, she reached up and cupped her cheek with her palm, surprised by the boldness of Saul's gentle touch, and decided being late was worth it. Tomorrow she would spend the afternoon alone with Saul, something she had wanted to do for as long as she could remember.

Mamm was sweeping the front porch when she parked the buggy, and she could see her three younger brothers out by the barn. Ben was carrying chicken feed inside, Elam had a shovel in his hand as he walked toward the barn, and little John was chasing an irritated rooster around the yard.

"You're lucky your cousin's flight was late, or she would have beaten you here." *Mamm* kept sweeping as she spoke, but finally looked up and gave Miriam a forgiving smile.

"I'm sorry, *Mamm.* But I'm here now." Miriam padded up the steps in her bare feet, feeling lighter than usual. "Can I help you with anything?"

Her mother pushed leaves from the porch with the broom, although most of them blew back in her direction. "No, I think everything is ready for your cousin's arrival. Your *daed* called on the phone, and Ben happened to be in the barn and answered. *Daed* said that Shelby's flight was late, but they were leaving the airport about an hour ago." *Mamm* pushed a big leaf off the porch with her foot as she shook her head. "It wonders me where all this wind came from. It wasn't windy until I started to clear the leaves from the porch." She pushed back a strand of gray hair, then tucked it beneath her *kapp.*

Miriam thought of Saul.

"They should be here any minute." *Mamm* leaned the broom up against the house, then put her hands on her hips and inspected the area before she turned to Miriam. "I'm making cheddar meat loaf, a recipe your

Aenti Lillian shared with me before they moved to Colorado."

Miriam thought about Aunt Lillian, Uncle Samuel, her cousins, and Aunt Katie Ann. They'd moved to Colorado in November to farmland that Lillian's *Daadi* Jonas had purchased before he died. "I miss them."

"*Ya.* I do too." *Mamm* sat down in one of the rocking chairs on the front porch, then crossed her legs. "But your *Aenti* Mary Ellen got a letter from Lillian just last week, and things are coming together for them there." *Mamm* gasped a bit. "Did I tell you that David is getting married? To a girl he met there named Emily."

David was a couple of years older than Miriam, and she missed him the most. "Will we travel to the wedding?" Miriam widened her eyes as she waited for her mother to answer. A trip to Colorado sounded exciting.

"We will see." Her mother smiled briefly, then her expression dropped. "I'm so glad that things are working out for Samuel, Lillian, and the *kinner,* but your *Aenti* Katie Ann is still having trouble adjusting to her new life there."

Miriam's heart hurt for Katie Ann. Her Uncle Ivan had left his dear wife shortly after moving to Colorado with the other members of their family. None of the family understood it, and her parents didn't talk about it much. And to make matters worse, Ivan had returned to Lancaster County and taken up with an *Englisch* woman they all knew. Her parents said they were not to speak to Ivan, and he was never invited to any family gatherings. That's how it was when you've been shunned.

"I don't know what's wrong with that *bruder* of mine." *Mamm* shook her head before she stood up and pointed to the end of the driveway. "There's a van pulling in. That must be them." She walked down the porch steps, raised a hand above her brow to block the sun, then called for Miriam's brothers to come up to the house.

Miriam strained to see the white van pull into the drive, then park beside the spring buggy. *Mamm* gathered Miriam's brothers around her in the yard, and they watched *Daed* slide a long door open and step out of the backseat. He turned and pulled out two large red suitcases and set them in the grass. As he slid his door closed, the passenger door popped open, and Miriam watched a brown boot land on the ground followed by a tall girl with flowing dark-brown hair.

Mamm leaned close to Miriam. "She's so *thin*."

Miriam studied the pretty girl who turned in their direction. She and Shelby probably weighed about the same, but her cousin stood at least five inches taller than Miriam's five-foot-five height. She nodded at her mother's comment, then smiled as Shelby walked toward them.

Her cousin was dressed in blue jeans, and her brown boots looked like something her brothers might wear to work in the fields, except hers were pointed at the toe. Cowgirl boots. Miriam wondered if Shelby could ride a horse. They had two suitable mares in the barn.

Shelby's dark-blue shirt was buttoned almost to the neck. Miriam knew that *Mamm* would appreciate the conservative clothing. Many times they'd hosted *Englisch* guests for supper, and *Mamm* was appalled when the tourists showed up in short pants, or worse, backless tops or ones that showed their stomachs. But *Mamm* continued to host the suppers, in conjunction with bed-and-breakfasts in the area. It provided some extra income, but the truth was, Miriam knew her mother loved to cook for others. Visitors went on and on about how good her mother's cooking was.

"Welcome, Shelby." *Mamm* gave Shelby an awkward hug, then stepped back and

31

pointed to Miriam. "This is our daughter, Miriam."

"Hi." Miriam didn't move. She was trying to decide if Shelby was happy to be here.

Her cousin said hello, but she wasn't smiling. She wasn't frowning either. Dark sunglasses hid her eyes, and her expression was confusing, rather blank.

Mamm introduced Shelby to the boys, then instructed Ben and Elam to carry her bags to Miriam's room as everyone else moved into the den.

"I will let you womenfolk talk. I think the cows are ready for milking." Miriam's father excused himself. Aaron Raber wasn't one for small talk, and Miriam suspected that he'd probably sat quietly in the backseat while the driver and Shelby talked on the way home from the airport.

Miriam watched her cousin eyeing her new surroundings. Shelby edged toward the couch when *Mamm* motioned her in that direction and told her to sit and rest, adding that she must be weary from her travels. As Shelby sat down on the tan sofa, Miriam saw her eyes darting around the room — to the two high-back rockers on the other side of the den, then to the hutch near the entryway. Miriam wondered what Shelby thought about their plain surroundings.

"I bet this is much different than what you are used to." *Mamm* sat down beside Shelby on the couch and twisted slightly to face her. Miriam sat down in one of the rockers, as did John.

"Not so much." Shelby showed the first hint of a smile. "It's nice."

Miriam breathed a small sigh of relief. Shelby had a soft, quiet voice, and when her brown eyes met with Miriam's, her smile broadened a bit.

John kicked his rocker into motion, his blond bob in need of a trim. "Do you have a cell phone?"

"Yes, I do." Shelby turned to *Mamm*. "Is that okay?"

"*Ya,* I think so." She paused. "If you wouldn't mind, we'd prefer if you use it outside. We have a phone in the barn. You're welcome to use that also."

Shelby nodded, then fumbled with the straps of the brown purse in her lap and bit her lip. Miriam wanted her to feel comfortable in their home.

"Do you want to see your room?" Miriam stood up from the rocker and smiled.

"Sure." Shelby rose, draped her purse over her shoulder, and waited for Miriam to motion toward the stairs.

"You girls get settled while I finish supper," *Mamm* said as she rose to her feet, then walked across the den toward the kitchen.

"We're the third door on the right at the end of the hallway." Miriam let Shelby walk in front of her, and her cousin's dark hair bounced against the middle of her back as she started up the stairs. Miriam's hair was just as long, although bound beneath her prayer covering. She thought about Saul again. *He'll see the length of my hair on our wedding night.*

Shelby stopped at the third door on the right. "This one?"

"Ya." Miriam reached around her and pushed the door wide. "Your bed is that one." She pointed to the bed on the right side of the nightstand. "I put fresh linens on it just this morning."

Shelby sat down on the bed and ran her hand across the quilt. "Thank you."

"I also cleared two drawers for you and made room for you to hang your clothes on those hooks over there." Miriam pointed to a dozen hooks running along a two-by-four on the far wall.

Her cousin glanced in that direction, then hung her head before she looked back up at Miriam. "I'm sorry you have to share this small room with a stranger."

Miriam sat down on her own bed and

faced her cousin, unable to ignore the sadness in Shelby's voice. "I don't mind at all. I've been looking forward to your visit." Miriam glanced around her room. She'd always thought it was a nice-sized room. "And you're my cousin, so not really a stranger." She smiled, and Shelby did so also, then quickly looked down.

When the silence grew uncomfortable, Miriam spoke again. "Tomorrow is church, but maybe Monday I can take you to town after we do chores."

Shelby nodded, then stood up and walked toward the window. She leaned her nose close to the screen and peered outside for a moment, then spun around. "Would we go in a buggy? Do you drive one of those?" Her eyes lit up, and Miriam silently thanked God at the glimmer of happiness in her voice.

"*Ya.* I drive the buggy. I've been driving by myself since I was twelve, but mostly on the back roads. I was sixteen before I started taking my little brothers and going to town." She paused as she walked to where Shelby was standing by the window. "Have you ever been in a buggy?"

Shelby turned to face her. "No. I've never even been in an Amish town or been around an — an Amish person." She bit her lip again as her eyes grew round.

Miriam recalled her mother's earlier comments but assumed Shelby must not remember her visit here as a young child. She leaned closer to Shelby and whispered, "I promise we don't bite."

Finally, a full smile. "Good to know."

Shelby sat next to Miriam at the large wooden table in the kitchen. It felt like eating at a luxurious picnic table with a long backless bench on either side, and the breeze blowing through three different open windows in the kitchen only added to the picnic effect. At each end of the table was an armchair. Aaron was already seated in one, and Rebecca was standing at the counter pouring glasses of iced tea. The boys waited patiently on the bench across from Shelby and Miriam. Shelby surveyed the offerings already on the table as her stomach growled. Aside from the meat loaf and potatoes, the rest was unfamiliar.

Rebecca placed the last two glasses of tea in front of Ben and John, then took a seat at the opposite end of the table from her husband.

"Shelby, we pray silently before and after a meal." Rebecca smiled before she bowed her head along with the rest of the family.

Shelby followed suit, but she didn't have anything to say to God. She lifted her head when she heard movement around her.

Miriam passed her a bowl first. "This is creamed celery."

Shelby spooned a generous helping onto her plate, trying to remember the last time she'd sat down for a family meal like this. She tried to recall when the problems had started between her parents. When had the two most important people in her life stopped loving each other and started screaming at each other?

"Do you like to cook, Shelby?" Rebecca passed a tray with bread toward Shelby, and Shelby nodded. She could remember spending hours in the kitchen with her mother when she was young. Mom would set her up on the counter, and together they would bake a variety of cookies. Shelby's job was to lick the beaters clean and be the tester for each warm batch that came from the oven.

She sat quietly, listening to the family talk about their day. The oldest boy, Ben, told a story about running into someone named Big Jake in a place called Bird-In-Hand. "He ain't ever gonna sell that cow now that everyone knows it birthed a calf with two heads." Ben laughed, then squinted as he leaned forward a bit. "I heard he even took the animal to Ida King, and —"

"Ben!" Rebecca sat taller in her chair and scowled at her oldest son. "We will not speak of such things at supper — or any time." She turned to Shelby and spoke in a whisper. "Ida King practices powwowing."

Shelby laid a fork full of creamed celery on her plate. "What's that?"

Rebecca shook her head. "Her practices are not something the Lord would approve of."

"She's like a witch doctor," Miriam whispered to Shelby.

"Enough." Aaron didn't look up as he spoke, but everyone adhered to his wishes and ate silently for a moment, then Elam commented that he saw a raccoon trying to climb the fence to his mother's garden. Shelby had noticed the large garden on the side of the house when the van first pulled into the driveway.

"I put a bowl of freshly cut vegetables right outside the fence for that fellow, hoping he wouldn't get greedy," Rebecca said with a laugh.

The youngest boy — John — chuckled as he told a tale about chasing their rooster around the barn. Shelby saw the boy's father grimace, but he didn't say anything.

"And what about you, Miriam?" Rebecca pinched a piece of bread and held it in her hand as she waited for her daughter to answer. "How was your time at the creek?"

Shelby wondered what they did for fun here. She used to love to swim. She turned slightly toward her cousin and waited.

"It was fine," Miriam said.

"She only goes there to see Saul Fisher." Ben reached across his brother and pulled back a slice of bread. Shelby was sure this was the best bread she'd had in her life, warm and dripping with butter. She took another bite of her own slice as Ben went on. "But you're wasting your time. I've heard it told that he ain't gonna be baptized."

"You don't know that, Ben." Miriam's tone was sharp as she frowned at her brother.

Ben's glare challenged her as he leaned forward in his chair. "That's what folks are saying."

"No talk of rumors, Ben." Once again Aaron didn't look up from his plate, but the conversation ceased immediately, and Rebecca started to talk about a new schoolteacher named Sarah who would be taking over when school started up again in September. When she was done, she spoke directly to Shelby.

"Will you be attending college next year, Shelby?"

Shelby took a deep breath as she shifted her weight. That had certainly been the plan, until she learned that her parents used up her college fund fighting each other in their divorce. "No, ma'am. I'll be getting a job when I go home."

Aaron lifted his head for the first time and looked directly at her. "Hard work is good for the soul. Too much schooling can turn a person from what is important — the love of the land and a hard day's work."

"Aaron, now you know that the *Englisch* often send their children to college, and it's not our place to judge." Rebecca smiled at Shelby. "I'm sure you will find a *gut* job suited to you when you return, Shelby."

She doubted it. *What kind of job can I get without a college degree?* But she didn't much care what kind of job she found. She was having trouble caring about much of anything. Over the past few months, she'd made sure that she wouldn't feel much, and she was never going to forgive herself for the things she'd done. Things she knew God wouldn't approve of. She used to care what God thought, but she'd stopped when she realized . . . God had given up on her.

These strangers, with their odd clothes and strange lifestyle, seemed nice enough, but her parents were only further punishing her by sending her to this foreign place. *Haven't they hurt me enough?*

Miriam walked into her bedroom with her hair in a towel and dressed in her long white nightgown. Shelby was already tucked into bed with her head buried in a book.

"What are you reading?" Miriam pulled the towel from her wet hair, then reached for a brush inside the top drawer of her nightstand. She sat on the edge of her bed and fought the tangles.

"Your hair is so pretty." Shelby looked up from her book, but Miriam noticed that she also had a pen in her hand, which she began to tap against the book. "Why do you keep it up underneath those caps?"

Miriam continued to pull the brush through her hair as she spoke. "We believe a woman's head should be covered, and we try not to show the length of our hair to a man until after we're married." She stopped brushing for a moment as she recalled past trips to the beach when most Amish girls shed their caps and pulled their hair into ponytails. "Some boys have seen our hair at the beach, though."

"You're kidding, right?" Shelby stopped tapping her pen and sat taller in the bed, then propped the pillow up behind her. "I'm sorry, I didn't mean that to sound —"

"No, that's okay. I'm sure our ways must seem strange to you."

Shelby closed the pink book in her lap and put the pen on the nightstand. "I'm sure everyone else seems strange to you too. Us *'Englisch'* as I heard your mom say."

Miriam pushed her hair behind her ears and put the brush back in the top drawer, glad that a conversation was ensuing. "No. We have many *Englisch* friends, so we know how different things are outside of our community."

"How much school do you have left, or did you already graduate?"

"I'm done with school. We only attend school through the eighth grade." Miriam was surprised that Shelby didn't seem to know anything about them. Miriam thought Shelby might have done a little research before she got here, but she didn't fault her for that.

Shelby leaned farther back against the pillow. She was wearing a long blue nightgown, and again Miriam thought about how that would please her mother. Maybe someone had told Shelby that it would be appreciated if she dressed conservatively.

Her cousin began to kick her feet together beneath the covers. Miriam had noticed that Shelby was always fidgeting and couldn't seem to be still. Even during supper, Shelby kept moving in her seat, pushing her food around, and she wiped her mouth a lot with her napkin. *She must be nervous.*

"Will you leave here, since you're eighteen? Or do you plan to stay here forever?" Something about the way Shelby said *forever* made it sound like a bad thing.

"I would never leave here." Miriam settled into her own bed and also kicked the covers to the bottom. "I plan to be baptized in the fall, and . . ." *And marry Saul someday.* She smiled as she thought about her future. "And someday I'll get married and start a family of my own."

"Aren't you curious, you know . . . about everything outside of here?"

"No. I'm in my *rumschpringe.* That means that at sixteen, we get to experience the outside world, then choose if we want to stay here and be baptized as a member of the community, or leave." Miriam fluffed her pillow as she spoke. "So I think I've seen enough of the *Englisch* world the past couple of years. It's not for me."

Shelby twisted to face Miriam, then

tapped a finger to her chin. "How many leave here?"

"Hardly any. I mean, a few do. But most of us stay." Miriam smiled slightly. "It's all we know, but what we know is *gut,* and I can't imagine living anywhere else."

"Who is Saul?"

Miriam sighed as she recalled the gentle way Saul brushed back a strand of her hair earlier that day, the feel of his touch. "A friend."

"You like him. I can tell." Shelby smiled a bit.

"*Ya,* I guess I do." She reached over and turned the flame on the gas lantern up since nightfall was upon them, then she eased down in the bed and propped herself up on one elbow. "What about you? Do you have a boyfriend in Texas?"

They both jumped when a gust of wind blew in through the screen and caused the green blind to bounce against the open window.

"I *did.* His name is Tommy." She shuffled in her bed. "He broke up with me when my parents were — were going through their divorce. I had thought . . . well, I thought we might get married someday."

"I'm sorry." Miriam had never had a real boyfriend. She'd been carted home by

44

plenty of boys following Sunday singings since she'd turned sixteen, but her heart belonged to Saul. She knew she would wait for him.

"It's okay. I really don't care."

Somehow Miriam didn't think that to be true. "Was he your boyfriend for a long time?" Miriam wanted to ask if they had kissed, but she didn't even know Shelby. That was something she might ask Leah or Hannah.

"About six months. Until things got bad with my family." She paused, then also propped herself up on one elbow and faced Miriam. They each strained to see each other over the nightstand in between them, so Miriam shifted upward a bit. Shelby did too. "Then he said I was sad all the time."

They were quiet for a while. "Are you still sad?" Miriam knew it was a dumb question. Of course she was sad. Her parents had recently divorced. "I mean, are you sad about *him?* Do you miss him?"

"No."

Again Miriam suspected otherwise.

"Did anyone tell you that breakfast is at four thirty?"

Shelby bolted upward, and Miriam could tell she was straining to see past the lantern in between them. "You're kidding, right?"

"No. We start our day early. The cows have to be milked, which *Daed* and the boys take care of. I usually go to the henhouse and collect eggs while *Mamm* gets breakfast started. Tomorrow is church service, so we will travel to the Dienner farm for that. We don't work on Sundays, but during the week, *Mamm* and I start the day by weeding the garden before the heat of the day is on us. Then we do our baking, and . . ." Miriam didn't want to overwhelm her cousin, so she trailed off with a sigh.

"I guess that's why everyone is already in bed, then." Shelby glanced at the battery-operated clock on the nightstand. "At eight thirty."

"*Ya.* Early to bed, early to rise." Miriam smiled, then turned the small fan on the nightstand toward Shelby. "Batteries. Sure saves us from the summer heat."

"It's not so bad."

Miriam chuckled. "Wait until August."

They were quiet again for a while, then Miriam reached over to extinguish the lantern. "Guess we'd best sleep. Morning will be here soon enough."

Shelby sat up in the bed. "Do you mind if we leave that on for just a little while longer? Will it bother you, keep you from sleeping?"

Miriam pulled back her hand. "No, I'll

just face toward the window. Just turn the knob to the left when you're ready for sleep."

"Okay. Thanks. I like to write in my journal before I go to bed." Shelby reached for the pen on the nightstand.

"Do you do that every day?"

"Most days."

Miriam noticed the tiny lock dangling from the side of the small book, and she wondered if Shelby locked it when she was done writing in it. Would Shelby ever share the contents with her like she assumed sisters would?

"Good night, Shelby."

"Good night."

Miriam closed her eyes and said her nightly prayers. She wondered if Shelby prayed before sleep. Just in case she didn't . . . *Dear Lord, I sense sadness inside my cousin. Please wrap Your loving arms around her and guide her toward true peacefulness, the kind of peace and harmony that only comes from a true relationship with You. May her time here help to heal her heart. Aamen.*

Shelby stared at the page for a long while. Her cousin was snoring before Shelby wrote the first word. She sat thinking about her parents, images she wished she could erase from her mind. So much screaming. Especially when Shelby's mother found out that her father had cheated on her. Shelby recalled that night with more detail than the other fights she'd seen her parents have. Her mother called her father names that she'd never heard spoken in her house. And from that moment, things went from bad to worse. And no one seemed to care how it was affecting her. It was as if the ground dropped from beneath her and she just kept falling, with no one to save her. She'd always relied on her father to protect her, to keep her safe — but he was the one who had pushed her into this dark place she couldn't seem to escape. Her mother was too distraught to notice and focused much of her energy on how to get even with Shelby's father. Then Tommy chose to break her heart in the midst of everything. "You're sad all the time, Shelby," he'd said. "I just can't be around you like this anymore."

Shelby glanced around at her new accommodations for the next three months. She could run away, she supposed. But she didn't have much money, so she wouldn't get far. And she didn't want to take up with the kind of people that she had in Texas, other lost souls like herself who eased their pain with alcohol and drugs. But what did she want?

She put the pen to paper.

Dear Diary,

I've been shipped to Pennsylvania to live with my Amish cousins — people I don't even know, who dress funny, don't have electricity, and who get up at four thirty to start their day. They seem nice enough, but I don't want to be here. The only family I have ever known sent me here against my will. If my parents love me, why don't they want me with them? They only care about themselves. They have destroyed my life with their stupid decisions, and I'm the one who has to suffer along with them. If Tommy loved me, why did he break up with me? I know I've made some mistakes in my life, but I don't think I deserve this.

Or maybe I do. Maybe I'm being punished. I don't know. I just know that I feel bad all the time. I want to be loved, but my heart is so empty, and my faith in life, in God, is gone. I don't have anything to live for.

3

Miriam gently nudged the huddled mass under the covers. "Shelby, breakfast is ready." It was already after five o'clock, but her cousin probably felt like she'd just gone to sleep.

"Already?" Shelby pulled the covers over her head. "It's not even daylight."

"It will be worth it when you see the feast *Mamm* and I have made for breakfast. *Mamm* always makes overnight blueberry French toast on Sunday, and we cook bacon and sausage."

Shelby poked her head from beneath the covers. "Blueberry French toast?" Then she sat up in bed and rubbed her eyes. "I love French toast."

"*Ya,* well . . . this is probably different from what you're used to, but it's a favorite around here." Miriam started to make her bed as she spoke. "*Mamm* makes the toast the night before in a casserole. It's got

50

cream cheese, fresh blueberries, and all kinds of *gut* stuff. Then she refrigerates it so that on Sunday morning, she can just put it in the oven."

Shelby eased out of bed and also began straightening the covers on her bed. "Is there anything I should do while you are at church?"

Miriam stopped smoothing the quilt, stood straight up, and faced her. "You don't want to go to church with us?"

Shelby turned to face her. "Should I?"

"There are usually one or two *Englisch* folks there, friends or family of others in the community, so I don't think you would feel out of place." Miriam watched her cousin's expression sour. "Did — did you attend church in your hometown?"

"Not for . . . a while."

Miriam knew it was none of her business, so she didn't press. "We don't worship in churches. The gathering is always at someone's house, or if the house isn't big enough, we have the service in the barn. Today it's at the Dienners' home, and they have a large farmhouse, so it will be inside."

Shelby went back to making her bed and didn't say anything, so Miriam did the same. When she was done, she turned to Shelby. "The church service is in High Ger-

51

man, so you might not understand any of it, but other *Englisch* folks say they enjoy the sense of fellowship."

Shelby grimaced. "I don't really have anything to wear." She opened the smaller of her suitcases on the floor by her bed and pulled out a brush. "And I'm not on good terms with God right now."

Miriam watched her run the brush through her hair and knew it was not her place to minister to Shelby, but her cousin seemed so unhappy, and being in a place of worship with so many others might help. "There's a wonderful offering of food following the church service." She smiled teasingly at Shelby. "And we play volleyball and other games outside this time of year."

Shelby slowed the brush through her long hair and seemed to be considering the idea.

"Better than staying here by yourself. You'll meet lots of folks." Miriam waited.

"I still don't have anything to wear."

"You can wear whatever you want. Did you bring a dress?"

Shelby twisted her mouth to one side. "Yes. But it's a short dress."

"How short?"

Her cousin unzipped the other suitcase on the floor by the bed. She pulled out a floral print dress with tiny straps, which was, indeed, short. "*Ya,* maybe too short." Miriam edged closer to where Shelby was squatting beside her suitcase. "What else do you have?"

Shelby held up two pairs of pants. "Which ones?"

Miriam studied the choices, then pointed to the pair of darker blue jeans. They were shorter than regular breeches, but not as faded as the longer pants Shelby was also considering. "What about those shorter pants, with maybe a nice blouse?"

Shelby held up a short-sleeved yellow pullover shirt. There was no fancy lace or low neckline. A little bright, but conservative.

"That will be just fine. I'll let you dress while I go help *Mamm* finish up breakfast."

Her cousin nodded, and Miriam closed the bedroom door behind her. When she returned to the kitchen, everyone was seated but her mother, who was placing a pitcher of orange juice on the table.

"Is she coming down for breakfast?" *Mamm* wiped her hands on her apron.

Miriam nodded as John propped his elbows on the table. "I bet she ain't used to gettin' up this early."

Mamm cut her eyes at him. "Elbows off the table, please."

They all turned when they heard footsteps coming through the den. Miriam thought Shelby was so beautiful. She didn't wear makeup like most *Englisch* girls, although this morning there was a shine on her lips. Miriam didn't long for makeup, nor had she experimented with it during her *rumschpringe,* but she was wishing for some of the gloss that Shelby was wearing. Especially for when she saw Saul this afternoon. Her cousin's thick, long hair was pulled back into a ponytail. She slowed as she neared the kitchen, as if waiting to be invited to sit.

"I poured you some juice, Shelby." Miriam smiled, then pushed back on the bench to make room for her cousin.

"*Guder mariye,* Shelby." *Mamm* took her seat. "That's good morning in Pennsylvania *Deitsch.*"

"Good morning to all of you." Shelby lowered her head when everyone else did for prayer. Miriam wondered what Shelby was saying to God, since she'd mentioned that she wasn't on good terms with Him.

Shelby enjoyed the buggy ride to the Amish farm where church service was being held. Miriam drove one buggy carrying Shelby, John, and Elam — a buggy with no top, which Miriam called a spring buggy. Aaron

54

drove another buggy with a top on it, and he took Rebecca and Ben. Shelby was glad to be in the spring buggy, the wind in her face, on this early Sunday morning as the sun barely peeked above the horizon.

It was a short trip from her cousins' farm to the Dienner farm, but Miriam told several jokes on the way. They were the cleanest jokes Shelby had ever heard, but still funny, and she'd found herself laughing out loud — something she hadn't done in a long time. She liked Miriam, and she appreciated the way Miriam seemed to be trying hard to make her feel comfortable. But Miriam didn't tell her that the church service was three hours long until she was parking the buggy. "You're kidding, right?" was all she said. Miriam just smiled.

Miriam kept close to Shelby's side, introducing her to everyone as they walked into the large home. Shelby was even related to some of them, but she couldn't keep everyone straight. They were all welcoming and thanked Shelby for coming to church with them, even though she'd already been told she wouldn't understand anything that was going on. And that was okay. She would just sit quietly and not have to feel guilty that she wasn't partaking in any sort of prayer. However, when she saw the backless benches set up in the large den, she thought about the three hours of sitting and wished she'd just stayed back at her cousins' farm.

"The men sit on one side, facing the women, who sit on the other side," Miriam whispered as they maneuvered through the crowd of about a hundred. "The bishop and deacons sit in the middle."

"Does it always last three hours?"

Miriam chuckled. "*Ya,* most of the time it does. Guess that's why we only have church every other Sunday."

Shelby followed Miriam, and they both sat down on a bench in the third row. Others were slowly filing into the room and taking a seat.

"Even though you won't understand the language, I think you will feel a sense of peace here." Miriam smiled.

Shelby didn't think so. Tiny distractions throughout her days provided her with brief reprieves from all that ailed her, but at the end of the day, when she laid her head down to sleep, life just seemed too much to bear. Her heart ached, and she missed the life she'd had before her parents' troubles. And if her parents loved her, they would have let her stay there to work through her problems. Especially her mother, whom she'd been living with before she was shipped away.

"You need a vacation, Shelby," her mother had said. "Far away from here. Away from those people you've been running around with and from the heartache associated with the divorce."

What her mother should have said was, "Shelby, I'm dating Richard Sutton and I don't have time to deal with your issues right now." That would have been a more honest reason to ship her only daughter to this foreign place. Her father had gotten on with his life, too, with the woman he'd left her mother for. Tina.

Shelby cringed. Yes, everyone was getting along with their lives just fine. She felt tears welling up in her eyes.

"Are you all right?" Miriam reached for Shelby's hand and squeezed. It was such a tender, endearing thing to do that a tear threatened to spill, but Shelby quickly blinked it back. She pulled her hand from Miriam's.

"Yes. I'm fine. I'm sorry." She hoped no one else saw. She was embarrassed enough.

Miriam smiled. "I'm so glad you're here, Shelby. So very glad. I know we're going to be like sisters."

Her cousin seemed so sincere, truly glad to have her here. *Why?* Shelby didn't have any brothers or sisters, and she wasn't sure

57

that was a bad thing. That would only mean more people to hurt her. She didn't respond.

Two hours into the service, Shelby straightened her back and sighed. She felt no sense of fellowship, and she felt emptier than she did before. This was a mistake. Her life was a mistake. She had no sense of purpose, no guidance, and no faith. Why did her parents bother taking her to church all those years if things were going to end up like this? Clearly her parents hadn't been listening. People fell in love, they got married, and they stayed together forever — through the good and the bad.

"You will like this part," Miriam whispered. "When there are several *Englisch* folks, like there are today, Bishop Ebersol says a few verses in *Englisch,* so that the entire congregation will understand the blessings."

Shelby forced a smile, wishing she could close off her ears to whatever was forthcoming. She was wallowing in self-pity, mixed with a heavy dose of anger, but knowing this didn't deter the sadness that threatened to suffocate her. She couldn't bear it.

When Bishop Ebersol started to speak in *Englisch,* she closed her eyes and tried to will away his words, but they entered her mind just the same — and played havoc with her heart.

"There hath no temptation taken you but such as is common to man," the bishop said. "But God is faithful, who will not suffer you to be tempted above that ye are able; but will with the temptation also make a way to escape, that ye may be able to bear it."

Shelby didn't hear anything else the bishop said after the Scripture reading. The words echoed in her head. *"But will with the temptation also make a way to escape, that ye may be able to bear it."* She clamped her eyes closed and held her breath for a moment. *I can't bear it.*

Shelby could see her parents yelling, her mother pounding her fists against her father's chest as she sobbed. As she tried to clear the image, Tommy's face showed up in her mind's eye, and she could hear his voice saying he didn't want to be around her.

She released her breath but kept her eyes closed as she pictured her circle of friends back home — the parties, the drinking, the drugs. All things she knew were wrong, yet she'd allowed herself to partake.

Slowly she opened her eyes and looked around at these strange people dressed so differently from the rest of the world. Sweat dripped down her spine from the lack of air-conditioning, and her back ached from sitting on the backless bench. She shifted her weight but couldn't get comfortable. *What am I doing here?*

"Are you all right?" Miriam leaned toward her as she whispered.

"No. I — I actually think I need some air. Excuse me." Shelby stood up and quickly moved past her cousin, then walked as briskly as she could toward the nearest door. She could feel everyone's eyes on her, but she didn't care. *I don't want to be here. God let me down.*

Miriam turned to her mother and waited for instruction. She saw Shelby dab at her eyes on the way out the door, and she wondered if *Mamm* saw too.

Mamm glanced past Miriam toward the window, then said, "*Ya.* Go see to your cousin."

Miriam bowed her head in a brief, silent prayer, then took a quick peek in Saul's direction. He didn't catch her glance, so she got up and hurried to find Shelby. She crossed the Dienners' front yard and made her way to where Shelby was sitting, in one of two swings that hung from a large branch of an old oak tree. She slowed down as she approached and saw that Shelby was crying.

"What's the matter?" Miriam asked softly as she squatted down beside her cousin. "Is there anything I can do?"

Shelby shook her head but kept it hung low as she sniffled. "No. I'm all right. I'm sorry." She finally looked up. "I shouldn't be here."

Miriam bit her bottom lip. She didn't know what to say. *Help me to help her, Lord.* She stood up and eased her way into the other swing beside Shelby, then twisted the point of her black shoe into the worn area below her as she stared at the ground. "Do you want to go home, back to Texas?"

Shelby turned toward her and brushed away a tear. "I don't have a home anymore." She stood up and paced in front of the swings. "I don't have a home. I don't have a boyfriend. I don't have any friends. I made bad choices, and . . ." She paused, then took a deep breath and said, "And God let all this happen." She sat back down in the swing.

Miriam had never felt the call to minister to anyone until now. It wasn't their way. But she heard the voice in her head loud and clear. *It is of My will that Shelby is here.* She squeezed the rope supports on either side of her and prayed she would speak the right words. "Sometimes things happen, and it's hard to understand how it could be God's will." She glanced at Shelby, but her cousin had her head turned in the opposite direction. "But I know your faith will see you through this, and if you want to talk about —"

"Faith?" Shelby swung her head around to face Miriam. Her teary eyes were now blazing with anger. "I don't have any faith." Then she shook her head back and forth over and over again. "Never mind. I shouldn't be saying this to you. My problems are my problems, and I'll get through this somehow."

Miriam wanted to tell Shelby that faith and prayer were the only ways to get through it, but she stayed quiet.

"I'm sorry," Shelby said after a few moments. "You can go back in, Miriam. You don't have to stay out here with me. I'm okay."

Miriam straightened in the swing. "No. That's all right. There isn't that much left." She smiled. "I'll just stay here with you."

Shelby gazed for a long while at Miriam. "You're a good person, Miriam. I can tell."

"Danki." Miriam twisted her mouth to one side. "But you don't even know me, so how

can you tell that I'm a *gut* person?"

Shelby smiled slightly. "Most of the time, I'm a good judge of character." Her smile faded. "Although I wasn't such a good judge of character before I left home."

Miriam didn't want to pry, but she couldn't imagine what Shelby did that was so bad. She seemed like such a nice person.

"Miriam?"

"Ya?"

"Do you think God forgives our bad choices?"

Miriam thought for a moment. She wanted to tell Shelby that she needed to reach out to God, to have faith, but instead, she said, "*Ya*. I do."

"Hmm . . ." Shelby paused. "I don't know."

"I believe that . . ." Miriam didn't feel qualified to speak with Shelby about this. She wished Shelby could talk to Bishop Ebersol, even though she was *Englisch*.

"What? What do you believe?" Shelby twisted the swing so that her body faced Miriam's.

Miriam took a deep breath and hoped she was saying the right things. "I believe that we have to forgive ourselves first. Only then can God reach us. I believe . . ." She paused, glanced at Shelby. Her cousin was waiting for her to go on. "I believe it's hard to hear God when we are angry, or can't forgive ourself for something." Miriam smiled. "God forgives everything if we ask Him to."

Shelby faced forward again and stared straight ahead. "I don't know about that." After a few moments, she said, "Besides, I think maybe I'm being punished by Him."

By God? Miriam wanted to tell Shelby that wasn't how it worked, but she heard the screen door close, and she looked up to see people starting to emerge from the service. "Church is over early today." She stood up from the swing when she saw her mother heading their way.

"Shelby, are you all right?" *Mamm* asked when she got within a few feet of them.

Shelby stood up. "Yes, ma'am. I'm sorry. I just needed some fresh air."

Mamm smiled as she put a hand on Shelby's arm. "I'm sure you're still tired from your travels, and I bet you aren't used to getting up so early."

"No. But I'm fine. Really. I'm sorry I left the service early."

"It's no problem. As long as you're all right."

Shelby smiled, but Miriam knew she wasn't all right.

■ ■ ■ ■

It was one o'clock when Miriam parked the buggy in front of their house. Shelby hadn't said anything on the way home, but she really didn't have a chance to. Little John was ribbing Elam about having a crush on thirteen-year-old Sarah King, and Elam spent most of the trip denying the accusation, though they all knew it was true. And Miriam spent the ride thinking about Saul and how she would meet him at the old Zook farm to go fishing soon. She'd only talked to Saul briefly after the service, and they'd confirmed plans. Miriam had also introduced him to Shelby. After they'd finished the meal, there was cleanup, so Miriam didn't see Saul again. She wondered if maybe he'd joined the men in the barn but suspected he'd left right after church, the way he usually did. Most of the younger folks had played volleyball that afternoon. Even Shelby joined in and played on Miriam's team. For a short while, Shelby seemed to be enjoying herself.

Miriam felt bad that she was going to have to leave Shelby this afternoon, but she'd waited so long to spend some time alone with Saul. Surely Shelby could occupy

65

herself for a couple of hours.

Miriam tethered the horse while Shelby excused herself to hurry to the bathroom, and Elam and John took off toward the barn.

She was walking up to the house when her mother came down the porch steps and met her in the yard.

"I got the sense that Shelby is upset. Did she tell you what's wrong?" *Mamm* wiped her forehead as she spoke, her eyes showing concern.

"She's upset about her parents getting a divorce." Miriam didn't feel the need to tell her mother any more than that right now.

"Hmm . . . Well, you stay close to her. Her mother didn't tell me much about what happened there, but I want us to be her family right now, help her any way we can." *Mamm* turned and started back to the house.

Miriam wasn't surprised that *Mamm* had agreed to take Shelby in. Her mother was known to care for others in their community who were in a bad way or just needed a place to rest. And Shelby was family — a distant cousin perhaps, but still family.

Miriam cleared her thoughts and returned to the subject at hand. *"Mamm?"*

Her mother turned around. *"Ya?"*

Miriam caught up to her before she

reached the porch. "Actually, I'm going to go meet Saul Fisher. We're going to go fishing at the old Zook farm. But I won't be gone for more than a couple of hours."

Her mother scowled, then softened her expression. "That's fine. You and Shelby have fun." *Mamm* turned again to head to the house.

What? She skipped across the yard to catch up with her mother again. "But, *Mamm* . . . I was going to go meet Saul by myself, and —"

Mamm turned around. "Why?"

"Why what?"

"Why do you need to meet Saul by yourself?"

Miriam took a deep breath, then let it out slowly as she shrugged. "I — we — it's like . . ."

Mamm put her hands on her hips and let out a sigh. "Miriam, your cousin just arrived yesterday, and I will not have you leaving her just yet."

So I have to babysit her? "But, *Mamm* . . ."

"No, Miriam. You take Shelby with you, or don't go at all." *Mamm* held up her first finger. "And no arguing." She turned to leave, and for the first time, Miriam considered how having Shelby here would alter her own choices.

■ ■ ■ ■

It was a half hour later when Miriam told Shelby about the fishing trip. They were upstairs in Miriam's room because Shelby said she wanted to change blouses. Shelby emerged from the bathroom wearing a brown T-shirt with a slogan for Texas barbeque on it. Miriam agreed that Shelby's choice would be better for fishing than her pretty yellow blouse.

"Aren't you going to change clothes?" Shelby seemed in a better mood since Miriam had mentioned the fishing adventure, so Miriam tried to be happy that her cousin was going with her to meet Saul.

"I already did."

"But you're still in a dress. Aren't you allowed to wear anything else?"

"I changed from my nice Sunday dress to this older, worn one."

Miriam couldn't help but notice the way Shelby's jeans and T-shirt showed off her curves, and for the first time in her life, Miriam wished she had her own blue jeans and T-shirt to wear.

"I love to go fishing. I used to go all the time with my dad, but . . ." Shelby sighed. "Anyway, thank you for inviting me."

"Sure. We'll have a *gut* time." Miriam felt a tad guilty for not wanting Shelby to go, but she'd try to make up for it by making sure her cousin had fun.

Saul maneuvered his buggy down the dirt road that led to the abandoned Zook farm. Brown and green weeds flanked the path, and in the distance stood the white clapboard house, its paint chipped from neglect. Part of the white picket fence surrounding the front yard was down, and several cows meandered through the yard as if it was a pasture. It was a sad sight, and Saul recalled the times he'd played with the Zook kids in that yard. But when Amos, the youngest of the Zook children, got cancer six years ago, the family had relocated to a place where there was a fancy medical center that could take better care of him. The property had sold right away to a local *Englisch* man who didn't care anything about restoring the farmhouse. He'd purchased the land just to run cattle on, but at least he'd given permission for them to fish in the pond whenever they wanted. Saul rarely saw the owner of the property and figured he must just come to check on the cows from time to time. It was hard on the eyes to see the house in such disrepair. Saul wondered whatever happened to Amos Zook, if he had been cured of the cancer.

He did a double take when he edged closer and saw two buggies near the pond. Saul was pretty sure one of them was Miriam's. He strained to see, and his chest tightened when he saw Jesse Dienner standing next to Miriam. And who was the other woman? As he got closer, he recognized the other woman to be Miriam's cousin whom he'd met at church.

Saul tensed even more when he thought about the way Jesse had lingered around Miriam earlier in the day. It was the only reason he stayed around after the service and gathered with the men in the barn — where Jesse should have been. Twice he'd poked his head out and saw Jesse in the yard with Miriam while she picked up glasses from the tables outside. He knew plenty well that jealousy was a sin, but seeing the two of them laughing and talking had sent his heart to racing. Saul knew that once he left, it was just a matter of time before Miriam settled on one of the many interested fellows in their district. Probably Jesse. He was a fine man, and he would make a good husband for Miriam. But, right or wrong, Saul wanted one summer with Miriam. And he knew she wanted it too, even if she didn't know that he would be leaving her in late August or early September. He cringed for a moment about the betrayal, but then he got a glimpse of Miriam's smile and knew he couldn't stop himself.

He stepped out of the buggy. "I see we have lots of company." He forced a smile as he tethered his horse to a nearby tree.

Jesse smiled. "*Gut* thing I stopped by the Raber place to return a platter Miriam's *mudder* left this morning. Otherwise I wouldn't have known that Miriam and her cousin were meeting you here to go fishing." Jesse chuckled. "Guess you were going to keep these two pretty *maeds* all to yourself."

"He didn't know I was bringing Shelby," Miriam said in a shy voice.

Good. Now Jesse knows this was supposed to have been a date. At least they could pair up — Saul and Miriam and Jesse and Shelby.

"Well, I'm glad you did." Jesse smiled, and Saul thought again about how Miriam would probably end up with Jesse, but for today, maybe Miriam's *Englisch* cousin could keep him occupied. She was a pretty girl, even if she was a bit thin.

Saul figured most women thought Jesse was handsome. He was tall and broad like

71

Saul, but his face was perfect. Perfect smile. Perfect teeth. And Jesse had never been in any kind of trouble.

Saul reached up and touched the scar that ran along his chin, then he ran his tongue along his not-so-straight front teeth. He disliked the fact that he felt inferior around Jesse just because of the man's looks. Besides, Saul knew he had gotten the scar on his chin in an honorable way, even if fist-fights were not allowed. But he'd seen the man nab Mrs. Perkin's purse. The elderly *Englisch* woman attended quilting parties with his mother, and she was a nice lady who didn't deserve to have her bag taken. The thief turned out to be almost more than Saul could handle. He'd gotten in one good punch before Saul stopped him. Then Bishop Ebersol had reprimanded Saul for his actions. Again.

"I went by my *haus* and picked up a couple of fishing poles." Jesse held up two cane poles.

"I brought three," Saul said as he reached into the back of his buggy. "I brought an extra one in case something happened to one of the other ones. So we have plenty."

Miriam smiled and batted her eyes at Saul, which caused him to once again go weak in the knees. "I brought my *own* pole," she said smugly. "It's my lucky fishing pole, and I catch fish every time I use it."

Saul couldn't take his eyes from hers for a moment. He recalled the way he'd pushed back a strand of her hair the day before. A vision he couldn't seem to shake, nor did he want to.

"Miriam, why don't you and me walk to the other side of the pond? We'll spread out a little." Jesse smiled his perfect smile, and Saul felt his temperature rise.

"Or . . . why don't we make this a competition, girls against the boys?" Shelby moved closer to Miriam. "Let's see who can catch the most fish."

"We don't usually compete against each other," Miriam said to her cousin. "Remember when we played volleyball after church? We didn't keep score."

Shelby looked toward the ground, her cheeks reddening, and Saul felt a little bad for her. "No one has to know," he said as he raised a brow playfully.

"Leave it to you, Saul." Jesse grinned, but Saul knew that his friend was hinting that he was always the one to break the rules. And maybe that was true. Another reason why he didn't belong here.

"But I'm in, if the girls are," Jesse added.

Miriam smiled. "I say let's do it." She

latched onto her cousin's arm, and they started to walk to the other side of the pond.

Saul let out a heavy sigh. This was not at all how he planned to spend the afternoon.

4

An hour later Miriam and Shelby gazed across the pond at Saul and Jesse. Miriam shook her head.

"I don't understand. That's at least the tenth fish they've pulled in." Miriam twisted another worm on her hook, then dropped her pole in the water.

"Maybe I'm bad luck." Shelby set her pole on the ground, then sat down on a grassy patch next to it and twisted a strand of hair between her fingers.

Miriam glanced down at her and frowned. "Of course you're not."

"One thing is for sure, though." Shelby put her elbows on her crossed legs, then propped her chin in her hands. "They both have a thing for you."

"A thing?"

"Sure. Clearly this was supposed to be a date for you and Saul." Shelby paused. "And I really shouldn't have come." Miriam started to interrupt, but Shelby went on. "I saw the way both Saul and Jesse looked at you all morning." Miriam was glad to see Shelby smile. "Yep, you're a popular girl."

Miriam knew that Jesse liked her. She'd known that for years. But Saul had always held the key to her heart.

"So Saul is the one you're interested in?" Shelby picked up her pole from where she was sitting, then tossed the line into the murky pond water.

Miriam sighed. *"Ya."* She dipped her pole up and down, hoping the action would attract a fish. "But Jesse is a *gut* man. He will be a fine husband for someone."

"Just not for *you?*" Shelby grinned.

"No. Not for me."

"Well, I think he's hot. Super good-looking."

Miriam glanced down at her cousin who was staring dreamy-eyed across the pond toward the men. While she was glad to see Shelby smiling and seemingly happy, her protective instinct kicked in. "He's going to be baptized in the fall, like I am. Then he'll be ready for marriage to someone in our community."

Shelby didn't say anything but continued to stare across the pond.

"Jesse is one of those who will never leave. Most of the boys here experience their *rum-schpringe* — running-around period — to the fullest. They drink beer, drive cars, and lots of other things I probably don't know about. Not Jesse, though. He's not like that. He'll be baptized, marry, and eventually take over his father's blacksmith shop."

"So he can date anyone while he's running around, right?"

"I — I guess so." This was unsettling to Miriam. She didn't want to marry Jesse, but she didn't want to see him get hurt either. Shelby was beautiful, and Jesse might be tempted to get involved with her — a girl who wasn't Amish and someone who was leaving in three months. Plus, Shelby was having some problems with God, and Miriam knew Jesse had an unquestionable faith.

Shelby set her pole down, then leaned back on her hands. "It doesn't really matter anyway."

"Why do you say that?" Miriam heard the sadness in her cousin's voice again.

"You've probably noticed, I have some issues. Lots of issues. I wouldn't want to subject anyone to that."

Miriam was glad that Shelby didn't want anything romantic with Jesse, but she also wanted her cousin to feel whole and happy.

"I think you will be fine, Shelby."

"How do you know that?"

"Because it's God's will for you to be here. He has a plan for you." Miriam would pray constantly that Shelby's faith would be restored, that she would feel close to God and trust His plan for her.

"I wish I could believe that. I feel like I'm being punished by being sent here." Right away Shelby looked up at Miriam. "I'm sorry. I didn't mean that the way it sounded."

"It's okay. I understand." Miriam couldn't imagine anyone not loving Lancaster County, its quiet people, simple ways, and love of the land and God. But Shelby was an outsider, and Miriam was sure she missed her home in Texas.

"I wish things were different for me." Shelby gazed out over the water with more unhappiness in her voice.

"They can be different. Things change according to God's plan, and we never know what time frame God is on."

"Oh, wow!" Shelby pulled back on her pole as her entire body fell backward onto the grass. "I've got one! And it's huge! Oh my!"

Miriam dropped her own pole when she saw Shelby struggling. She helped her cousin pull as they both scooted backward on their behinds, pulling the cane pole and line through the tall weeds.

"I've never worked so hard to pull a fish out of this pond!" Miriam screamed as they watched the enormous fish surface. "Keep pulling!" They both kept hold of the pole and stood up. Miriam could see Saul and Jesse out of the corner of her eye running along the bank.

"We have to get it in before they get here and try to help us." Shelby was laughing, then Miriam started laughing, and together the girls pulled the fish onto the bank right before the men arrived, breathless — and speechless.

Shelby and Miriam looked on as Saul carefully picked up the large catfish. He held it by the mouth at arm's length and shook his head. "Can't believe a *girl* caught this." He chuckled as he tossed it back into the pond. Shelby was proud of her catch and wished she had a camera with her. She hadn't even bothered to bring hers from home, and Miriam told her that the Amish people didn't take pictures, something to do with their religion.

As the fish met with the water, it immediately disappeared. Shelby pulled the band that held her hair, then picked up the loose strands and twisted it back into a ponytail. "Yep, you boys were beat by a girl." She dropped her hands to her side. "I still say it's a shame not to have a picture."

Saul looked at Jesse. "I don't have a camera with me. Do you?"

Jesse shook his head, but Shelby was confused. She turned to Miriam. "I thought you said that no pictures were allowed."

"We're in our *rumschpringe,* running-around time," Miriam said. "So some people our age have cameras, cell phones, things like that."

"Oh." Shelby raised her brows. "Couldn't we have eaten it? I love fish."

"We throw most of them back." Jesse wiped his hands on his black pants, then looped his thumbs beneath his suspenders. His dark-green shirt brought out his eyes, and Shelby couldn't seem to look away from him. She reminded herself that Jesse liked Miriam, but her cousin had eyes for Saul. "Me and Saul threw ours back too. We'll let them all get bigger," Jesse added.

"Of course you threw yours back." Shelby giggled. "Because none of yours were even close to being as big as ours."

"The contest was to see who could catch the *most* fish," Jesse said, then chuckled.

"And the men are the winners." He stood tall and smiled. "But you girls gave it your best try."

As the four of them stood at the bank's edge, Shelby glanced at Miriam, then at Saul. She'd ruined her cousin's date, so maybe she could make it up to Miriam, and also get to know Jesse Dienner a little better. Jesse carried his fishing pole and a bait bucket to his buggy, and Shelby followed him. As Jesse stowed the items in the back of the buggy, Shelby whispered, "Maybe you could take me home so they could spend some time alone together. I think I sorta barged in on their date."

Jesse grimaced instantly, and Shelby felt foolish to think that she could sway his feelings for Miriam. Miriam was very pretty and one of his own people. But Jesse was the first thing to pique Shelby's interest in a long time. She could knock out two things here, if Jesse would go along with her. Jesse glanced toward Saul and Miriam. They'd edged closer together and were talking. Jesse's scowl hardened, but then he took a deep breath and turned back to Shelby.

"Sure. I can take you home."

They walked back to where Miriam and Saul were standing, and Jesse told them that he was going to give Shelby a ride home.

He didn't offer any additional information, and both Miriam and Saul nodded. Shelby winked at Miriam as she walked away. Her cousin winked back. Shelby hoped it went well for Miriam and Saul, though she didn't understand why Miriam would choose Saul over Jesse. Saul seemed quieter, and he wasn't nearly as good-looking as Jesse. Jesse smiled a lot and was much more outgoing too. But this worked out well for Shelby. She thought Jesse would be a great catch, and Miriam did say that a small percent of the Amish people did leave to go out into the real world. She hopped into the passenger side of Jesse's buggy, anxious to learn more about him on the way back to her cousin's farm.

Miriam helped Saul load the rest of the fishing equipment into the back of his buggy. She had her own ride, so she wasn't sure whether to say good-bye. After an awkward few minutes, Saul asked her if she wanted to go sit on the porch swing. Miriam glanced at the cows grazing in the yard, then up to the porch, which was barren except for the old swing.

"Okay." She followed him through the overgrown yard as he cleared the way and motioned with his arms to clear two cows in their path. He stepped carefully up the creaky wooden steps, then motioned to her with his hand.

"It's a mess but seems safe enough."

Miriam sat down on the small swing built for two. She eased as far to one side as she could, but even then, Saul's leg brushed against hers when he sat down, sending a rush of adrenaline through her body, and she could feel her cheeks reddening.

"That was fun, fishing." She twisted the string on her prayer covering. "Shelby sure was excited to catch that big fish."

Miriam jumped when Saul shifted his weight slightly to face her, pushing his leg against hers. "How long is she here for?"

"For the summer, until August. Her parents got a divorce, and I think she got in some trouble back home." Miriam paused. "But she seems so nice, so I can't imagine what trouble she could have gotten into."

"Is it strange having an *Englisch* girl living with you?" Saul cocked his head to one side. "It's gotta be really different for her here."

Miriam shrugged. "She only arrived yesterday, but it doesn't seem so strange. It probably does to her, though."

Saul's body was still turned toward her, and when she turned her head to face him, there were only a few inches between their faces. His bobbed cut was longer than it should be, his light-brown hair boasting sandy-red highlights and brushing against his brows. Dark eyes stared into hers, and she watched him take a deep breath. *Is he as nervous as I am?*

Saul was lost in Miriam's blue eyes for the few moments that their eyes locked and held, but within seconds she turned away from him. And that was probably a good thing. Saul might have kissed her, and that would be moving too fast for Miriam. Why, after all these years, did she approach him? He could have just slipped away in a few months without hurting her. Saul knew that the right thing to do would be to avoid any more of these private times together, but he feared he didn't have the strength. Even though he'd often seen Miriam watching him, smiling at him, and whispering to her girlfriends when he was around, she always seemed out of reach for him. Miriam was a good girl, perfect for marrying and raising a family here in Lancaster County.

She turned to face him again and opened her mouth to say something. But she quickly snapped her lips together and looked away.

"What?" Her hand was on her leg, and without much thought, he stretched one of his fingers out and touched the top of her hand. "What are you thinking about?" He felt her hand tense beneath his touch.

"I — I don't know."

Saul eased his hand away from hers, and they were both quiet for a few moments.

"Miriam?"

She kept her eyes cast down and bit her lip for a moment. *"Ya?"*

He waited until she looked at him, then rubbed his chin. "Do you want to go on a date with me? I mean, a real date. Maybe to supper . . . and a movie?"

She bit her bottom lip, then grinned. "Sure. I've only been to a movie a couple of times."

"We're in our *rumschpringe.* Better see as many as you can," he said, even though he knew there would be plenty more opportunities in his future.

She faced him, the corner of her mouth curled upward. "I'd like to see a movie with you."

Saul pictured them in a dark movie theater and wondered if they would hold hands. Would he kiss her at the end of the night? "Do you want to go Friday night?"

She frowned. "I can't on Friday. *Mamm* hosts suppers for the tourists on Friday nights, and I'm expected to help."

"Okay," he said, trying not to sound as disappointed as he was. "Maybe some other time."

"When?" Her eyes widened as she faced him, and Saul didn't think he'd wanted to kiss anyone more than right now. He froze for a moment, then blinked his eyes a couple of times and forced himself to look away from her.

"*Mei daed* will expect me to work in the fields, then do chores on Saturday. But I could go Saturday night." He looked back at her. "Think your folks would let you go?"

Miriam dabbed at the sweat beading up on her forehead. Saul wondered how her parents would feel about him taking her to supper and a movie. But most of the teenagers in their district did things normally forbidden by the *Ordnung,* and parents just looked the other way while they were in their *rumschpringe.* This was the time to experience the outside world, but Saul suspected Miriam had never taken full advantage of her freedom.

"I'm sure it will be fine," she finally said, smiling.

Saul felt warm inside as he smiled back at her.

Shelby thanked Jesse for the ride home as

he pulled to a stop in front of Miriam's farmhouse. Jesse had been polite enough, but when Shelby mentioned twice how much she enjoyed going fishing, he never suggested a return trip to the Zook farm. And he talked about Miriam a lot. Shelby didn't even think he realized it. Miriam's name just seemed to slide off his tongue in almost every conversation. Jesse was Amish anyway, so what was the point? But his stunning good looks had been a nice distraction today. For a while this afternoon, she hadn't thought about her parents or Tommy.

She waved to Jesse, then headed across the front yard.

"Where's Miriam?" There was an urgency in Rebecca's voice, and it caught Shelby a little off guard.

"She's still with Saul. I think they wanted to spend some time alone together. I think maybe today was supposed to be a date, but I ruined that for them." She smiled but quickly stopped when Rebecca's eyebrows drew into a deep frown.

"Did Miriam say when she would be home?"

"No, ma'am." Shelby regretted that she had apparently gotten Miriam in trouble. Maybe Amish girls weren't allowed to date. Maybe Shelby shouldn't have used that word. She'd talk to Miriam later when she got home. Besides, she had something to tell Miriam. Something Jesse told her that she didn't think Miriam was going to be happy about.

Rebecca lifted her chin and sighed. "Well, I'm sure she'll be along shortly. Why don't you go in and get yourself a glass of iced tea. Miriam knows to be home to help with supper, so she'll be here soon."

Shelby nodded and slid past Rebecca. She was hot and tired, and a glass of iced tea sounded wonderful.

Rebecca stood in the front yard and watched her husband washing his hands at the pump by the barn. When he was done, he slowly made his way toward her.

"Aaron, Miriam is with Saul Fisher." She clenched her hands at her sides. "And they are alone together."

Her husband took off his straw hat, then ran his sleeve across his forehead. He slowly put his hat back on as he let out a heavy sigh. "*Ach,* we've known this was coming. She's liked that boy for years."

"Aaron, how can you be so calm about this? Saul Fisher has been in more trouble than any other boy in this community." She folded her arms across her chest. "And you heard what Ben said at supper last night, that he heard Saul wasn't going to be baptized."

Her husband lowered his head, then lifted tired eyes to meet hers. "Now, Rebecca, those're just rumors."

Rebecca reached up and pulled a piece of fuzz from Aaron's black beard, speckled with gray. "I don't want her seeing that boy, Aaron." She knew it was wrong to judge another person, but Miriam was her only daughter.

"Rebecca." Aaron put one hand on his hip, then rubbed his forehead with the other. "She's in her *rumschpringe*. Let the *maedel* have some freedoms. We've raised Miriam well. She will make *gut* choices."

"I never said that Miriam shouldn't experience her *rumschpringe*." She sighed with irritation. "It just gives me worry that she might be thinking of dating Saul Fisher." She shook her head. "He's not right for her, Aaron."

"Who are we to decide that, Rebecca?" He sighed, and Rebecca knew her husband was ready to get into the house and have something cold to drink, but worry consumed her.

"We are her parents. That's *who* we are." Rebecca raised her chin and faced off with her husband.

Aaron kissed her on the cheek. "I'm goin' in the house, Rebecca. I'm hot and tired." He eased past her, and she spun around.

"Pray about this, Aaron! I will be."

He didn't turn around but waved an acknowledgment as he made his way up the porch steps.

Rebecca shook her head. Like her husband, she'd known for years that Miriam had a crush on Saul Fisher, but she'd always hoped that her daughter would have the good sense not to get involved with a boy like that. She recalled Miriam's hesitancy to take Shelby with her today, which certainly set off alarms. Now, after hearing what Shelby had to say about Miriam and Saul wanting to be alone, Rebecca felt her stomach clench with worry.

Miriam wished she could sit on the porch swing with Saul well into the evening, but she knew she was already going to be late getting home. *Mamm* wasn't going to be happy if she didn't arrive in time to help with supper.

Saul was a man of few words, but Miriam stayed persistent and eased him into a conversation, and during the past half hour, she'd learned a little bit more about him.

All food related. It was a subject he was passionate about. He was allergic to shellfish, didn't care for whoopee pies, and once ate seven cheeseburgers on a dare from a friend. He also knew how to cook and told her that he could make a better shoofly pie than anyone in the district. She'd stifled a grin more than once as he spoke. *Saul Fisher can cook?*

Miriam remembered that Saul's mother and only sister had died in a buggy accident about five years ago. Since then, Saul had helped his *daed* raise his two younger brothers, and he'd probably learned to cook out of necessity. She couldn't believe how many different things he knew how to prepare, and she found herself sharing some of her secret recipes with him.

"Okay, Saul. I told you how to make cream of carrot soup. Now . . ." Miriam nudged him with her shoulder. "I want to hear about this ultimate grilled cheese sandwich."

Saul chuckled. "No way."

"That's not fair, Saul Fisher. That cream of carrot soup was my great-*mammi's* recipe, and no one in the district knows how to make it but me and *Mamm*."

"Not true. I've had cream of carrot soup before. *Mei mamm* used to make it before

—" He took a deep breath. "Before the accident."

Miriam wasn't sure how much Saul wanted to talk about his mother, and they'd been having so much fun, so she just nodded.

"Fine." He shifted his weight in the swing, turning to face her even more, and grinned. "I'll tell you how to make the ultimate grilled cheese sandwich."

Miriam kept her eyes on his, but she was acutely aware of his knee pressed up against her leg. "*Gut.* Let's hear it."

Saul described preparation of the sandwich as if he was creating a work of art, talking with his hands as he spoke, but Miriam couldn't stay focused on anything but his mouth, his lips. It took everything in her power not to thrust forward and press her mouth to his. *How completely inappropriate!* She blinked a few times to refocus and caught the tail end of his explanation.

"You mix the cream cheese and mayo until creamy, and then you stir in the cheddar, mozzarella, garlic powder, and seasoned salt, and —" Saul stopped midsentence, and his dark-brown eyes locked with hers. "Do you think it's weird that I like to cook?"

Miriam was careful not to blurt out the first thing on her mind, since the truth was she thought it made him a thousand times more attractive. She didn't know any men who could cook, and she found this new information about Saul fascinating. "No, I think it's wonderful that you cook!" She stared into his eyes and pictured the two of them in their own kitchen, cooking together and trying new recipes. It was a very non-Amish scenario, but Miriam had the vision just the same.

Saul's smile broadened. "Well, I like to eat, so I had to learn to cook. After *mei mamm* and Hannah died . . ." His smile faded as he momentarily pulled his eyes from her, then looked back up. "*Mei mammi* used to come cook for us. But then she got sick and wasn't able to come so much." He paused, then rubbed his chin as he spoke. "I just kinda taught myself."

This was the most she'd talked to Saul, and she wasn't ready for it to end. But her mother would start to stew if she didn't get home soon. "I guess I need to go," she said as she watched the sun begin to set.

"*Ya.* Me too." He smiled at her as they both stood from the swing. "Guess what everyone at my *haus* will be having for supper?" He rubbed his hand in a circular motion on his stomach.

Miriam giggled. "I'm guessing ultimate

grilled cheese sandwiches."

Saul nodded, then they both headed down the creaky porch steps. "Watch that cow patty." He latched onto her arm and guided her around it, then let go and waved an arm at two cows in the yard. "Go on, now! You don't need to be in the front yard."

"This is so sad," Miriam said as they eased their way through the overgrowth in the yard. "This place was so pretty at one time."

"*Ya.* I know." Saul shook his head as he let Miriam go ahead of him through the rickety gate at the end of the sidewalk. He opened the door of Miriam's buggy, and she climbed in. Then Saul untied the reins and handed them to her.

"This was fun today." Miriam was sad to see it end, but she would have Saturday to look forward to.

"*Ya.*" Saul stuffed his hands in his pockets. "I guess I'll pick you up on Saturday. Seven o'clock?"

Miriam nodded but then said, "Why don't I meet you in town? On Saturday, I run errands in the afternoon, so I'll already be on Lincoln Highway. I could meet you at Yoder's Pantry. They stay open late." She paused, wondering how her parents were going to feel about her going on a date with Saul. "Can we make it eight o'clock?" She crinkled her nose, then grinned. "It's Saturday night."

"Sure."

She pulled back on the reins and clicked her tongue until her horse started to back up the spring buggy. She'd backed up a few feet when Saul walked briskly up to her.

"Miriam, wait!"

She stopped, raised her brows. *"Ya?"*

Saul cocked his head to one side and stroked his stubbly chin. "What made you come talk to me yesterday at the creek?" He captured her eyes and gazed at her, one side of his mouth hinting at a grin. "I mean, after all these years."

Miriam bit her lip and pulled her eyes from his. Then she looked back at him and held his gaze. "Don't you think it was time?"

His grin eased into a big smile. *"Ya.* I guess it was."

Miriam started backing the horse up again, and Saul walked to his own spring buggy. Then she stopped again. "Saul?"

He turned, took a few steps toward her. *"Ya?"*

Miriam brushed loose strands of hair away from her face, then found Saul's eyes. "Would you have come and talked to me?"

Saul lifted his eyes to hers. "No."

Miriam's heart thudded with disappointment, and she hung her head. A moment later Saul's hand was gently lifting her chin until her eyes met his again. "I'm not good enough for you, Miriam Raber." His finger brushed her cheek as he spoke in the raspy whisper that always sent her senses soaring.

She reached up, put her hand on his, then closed her eyes. "I think you are perfect for me, Saul Fisher."

Saul prayed all the way home. He knew what he was doing was as wrong as it could be, but nothing had ever felt more right to him. Being around Miriam, actually talking to her, getting to know her — it made his heart flip in his chest. But getting too close to her would only hurt them both in the end. And poor Miriam was going into this blind. Saul knew he would leave in August for the *Englisch* world, forgoing baptism and a future here in Paradise. When he visited Pittsburgh a few months ago, he never could have imagined how that trip would change his life. He'd answered the ad for an apprentice chef with little hope of landing his dream job. But soon after his trip and meeting with the owner of the restaurant, the letter came . . .

He'd saved enough money, and his brothers were old enough to fend for themselves.

He'd taught them as much as he could. At fifteen and thirteen, Ruben and James both knew how to prepare some basic meals, tend to the fields, and handle the tools in the barn. Ruben was turning out to be a fine carpenter, and now that James was graduated from school, Saul knew he would find his calling too.

He tried to ease his guilt through prayer. It was bad enough that he would be leaving his father and brothers, but now he would be leaving Miriam too. Their feelings for each other would only grow if they dated through the summer, setting them both up for heartache. But he'd worked so hard to save his money, and *Daed* was on the mend. Surely everyone would be all right when he left.

Miriam would go on to find someone who deserved her. She'd been raised to be the perfect Amish *fraa,* and some lucky man would win her heart after Saul was gone. He promised himself that he would not break her heart. They would have fun, enjoy each other, but not get too close. But if that was true, then why couldn't he stop wishing he could just kiss her, hold her in his arms one time . . .

He pulled up his driveway. Ruben and James were sitting on the front porch, dangling their feet over the side. Ruben had his head in his hands, but James looked up when Saul pulled closer. His brother swiped at his eyes, and Saul knew immediately what was going on. This scene had played out a hundred times, but Saul thought they were past this. He walked across the yard and stood at the edge of the porch. Both his brothers locked eyes with him. Saul waited.

"It's worse than ever before," Ruben said as he stifled tears. "Go see for yourself."

5

Miriam's mother was more than a little mad when Miriam showed up too late to help with supper. *Mamm* had barely spoken to her, and Miriam was relieved when it was time to head upstairs for bed.

"I hope I didn't get you in trouble, Miriam. Are you not allowed to date?" Shelby fluffed the pillow behind her.

"*Ya*, I'm allowed to date." Miriam ran her brush the length of her hair. "I just think *Mamm* would prefer that I date Jesse." She rolled her eyes.

"Well, I gotta admit, I'm a little confused about that too. Jesse is so hot, and I could tell on our ride home how much he likes you. Your name came up in every conversation."

Miriam put the brush in the drawer, then got comfy in her bed. "Jesse is very nice, and *ya*, he's handsome. But Saul . . ." She smiled with recollections of their time alone sitting on the porch at the Zook farm. "He's just special."

Shelby sat up, hung her legs over the side of the bed, and faced Miriam. "He does seem nice, but . . ."

Miriam sat up, turned toward Shelby, and crossed her legs beneath her. "What is it?"

Her cousin looked down for a moment, then met eyes with Miriam. "Jesse said Saul is leaving here, that he's not going to be baptized." She paused. "And isn't that what your brother said too?"

Miriam was tired of these rumors. "I don't know why people are saying that. I'm sure it's not true." She leaned back on her palms. "Otherwise he wouldn't have asked me out on a date for this Saturday night."

"I take it this will be your first official date with him?" Shelby smiled.

"It will be my first official date with *anyone.*"

Shelby bolted upright. "You're kidding me, right?"

Mirriam giggled. "You know, you say that a lot. But no, I'm not kidding. I've been waiting for Saul." She wrapped herself in a hug. "He's the one. I've always known that."

Shelby reached for her pink book and pen on the nightstand. "I just wouldn't want to see you get hurt." Her cousin leaned over

100

the side of the bed and reached into her purse. Miriam watched her retrieve a key, then twist it in the tiny lock. She dropped the silver ring that held the key back into her purse.

Miriam lit the lantern. "I won't get hurt. Saul's not going anywhere. He belongs here." She smiled at Shelby as she leaned forward. "Here with *me.*"

"Just be careful. Guys can be total jerks, and just when you think you've found the right one, they go and break your heart." Shelby opened the small book in her lap.

"Not Saul. He won't break my heart." Miriam hadn't always been right about everything, but this was one thing she was sure of. She saw the way he looked into her eyes today. "I'm going to go to sleep. You should too. Tomorrow is Monday, wash day. It always makes for a long day."

Shelby sighed. "I guess we get up again at four thirty tomorrow?"

"Every day." Miriam smiled as she rolled onto her side to avoid the soft glow of the lantern.

Shelby pressed the pen to the paper.

Dear Diary,
  Today I went fishing with my cousin

101

Miriam and two of her friends. It was the first time that I forgot about Mom and Dad and Tommy for a while. But now, as I try to calm my thoughts and get some sleep, images of the past are all over the place. I miss Tommy so much. And I'm so angry at Mom and Dad for the choices they made — choices that landed me here in Amish Country where I don't have any friends.

Shelby wiped sweat from her forehead, then turned the battery-operated fan more in her direction. She leaned closer to the breeze and thought about her friends back home.

I guess maybe they weren't true friends after all. I'm not sure I want or need any friends anymore. But I do like Miriam, even though I don't want to get too close to her. First of all, she's different. She's eighteen years old and she's just now going on her first date this Saturday night. Weird. Or maybe it's kind of sweet in a way. I don't know.

I met a guy. An Amish guy. His name is Jesse, and he is the hottest man I've seen in a long time. He seems to like Miriam a lot, but Miriam likes a guy named Saul. So, I don't know. We'll see what happens. But Jesse is easy on the eyes and seems so nice. Gotta watch it though — I don't want to get too close to him either.

Everyone I get close to hurts me. Even God.

Saul closed the door to his father's room after helping him into bed. *Daed* was snoring the minute his head landed on the pillow and before Saul even had a chance to pull his father's boots off. His father would wake up in the morning with all his clothes on and know what happened. But no one would mention it. That's the way it always was. Zeb Fisher was a kind, gentle man when he wasn't drinking. He loved the Lord, and he loved his sons. Maybe he'd loved their mother and Hannah more. Saul wasn't sure. But that's when the drinking started, after the accident, and it had gotten worse every year. Until three months ago. *Daed* just stopped drinking in the evening hours. *What made him start again?*

Ruben and James were cleaning up the mess when Saul walked into the den, the smell of red wine hovering in the air around them.

"What set him off this time?" Saul asked

as he made his way to a spilled bottle of wine. He picked it up and recognized the brand to be none other than their own. For as long as Saul could remember, his father made his own wine from the muscadine grapes that grew along the back of their property. They grew wild and abundantly, and once Saul had taken a machete to the flourishing vines, hoping to banish them forever. But they came back even fuller the next year, along with *Daed's* appetite for the drink.

Saul glanced around the room at the toppled coffee table, overturned rocking chair, and slivers of glass surrounding the brick outlay of the fireplace. As he grew closer, he recognized the stems on the broken glasses at his feet. He squatted down and picked up one of his mother's favorite glasses that had remained housed in her china cabinet until tonight — glasses that she'd never used, a gift from an *Englisch* friend. *Mamm* said they were too fancy, but she kept them displayed so that her friend, Ida, would see them when she came to visit.

Ruben edged closer. "I don't know, Saul. Me and James were cleaning things up in the barn, and we heard *Daed* yelling and glass breaking. I went in, but when I saw the fire in his eyes again, I went back to the barn." Ruben hung his head. "I wasn't sure what to do. I told James I thought we should stay in the barn until *Daed* passed out." He looked back up at Saul. "I ain't ever seen him throwing things like that, and I just . . ."

Saul was glad his father had passed out on the couch, instead of just falling down on the floor. It was so much harder to get him off the floor. "You did the right thing. When he gets to that point, there's no reckoning with him, and he usually passes out not long after that."

Ruben picked up a piece of glass. "*Mamm* loved these glasses, even though she never would use them."

Saul picked up the two green blinds that were in the middle of the floor, window coverings ripped from the walls. He shook his head. "*Daed's* been doing so *gut*. I thought we were done with this."

James brushed by Saul and Ruben carrying a plate that he'd picked up from the other side of the room. Spaghetti and meatballs left over from the night before covered the whitewashed wall to the right of the fireplace. "I don't know how this plate didn't break," James said as he moved toward the kitchen.

"Well, we best get this cleaned up and try to make things look as back to normal as we can." Saul shook his head as he went to the mudroom to get a broom.

When he returned, he started sweeping up broken glass while Ruben scrubbed tomato sauce from the wall. He dreaded the next morning. They'd all eat breakfast together and no one would say anything. *Daed* would eat very little and head to the fields early, then he'd stay out later than usual, as if the extra hard work would in some way make up for what he'd done. He'd know what happened, even if he didn't remember all the details. Saul thanked God that his father had never laid a hand on any of them when he was in a drunken rage.

"It ain't ever gonna be normal," Ruben said as he carried a white rag soaked in red to the kitchen.

Saul sighed. He'd been counting on it being normal. Finally. So that he could leave in August knowing that his brothers wouldn't have to go through this in his absence. Ruben might be able to handle it, but James still cried after *Daed* had one of his fits like tonight.

Two hours later Saul set the lantern on his nightstand, then sat on the edge of his bed. He still needed to take a shower, but he'd told Ruben and James that they could bathe first. It was going to be late when they all finally got to sleep. He opened the drawer to his nightstand and pulled out the white envelope hidden beneath his Bible. He didn't need to read the letter since he knew it by heart. Instead, he opened the Bible and read for a few minutes but decided he needed some direct communion with God. He closed his eyes and bowed his head.

Dear Lord, please help me to help him.

Saul opened his eyes and questioned his plea. Was it selfish to want his father to be a well man so that he could leave and pursue his dreams?

He closed the Bible, set it on the bed next to him, then pulled the letter from the white envelope. As he moved the lantern closer to him, the words danced on the page in the dimly lit room.

Dear Saul,

I would like to extend a formal invitation for you to join me at my new restaurant in Pittsburgh. Our meeting confirmed your willingness to learn more about what it takes to be a chef, and you asked some fine questions. The dishes you prepared were delicious and distinct, and I enjoyed some of the other recipes you left with me too. Your pumpkin cinnamon rolls with caramel frosting were amazing, and the recipe you referred to as Heavenly Chicken was — indeed — heavenly. The ground ginger was a great touch. I look forward to tasting your traditional Amish recipes — shoofly pie, whoopee pies, and creamed celery.

I would like to offer you the position of apprentice chef if you are still interested in working with me. As we discussed while you were here, my bistro will open for business in September.

Warmest regards,
Phil Ballentine,
Owner and Head Chef,
Ballentine's Bistro

Miriam spent the week trying to get Shelby used to the family schedule, but her cousin still couldn't seem to get up and going in the morning. She'd thought that after almost a week, maybe Shelby would come help with breakfast, and today would be a busy day. Like Mondays, there was always more to do on Fridays because *Mamm* hosted supper for tourists. Their *Englisch* friend Barbie always suggested *Mamm's* suppers to the guests at her bed-and-breakfast, and tonight eight people were coming.

Miriam fought her irritation with Shelby as she marched up the stairs to tell her breakfast was ready. As expected, her cousin was still in bed with the covers over her head. Miriam didn't know how Shelby didn't burn up underneath those covers this time of year. She put one hand on her hip, shined the flashlight toward the bed, and prepared to speak loudly to her cousin and remind her that there was much to do today. But as she opened her mouth to speak, she noticed Shelby's pink book on the night-stand, her pen resting between the opened pages. She moved the flashlight toward it.

Every night Shelby would pull her book from the drawer, then pull the tiny key from her purse. It was always about that time when Miriam would roll over, face away from the lantern light, and fall asleep. Each night the book was tucked safely back in the top drawer. Locked. Miriam only knew this because she kept her hairbrush inside the drawer too, along with a spare *kapp* and a scarf for trips to the barn. There was only one drawer in the nightstand, so she couldn't help but notice.

From where she was standing, she could see blue ink scrawled across the pages, and there was not a doubt in her mind that Shelby kept the book locked for a reason.

But Miriam could practically feel the Devil himself pushing her closer to the book as she tiptoed around Shelby's bed toward the nightstand. She held her breath for a moment, heard Shelby lightly snoring, then leaned her head down and pointed the flashlight toward the words on the page.

Dear Diary,

I'm so lonely. My cousins are doing their best to make me feel welcome, but I can tell that I just don't fit in here. Not surprising. Nothing is the same as back home, and I hate getting up at four thirty in the morning. I'm not missing Tommy as much. Now I'm just mad at him for hurting me. But I'm even madder at my parents. Neither one of them have called to check on me or anything. What kind of family is that? My cell phone has been dead for days because there is no electricity, another thing that I could never get used to. But there is a phone in the barn and Mom and Dad could have called. They've just written me out of their lives and moved on. Hope they're both happy.

Since I don't talk to God anymore, this journal is all I have. I wish I could talk to Miriam, but I don't think she'd understand any of this. We're just too different. Her parents are different. This whole family is different. In some ways, that's good, I guess. They are all nice to each other. There's no screaming or yelling.

I miss television. I wish I had a car here. I wish I had someone to love me.

Miriam didn't move or breathe when Shelby twisted beneath the covers in the bed. Then she eased her way back to the open doorway of the bedroom. She felt guilty for reading Shelby's private thoughts, but she immediately began to think of ways to help her cousin. *Doesn't she realize that God loves her?* Miriam knew that if Shelby didn't find her way back to God, it would be hard for her to come to peace with the other things bothering her. She tried to put herself in Shelby's shoes, although it was hard. *What if my parents didn't live together? What if I was cast out among the* Englisch *to live? What if my parents didn't check on me? What if Saul broke my heart?* Maybe it was okay that Shelby didn't get up early to help make breakfast.

"Shelby." Miriam shined the light at the foot of her bed. "Time to get up and eat. Breakfast is ready."

Her cousin pulled the covers back but didn't open her eyes. "Okay. I'm coming."

Miriam glanced at the book on the nightstand, then turned and left the room. By the time she returned downstairs, everyone was seated at the table.

"Is everything okay?" *Mamm* spread her napkin on her lap. "Is Shelby coming?"

Ben let out a heavy sigh. "She's always late to breakfast."

"Hush, Ben," *Mamm* whispered as they all waited.

Miriam glanced at her father, his arms folded across his chest, then at each of her brothers who were eyeing the eggs, sausage, and biscuits. *Come on, Shelby.*

After a few moments, Miriam said in a whisper, "I think Shelby's sad, and I think she misses her family."

Mamm nodded. "I'm sure she does." She sat taller and gave her head a taut nod. "This morning everyone at this table is going to do our best to include Shelby in conversation and make her feel like part of this family. Understood?" *Mamm* glanced around the table.

"Elam can tell some of his *dumm* jokes." Ben chuckled.

"No joke telling at the breakfast table." Their father unfolded his arms and stretched. "Where is that *maedel?*"

"Sorry I'm late." Shelby scurried into the kitchen with sleepy eyes, her hair still tangled. She eased onto the bench next to Miriam.

"It's no problem, dear. Let's bow our heads."

Miriam was sure the prayer was the shortest on record. They always took a cue from their father. When he cleared his throat and lifted his head, so did everyone else. This morning *Daed* must have just said, "Thank You, Lord, let's eat."

Shelby dished out a small spoonful of eggs, one piece of sausage, and half a biscuit onto her plate. No wonder Shelby was so thin. She didn't eat enough. Miriam helped herself to a much larger helping of eggs, two pieces of sausage, and an entire biscuit.

Everyone was quiet for a few moments, but then Miriam was surprised when Shelby helped herself to more eggs. Barely a minute or two later, she spooned even more eggs onto her plate. Miriam realized that this was the first morning her mother had made what little John called "special eggs."

"These eggs are different, Rebecca." Shelby swallowed, then filled her fork again. "I love them."

"*Ya,* they're different all right," Elam said

with a smile.

"Why, *danki,* Shelby." *Mamm* smiled, then shot a warning look to everyone at the table. "Let Shelby enjoy her eggs." She turned to Shelby. "This is the most I've seen you eat since you arrived."

Shelby nodded with a mouthful.

Ben put his hand over his mouth to stifle a giggle. Miriam knew why he was laughing, and she was fighting the urge to grin as well. Most *Englisch* folks didn't care for *Mamm's* secret ingredient in her "special eggs," but Shelby sure did.

Little John leaned forward across the table, his eyes wide with wonder as he spoke. "You're the first *Englisch* person I ever saw who liked head cheese."

Miriam held her breath as she watched Shelby stop chewing. "What?" Shelby asked with a mouthful.

"Mmm." John rubbed his small belly as he talked. "I seen *Mamm* make that cheese too. She takes them hogs' heads and scrapes 'em clean, then she pokes out their eyes and dumps 'em in a kettle —"

"John! I'm sure Shelby doesn't need to know how I make my special eggs." *Mamm* forced a smile, but the damage was done.

No one moved as they watched Shelby slap a hand across her mouth, which was filled with those special eggs.

Mamm let out a heavy sigh, then cut her eyes at Miriam's youngest brother. "See what you've done." Then she turned to Shelby and pointed at the trash can. "Go ahead, Shelby, dear. You won't be the first."

Shelby bolted from the chair, ran to the trash can under the sink, and spit *Mamm's* special eggs into the garbage. When she looked up at everyone, the expression on her face was totally blank.

Miriam couldn't help it; she burst out laughing, followed by her brothers. Then Shelby started laughing so hard that she bent over at the waist, and Miriam was sure her cousin was going to cry.

Her mother just shook her head and grinned. *Daed* shook his head too, but he smiled from ear to ear.

This was probably the last thing *Mamm* had on her mind to cheer Shelby up, but Shelby laughed longer and harder than any of them.

Which made her seem just like part of the family.

It was late morning when Rebecca sent Miriam and Shelby to the market to pick up a few things she needed to prepare supper that evening. Despite plans to go earlier in the week, this was Shelby's first time to visit the town of Bird-In-Hand, so she scanned her surroundings while Miriam parked the buggy.

"I'm sorry I haven't brought you sight-seeing before now. This isn't where I would normally go shopping for groceries, but it's a fun place I thought you might like to see. The Bird-In-Hand Farmers Market is popular with the tourists." Miriam pulled back on the reins once she had the buggy parked next to another one in the parking lot. "We won't have much time today, but I promise soon we'll take a day so I can show you around."

Shelby stepped out of the buggy, then looked across the street from where they were parked. Bakeries and gift shops lined streets filled with bustling tourists. She walked around to where Miriam was tethering the horse and waited.

"Ready?" Miriam smiled, then took a few steps across the parking lot. Shelby followed, but she stopped abruptly when Miriam did. Her cousin raised her hands to her face, then sidestepped four women whose cameras flashed in their direction. Shelby felt unusually protective. Miriam had told her earlier in the week that they didn't take or pose for pictures. It was actually against their religion, for reasons Shelby didn't totally understand. Miriam also told her that most of the non-Amish people knew this, but that they took pictures anyway.

"Don't get *her* in the picture," said a woman with dark curls, toting several bags and pointing at Shelby. "She's not Amish."

Shelby glared at the women as she and Miriam passed by them and continued across the parking lot. She waited until they were out of earshot from the women, then turned to Miriam. "Doesn't that aggravate you?"

"Huh?" Miriam crinkled her nose.

Shelby had noticed throughout the week that Miriam's entire family had a limited vocabulary. "Doesn't that make you *mad*? People always snapping pictures and staring."

Miriam shrugged as they neared the entrance of the market. "No. We're used to it."

"Well, I think it's rude."

Miriam grinned. "I didn't say we liked it. We're just used to it." Miriam held the door open and let Shelby walk ahead of her. Then her cousin pulled out a handwritten list that Rebecca had given them. "It's a short list. Normally we go to Zimmermann's grocery store in the town of Intercourse. We'll go there next week to do our heavy shopping."

Shelby eased down the aisles with Miriam, where Amish and non-Amish vendors on both sides sold quilts, dolls, jewelry, baked items, canned vegetables, jams, jellies, and a hodgepodge of other things. Shelby could stay there all day looking and shopping, she thought. She pulled her purse up on her shoulder and remembered the small amount of money she had to last her for three months. Not enough to do any real shopping. She eyed a jewelry rack to her left, silver earrings and matching necklaces. Then she breathed in the aroma of freshly baked goods and decided that if she splurged, it would be on something to eat. Something safe — without head cheese in it. She grinned at the recollection. Her parents would have come unglued if she'd spit food into the trash and certainly not laughed about it. Shelby loved the laughter in Miriam's house.

Most of the people shopping were non-Amish, she noticed. She also took note of two men walking her way. Nice-looking guys about her age. For some reason Jesse popped into her head, but the vision vanished when one of the young men mumbled something in Pennsylvania *Deitsch* to Miriam as they walked by. Her cousin scowled but didn't say anything.

"Why were they speaking in Pennsylvania *Deitsch?* They weren't Amish." Shelby turned around in time to see the men round the corner to the next aisle.

Miriam reached into a large wicker basket on a nearby counter and pulled out a large bag of homemade noodles, then blew a loose strand of hair that had fallen across her cheek. "No, they're not Amish. They're just *dumm.*"

Shelby's jaw dropped momentarily. This was the first time she'd heard her cousin speak harshly of another. "What did they say?"

"*Schee beh.*" Miriam shook her head, then started walking again. "It means nice legs, and non-Amish boys and some of the younger men say that to us. I don't know who first taught them to say that in Pennsylvania *Deitsch,* but it stuck." She shook her head. "We hear it all the time."

Miriam stopped abruptly, almost dropping the bag of noodles.

"What's wrong?"

Her cousin spun around. "Hurry, let's go the other way."

Shelby looked over her shoulder. There was a man about her father's age holding hands with a pretty woman with blond hair, and there were also three women huddled together by one of the jewelry racks.

"Who are you avoiding?"

They both rounded the corner, and once they were halfway down the next aisle, Miriam stopped and took a deep breath. "That was my *Onkel* Ivan and his . . ." She scowled as she lifted her chin. "His *Englisch* girlfriend, Lucy Turner."

"Oh. The *bad* uncle." Shelby pressed her lips together. "Want me to go pull that woman's hair or something? Then I could kick your uncle in the shin."

Miriam's eyes grew wild and round. "We don't do things like that, Shelby!" She spoke in a harsh whisper.

She was so serious that Shelby couldn't help but laugh. "Miriam, I'm kidding."

Miriam grinned. "*Ya,* well . . . I wasn't sure." They slowly started walking again. "I've only seen *Onkel* Ivan once since he's been back. It was in a restaurant, but he didn't see me. I almost didn't recognize him. He looks different now." She faced Shelby with squinted eyes. "We're supposed to avoid him, and I didn't want it to be awkward."

"Where's your aunt?"

"*Aenti* Katie Ann is in Colorado with some other family members."

"Did that woman who was with your uncle break them up?"

Miriam sighed. "I think so."

Miriam paid for everything with the money her mother had given her, then looped the small bag over her wrist. They were almost out the door when she heard her name. She recognized the voice and slowly turned around.

Uncle Ivan eased ahead of Lucy and gazed down at Miriam with soft gray eyes, his lips parted slightly in a smile. His tan trousers were held up with a black belt instead of suspenders. His short-sleeved shirt was bright yellow, not dark brown, blue, or green, like she was used to seeing him wear. He seemed thinner and different in more ways than just his appearance. He seemed to stand taller, almost . . . proud. It was unsettling to see him this way, since pride was to be avoided, and it worsened as Lucy cozied up to his side and looped her arm through his.

She'd been praying for her uncle to see the wrong in his ways and return to the church. But based on this new look, she didn't feel hopeful.

Lucy's hair was so blond that it was almost white, and her wavy locks rested on her shoulders. She wore blue jeans that hugged her body in a way that made the pants look much too small, and her tight white blouse was cut low on her chest, so low that Miriam felt uncomfortable. Her pink lipstick matched the beaded belt around her waist.

"Wie bischt, mei maedel?" At the sound of his voice, memories filled Miriam's mind, but her heart beat with regret over Uncle Ivan's choices. Lucy scowled, as if maybe she didn't like him speaking their native dialect.

"I'm *gut, Onkel* Ivan." Miriam fought the tremble in her voice as she glanced at Lucy. "Hello, Lucy."

They'd all known the *Englisch* woman for years. Lucy's mouth turned up at one corner. "Hello, Miriam. Who is your friend?"

Miriam looked at Shelby, whose arms were folded across her chest, her chin lifted higher than usual. Her cousin spoke before Miriam had a chance to. "I'm Shelby," she said as she eyed Lucy with a critical squint. She looked back at Miriam. "We're late. Don't we need to go?"

"Uh, *ya.* We do."

Whatever pride Miriam thought she saw moments before seemed to fade from her uncle's expression. His eyelids drooped, and his shoulders slumped somewhat. He rubbed his shaven chin, and Miriam wondered if he was thinking about the times they'd spent together, regretting that he could no longer be a part of her life. *Onkel* Ivan was the first person to take her fishing when she was young, and they'd continued going as often as they could up until he left for Colorado. She'd missed those times together since he'd been back in Paradise. He locked eyes with her, and Miriam didn't look away. *Come back to us,* Onkel *Ivan.*

"Take care, *mei maedel.*"

Miriam gave a quick nod, then turned away. She could hear Shelby's boots clicking behind her as they moved through the door and to the parking lot. Miriam didn't look back. She was sure Ivan and Lucy wouldn't be there anyway, but she didn't want Shelby to see her crying.

6

Shelby had just finished setting the table when the first guests pulled into the driveway. Today she'd learned to make stromboli. One thing she had to admit, the food here was always great. Rebecca and Miriam were both good cooks, and Shelby thought she'd gained a pound or two over the past week. Though she enjoyed helping with supper, she still couldn't seem to get out of bed early enough to help with breakfast.

"So they each pay fifteen dollars for the meal?" Shelby carried a loaf of buttered bread to the table and placed it between a jar of rhubarb jam and a bowl of chow chow. She loved the sweet rhubarb jam, but she wasn't fond of the pickled vegetables they called chow chow.

"*Ya,*" Rebecca answered as she scurried past Miriam, toting a bowl of paprika potatoes.

Miriam placed the stromboli on the table

next to a chicken casserole. There was also a bowl of creamed celery on the table, a plate of saucy meatballs, and something Miriam referred to as "shipwreck" — a casserole layered with potatoes, onion, ground beef, rice, celery, kidney beans, and tomatoes. It seemed an odd combination of offerings to Shelby, but her cousin had said that non-Amish folks expected to be served a variety of Amish dishes. And Rebecca had said these recipes were handed down from her mother. Even though Miriam told Shelby that pride was avoided in their community, Shelby could tell that Rebecca was proud of her cooking.

A spread of desserts beckoned from the counter: shoofly pie, whoopee pies, glazed apple cookies, and some molasses sugar cookies. Rebecca had been baking most of the day. Shelby wondered if it was worth it and quickly calculated fifteen times eight. She decided it probably was.

She heard footsteps coming up the porch steps.

"Don't forget. As soon as the meal is over, show them to the den." Rebecca gave instructions to Miriam as she pointed around the corner to the family room. Jams and jellies decorated with quilted doilies covered a long table against the far wall of the den.

Shelby also noticed handwritten cookbooks, quilted pot holders, and individually wrapped whoopee pies.

"The *Englisch* love all that," Miriam said to Shelby before she turned to her mother. "I will, *Mamm.*"

Rebecca crossed through the den and opened the door for the first of their guests. Shelby stayed in the kitchen with Miriam. She liked the way the kitchen was large enough for the long wooden table, unlike most homes she'd been in that had a separate dining room for such a large crowd. Their kitchen was the largest room in the house, much bigger than the family room, or den, as Rebecca called it. Shelby counted fifteen place settings. Each white china plate had a smaller white plate on top of it, a cloth napkin and silverware, and a glass already filled with ice water.

"Welcome to our home," Shelby heard Rebecca say as she ushered the first two dinner guests to the kitchen. "This is my daughter, Miriam, and our cousin, Shelby." *Mamm* paused as she turned to the older couple. "And, girls . . . this is Frank and Yvonne."

"Nice to meet you," Shelby said in unison with Miriam.

Rebecca excused herself when there was

another knock at the door, and she returned with the other six dinner guests — two couples who looked to be in their thirties, and two older women who appeared to be together. Rebecca made introductions, then asked everyone to have a seat.

Shelby wasn't sure what to do next, so she eased closer to Miriam and whispered, "What now?"

"*Daed* and the boys should be washing up outside at the water pump, then when they're seated, we'll sit down."

Shelby nodded as she checked out their company. One of the younger couples began to sit down. Both were well dressed, the woman in a peach-colored skirt and matching blouse that looked more appropriate for church, and the man in black slacks, a starched white shirt, and a black and white tie with tiny red dots. Her eyes drifted to the younger couple already seated. Both wore blue jeans and matching red T-shirts that said *Amish Dutch Country* on the back with a picture of a horse and buggy. The man had been introduced as Bruce, and his dark hair was pulled back in a ponytail that hung a few inches down his back. His arms were folded across his chest as he eyed the offerings in front of him. Frank and Yvonne took their seats, as did the two older women who'd arrived together.

Shelby stepped aside when Miriam brushed past her carrying another plate of buttered bread, and a few moments later Aaron and the three boys joined them.

"If we could please all bow our heads for silent prayer," Rebecca said after everyone was seated.

Shelby bowed her head, but she didn't close her eyes and instead glanced around the table. Bruce didn't bow his head or close his eyes, and when his eyes locked with Shelby's, a chill ran up her spine. She was relieved when his wife raised her head and began talking to him, pulling the man's dark, icy eyes away.

Rebecca identified the various dishes for their guests, then started passing bowls and platters to her left. "And please try some rhubarb jam on your bread if you'd like," she said, smiling.

"This looks delicious, Rebecca." Yvonne smiled as she passed the creamed celery to her husband.

Her sentiments were echoed throughout the group. All except for Bruce. There was something unsettling about him, and Shelby's eyes kept veering in his direction. Bruce's wife whispered to him several times, but she also commented to Rebecca about how good everything tasted.

"Why aren't you dressed like them?"

Shelby almost lost her grip on the bowl of potatoes at the sound of Bruce's gruff voice. "I'm not Amish. I'm their cousin, just visiting."

He narrowed bushy brows as one corner of his mouth twitched. His wife elbowed him to accept the plate of bread that she was holding, and he looked away. She was relieved when the two elderly women took over the conversation and began asking lots of questions about Amish life.

"I read somewhere that Amish children only attend school through the eighth grade. Is that true?" The gray-headed woman named Mary smiled as she posed the question to Rebecca.

Rebecca swallowed and took a moment before she answered. "*Ya.* It's true. We feel like that is enough education to prepare our young people for the type of work that we do."

Mary nodded, then spoke directly to Miriam. "Honey, are you in your *rumschpringe?*"

Even though the woman seemed pleased with her use of the Pennsylvania *Deitsch* dialect, Shelby recognized the fact that she mispronounced the word. But Miriam just smiled and said, "Yes, ma'am. I'm eighteen, and at sixteen, we are given the freedom to explore the *Englisch* world so that when we choose to stay here, it's not because we don't know what life outside of our community is like."

Bruce's throaty chuckle reeked of cynicism before he said, "Surely you all get out of here as soon as you can." He glanced around the room. "I mean, really. Who'd choose this life if they had a choice?"

His wife, a woman with shoulder-length blond hair, lowered her head, but Shelby saw her cheeks redden.

"I think I'd enjoy this life," the woman in the peach-colored outfit said. "It's so peaceful and without the distractions of our life — cell phones, tight schedules, and . . ." She paused and sat taller. "And the Amish have a strong faith in our Lord."

"Whatever," Bruce mumbled as he reached across his wife and scooped a large spoonful of chicken casserole from the dish. Rebecca shifted her weight in her chair and glanced at her husband. Shelby saw Aaron nod at her, as if they were having a secret conversation . . . one that perhaps they'd had before.

"Boys, finish up. You still have chores to finish." Aaron spoke with authority to Elam,

Ben, and James, who all nodded and began to eat faster. A few minutes later all three boys excused themselves and headed outside.

"Uh, excuse me . . ." Bruce's wife glanced over Rebecca's shoulder toward the den. "Is the bathroom that way?"

Rebecca pushed herself away from the table. "*Ya.* Of course. Follow me."

"Nah, don't get up. I'll find it." The woman hurriedly stood up, lifted one leg over the bench, then the other, and was heading across the den before Rebecca could argue.

Mary cleared her throat. "You have a lovely home, Rebecca. Thank you for having us for supper." She smiled. "And this food is *wunderbaar gut.*" She nudged her friend, again proud of her use of the dialect.

"Danki," Rebecca said as she glanced at Miriam, who lowered her eyes and grinned. Shelby would remember to ask both of them what was so amusing, even though Mary didn't seem to notice.

When the main meal was over, Shelby and Miriam helped Rebecca clear the table, then they placed the desserts in the middle. They supplied fresh plates for everyone and served hot coffee. Shelby noticed that Rhoda — Bruce's wife — wasn't back from the bathroom.

"Do you think your wife is all right?" Shelby avoided the man's eyes and glanced into the den.

"She's fine." He didn't look up but instead helped himself to a generous supply of each dessert offered.

It was at least another five minutes before Rhoda returned, and she slipped in beside her husband. "You got enough there on your plate, Bruce?"

"For fifteen dollars, I'm having everything they put out." He scowled at his wife.

"Everything is wonderful, Rebecca," Mary said as she daintily picked at a piece of shoofly pie.

"*Danki,*" Rebecca answered again, smiling. "I'd like to invite you all into the den to look at our homemade jams and jellies. We also have cookbooks that include the recipes for everything you have eaten here tonight. And there are some other things that might interest you." Rebecca motioned toward the table in the den.

"Don't even think about buying any of that junk," Bruce said to Rhoda, his forehead creasing as he spoke. Shelby watched Aaron take a slow, deep breath, but he didn't say anything. Miriam lowered her eyes but stood by her mother as everyone but Bruce and Rhoda walked into the den.

Aaron stayed at the table with Bruce and Rhoda while Bruce loaded up on another round of desserts. Everyone else was gathering up jams, jellies, cookbooks, and quilted pot holders in the other room.

"Thanks for dinner," Rhoda said a few minutes later as she and Bruce made their way across the den and toward the front door.

Rebecca quickly joined them, smiling. "Thank you for being a guest in our home."

"Yeah," Bruce said as he opened the door. "Come on, Rhoda."

Rhoda gave Rebecca a weak smile and followed her husband.

After Bruce and Rhoda were out the door, Shelby whispered to Miriam, "I'm glad they're gone."

Aaron followed the couple out the door, and it wasn't until tires met with the gravel road that Aaron came back in the house. He excused himself and thanked everyone for coming, then headed to the barn.

"I'm glad too," Miriam finally said.

Once everyone had paid for their goods, they thanked Rebecca and headed to their cars. Rebecca dropped onto the couch the minute everyone was gone. She put her head in her hands, and Miriam sat down beside her mother. "What's wrong, *Mamm?*"

Her mother didn't look up but pointed to the oak china cabinet on the far wall, next to the table of jams, jellies, and such. Miriam stood up and walked toward the cabinet, then hung her head for a moment. "It's okay, *Mamm.* We'll get another one."

"What?" Shelby walked to where Miriam was standing. "What's wrong?"

"*Mamm's* silver letter opener is gone."

"Someone stole it?" Shelby was sure who the culprit was. "Was it worth a lot?"

Rebecca pulled her hands away from her face, then joined Miriam and Shelby by the china cabinet. She let out a heavy sigh. "No. It was only silver-plated, but it was a gift from my grandmother years ago. It was inscribed to me, from her. It said, 'May all your letters be received with an abundance of love.' "

"Well, clearly that Rhoda woman took it when she went to the bathroom." Shelby shook her head, then looked up at Rebecca. "Is anything else missing?"

Rebecca glanced around the den. "No." She bit her bottom lip. "But the woman had to go down the hall to get to the bathroom, and she was gone a long time." She started down the hallway, Miriam and Shelby following. All the bedrooms were upstairs. The downstairs consisted of the large kitchen, a nice-sized den, a mudroom, and a hallway to the bathroom with a closed door on each side. Shelby knew that one room housed a pedal sewing machine and quilting supplies, but she'd never been in the other room.

"There's nothing missing in here," Rebecca said after she scanned the sewing room. Then she went to the door on the other side and pushed it open. "Oh no."

"What?" Shelby slid into the room with Miriam. "Rebecca, what is it?"

Rebecca walked to the middle of the room. There were racks and racks of jams, jellies, cookbooks, quilted pot holders, and other items marked with white price tags. "I left the cash box on the shelf." She walked to a cigar box and lifted the lid, then slowly closed it.

"How much did they take, *Mamm?*"

Rebecca turned around, tears in her eyes. "Your *daed* told me I needed to get the money to the bank last week after the Mud Sale, but I just didn't have time."

Miriam put a hand on her mother's shoulder. "How much, *Mamm?*"

Rebecca leaned her head back against her neck and closed her eyes. "A little over two thousand dollars."

"We need to call the police. I'll do it from

the barn because my cell's dead." Shelby turned to leave the room.

"No, Shelby." Rebecca's voice shook, but the tone was firm. "We have no proof, and it's God's will. Perhaps whoever took the money needs it more than us."

"You're kidding me, right?" Shelby glanced at Miriam, recalling how her cousin said she overused the phrase, but in this case, she couldn't believe what she was hearing. "God's will? Are you saying that it's God's will for you to be robbed by people in your own home? People you served dinner to. You need to call the bed-and-breakfast where they are staying, let the owner know, then call the police."

Rebecca just shook her head, but she finally said, "I will call Barbie Beiler because she needs to know that someone in that group took things from our home. She needs to know that since those folks are guests at her place."

"*Mamm,* the only one who went this way was Rhoda. Where would she have put the letter opener? The cash she could put in her blue jean pockets, but not the letter opener." Miriam turned to Shelby. "The letter opener was long, maybe seven or eight inches long."

"In her sock," Shelby answered without hesitation, ashamed that she knew where the woman would conceal something she'd stolen. "She had on tennis shoes . . . and socks. She probably put it in her sock." Shelby's past flashed before her — a trip to the police station, a stolen necklace. She took a deep breath as she recalled how easy it was to steal the silver chain from the rack at the department store. Or so she'd thought. That's how it is when you're high — a false reality. Shelby was forced to watch the security tape later when she wasn't under any influence, and she'd cried hard, begging her parents for forgiveness. The department store went easy on her, but forgiveness never came from her parents.

Who was I back then? She wondered if she would be released from the guilt she felt about her shoplifting, especially now as she watched Rebecca close the door and dab at her eyes.

Shelby followed Miriam and Rebecca to the kitchen.

"I still think we need to call the police."

Rebecca walked to the table and began clearing the dessert plates. "No, Shelby. I will call Barbie from the phone in the barn, but not the police."

Shelby put her hands on her hips. "Rebecca, this just isn't right. We know who took that money, and this isn't God's will."

Maybe it was the way she said "God's will," but Rebecca's expression turned sour quickly. "Everything that happens is God's will." She lifted her chin and sniffled. "I'd like no further talk of this."

Shelby glanced at Miriam, then sighed. "Okay." She walked to the sink and started placing the dishes in soapy water. "I'm sorry, Rebecca. I didn't mean to upset you."

Rebecca grabbed a towel and accepted a washed plate from Shelby. "You didn't upset me, Shelby. It upsets me that folks would come into our home and do this, but instead of calling the police, we handle things a bit different. We will pray for them every day and hope that they will find their way to God, and we'll ask God to forgive them for this."

Shelby momentarily wondered if anyone had prayed for her when she was making bad choices.

"I'm *not* praying for them." The words slipped out, and it was too late for Shelby to take them back. She glanced at Rebecca, then at Miriam. "I'm sorry. I just can't."

By Saturday afternoon Miriam couldn't stop thinking about her date with Saul.

"You never did tell me why you and your mother were grinning last night when that woman said *wunderbaar gut*." Shelby ran the sweeper across the wooden floors in their bedroom.

"Because Amish folks don't really say that." She laughed. "Unless we're being funny, or making fun of the *Englisch* for saying it. The *Englisch* seem to think we say that all the time, but we don't."

Shelby just nodded, then she leaned the sweeper up against the wall. "Are you excited about your date?"

Miriam's insides warmed. "*Ya.* I am."

"What date?"

Miriam spun around at the sound of her mother's voice. "Uh . . . I meant to tell you . . . I have a date with Saul tonight. We're going to eat after I run my weekly errands in town." She held her breath when she saw the pained look on her mother's face, a squinting of her eyes as she pressed her lips together.

"Miriam, Shelby has just been here a week, and I don't think you should be off on a date when your cousin is —"

"It's okay, Rebecca." Shelby plopped down on her bed. "I'm fine. Really."

Miriam smiled at Shelby, then turned back to her mother. "See?" She raised her brows and waited.

Mamm shook her head. "Not tonight, Miriam. I need to wait another week or so before you make the weekly run to town, until I have — have more money." She held up a finger the way she was known to do when Miriam opened her mouth to argue. "And there might be a storm coming later. It's best you stay home tonight."

Miriam felt her heart sink to the pit of her stomach. "But, *Mamm* . . . I already told Saul that I would meet him in town. I don't have any way to tell him I can't be there."

"I'm sure the Fishers have a phone in their barn like everyone else." *Mamm* slapped her hands to her sides. "Please, *mei maedel,* don't argue with me. This is just not a *gut* night for you to be going out."

Miriam took a deep breath, then let it out slowly. She didn't say anything but nodded.

When she heard her mother's footsteps going down the stairs, she turned to Shelby. "That is not fair."

"Maybe your mom just can't accept that you are plenty old enough to date." Shelby leaned back on her elbows. "I remember when I went on my first date when I was sixteen. I thought my dad was going to have a heart attack about it."

Miriam sat down on her own bed and faced Shelby. "She doesn't think Saul is right for me. I'm sure that's it." She leaned back on her palms. "She just doesn't know him very well. He's quiet around most people, and . . . he's been in a little trouble before. Nothing serious. But I think *Mamm* thinks he just isn't the right person for me." She sat up again. "But that is not her choice."

"Maybe your parents are worried that Saul will leave and that you will get your heart broken, or worse yet . . . that you'll leave with him."

Miriam shook her head. "Saul isn't leaving. Those are just gossipy rumors."

"I hope so, for your sake." Shelby rolled onto her side, then propped herself up on one elbow. "So are you going to go call Saul?"

Miriam thought for a few moments before she answered. *"Ya."*

"It's a shame you have to cancel, but maybe you can reschedule for another time."

"*Ach,* I'm not canceling." She grinned at Shelby. "I'm just going to tell him that I will meet him at nine thirty. After my parents are asleep." She tucked a loose strand of hair beneath her *kapp.* "This is *Saul Fisher.* I have been waiting for this night my entire life. I am not going to miss it."

7

Saul listened to Miriam's message twice, just to make sure he'd heard her correctly. He didn't understand why she wanted to meet so late at night, but that might be better anyway. He could make sure *Daed* was sound asleep by the time he left, and he wouldn't have to worry about there being trouble while he was gone. After his father's outburst a few days before, the rest of the week had gone fine. No drinking. And as Saul had suspected, his father never brought that night up. He merely went to the fields earlier on that day, and he stayed out working later . . . well past the supper hour. Saul wondered what time his father would come in tonight.

Saul had prayed extra hard every night that his father would stop drinking, and every night he would read his employment offer and ask God if he was doing the right thing by leaving his family and friends, particularly about leaving his brothers. He thought about the speedy response he'd sent to the owner of the bistro, and the way his hand had shook as he wrote the letter.

He pulled the lever on the water pump until the cool water splashed at his feet, then he ran his hands underneath. He caught a glimpse of his brothers as they walked toward the barn. James would collect eggs from the hens while Ruben brushed down the horses. Saul knew they were both going to be fine. They were strong and level-headed. *They have to be fine.*

He strolled into the house, tired from a hard day's work in the fields but excited about his date with Miriam. Just the thought of holding her hand or putting his arm around her at the movies gave him a burst of energy he wouldn't normally have this time of day. When Saul walked into the den, his father was pulling off his work boots.

"It was a hot one today, no?" *Daed* dropped into his chair by the window, then fumbled for his glasses on the table next to him. Once he had the gold-rimmed glasses situated on his nose, he reached for *The Budget.*

Saul pulled off his own shoes, hung his hat on the rack, then let his suspenders drop to his sides. He sat down on the couch across from his father, one of the best men he'd ever known in his life. *Daed* was strong in his faith, and he went out of his way to help others. He just had this one problem. Saul leaned back against the couch, wishing he had the courage to tell his father about his plans in Pittsburgh. Since Saul hadn't been baptized yet and wouldn't face a shunning, maybe *Daed* would bless Saul's choices. He didn't realize he was staring until his father looked over the top of the newspaper at him.

"Something on your mind?" *Daed* pushed his reading glasses down on his nose.

If you only knew. Saul shook his head. "No, not really." His father seemed to be waiting for more. "I'll be going out later. I'm taking Miriam Raber for a late supper."

His father nodded as he pushed his glasses up and returned his eyes to the paper. "*Gut* folks, the Rabers." He lowered the newspaper. "Think she might be the one you'll settle with?"

Guilt tugged at Saul's heart as he shifted his weight. "I dunno." He leaned his head back against the couch and stared at the ceiling. He should never have set this date with Miriam.

But being with her was all he could think about.

■ ■ ■ ■

Miriam closed the bedroom door behind her, then whipped the towel from her head. She leaned down and began to dry her hair in front of the small fan on the nightstand.

"What's that smell?" Shelby closed her pink book, locked it, then dropped the key in her purse like she always did, and Miriam wondered if she was writing about happier thoughts.

"It's vanilla lotion." Miriam held her arm up for Shelby to sniff. "I bought it at the market a few weeks ago."

"You smell like a candle." Shelby reached into her purse. "Here, try this. It's perfume, and you'll smell much better to Saul wearing this."

Miriam reached for the glass bottle. "Thank you, Shelby."

Shelby sat up and crossed her legs beneath her. "Miriam, sneaking out like this will only get you in trouble down the line, in one way or another." She shook her head. "Trust me. I know. Plus . . . don't you think your parents will hear you sneaking out? Those steps creak. . . . Then you'll have to hitch up the horse. They'll hear you leaving." She tapped a finger to her chin. "Do the Amish

145

ground their kids? Because if so, I can already see you getting grounded for a long time."

"*Ya,* we get punished. But no worries. I have everything covered." Miriam knew her hair would never be completely dry by the time she needed to leave, so she wound it atop her head, then secured her prayer covering. She turned to Shelby. "Have you seen that huge fan in *Mamm* and *Daed's* room? It's run by the generator, and that thing is so loud that *Mamm* and *Daed* don't hear anything outside of their bedroom. They'll never hear the steps creak, and they won't hear me leaving."

"This has trouble written all over it, Miriam. I don't think you should go."

Miriam folded her arms across her chest. "Why? I'm not going to get caught. And I'm not exactly lying either."

Shelby twisted her mouth from side to side for a moment, then she sat up and dropped her legs over the side of the bed. She leaned closer. "Miriam, I kinda got in some trouble back home."

Miriam knew this, but she'd never known what kind of trouble. She eased her hands into her lap and folded them together. "What kind of trouble?"

Shelby took a deep breath, then blew it

146

out slowly. "After my parents' divorce, and after Tommy broke up with me, I was sneaking out . . . and doing some things I shouldn't have done."

Miriam waited a moment to see if Shelby was going to share any details, but she didn't. "Saul is a wonderful person. My parents just don't know him, and they're judging him . . . My mother is, anyway. And *Mamm* knows that only God can judge."

Shelby let out a heavy sigh. "Maybe, Miriam. But I was running around with some people that my parents didn't like, and they ended up dragging me into a bunch of stuff that wasn't good for me."

"Have you heard from your parents?" Miriam wanted to change the subject.

Shelby frowned. "Your mom said my mom left a message on the phone in the barn day before yesterday, saying that she couldn't get hold of me on my cell." Shelby rolled her eyes. "Duh. My cell phone has been dead, and Mom should know that." She raised one shoulder, then dropped it slowly as she spoke. "Whatever. Obviously, my mother wasn't in that big of a hurry to check on me."

Miriam didn't understand much about divorce, but she could tell that Shelby was bitter, and she hoped that her cousin would reach out to God for comfort. She wasn't sure what to say.

"I'm mad at my parents for getting a divorce, for ruining my life. But if they did anything right, it was pulling me away from the kids I was running around with before they shipped me here." Shelby turned away from Miriam and looked at the wall. "I wasn't exactly thrilled to come here." She turned to Miriam. "I'm sorry. It's just that everything is so different. I don't really know anyone. And I figured it would be like this. But . . . I do have to say . . . I was running around with a pretty rough crowd, and I was sneaking out all the time. Looking back, I should have made smarter choices, even if things were really bad at home."

"Saul is a *gut* man. The best. When *Mamm* and *Daed* get to know him, they'll see that."

"I hope you're right. But I'm going to get my two cents in, and I don't think you should be sneaking out at nine o'clock at night to go meet someone. It's not safe."

"Around here it is."

"How can you say that? Just yesterday a woman stole from your home." Shelby shook her head. "The world is not a safe place, Miriam. And your people aren't exempt just because they are Amish and live in the country." She paused. "And your mom said there might be a storm. Please don't go."

Miriam was touched by Shelby's concern. "I feel like we're sisters right now." She smiled. "But no worries. It's not like this is the first time I've snuck out of my house."

Shelby stiffened. "Huh?"

Miriam giggled. "I'm eighteen, Shelby. I've been in my *rumschpringe* for two years."

"But this is your first date?" Shelby's voice rose an octave as she spoke.

Miriam shrugged as she smiled. "That's just because I've been waiting for Saul. But I've snuck out to meet Leah and Hannah before."

"What in the world for?"

Miriam wasn't proud of her actions, but she wanted Shelby to stop worrying so much. "There was a country gospel band playing at a restaurant in Lancaster. That rarely happens, and we wanted to go. We all felt like our parents would forbid it because it was on a Thursday night and the music didn't start until ten o'clock." She shrugged again. "So we snuck out, met on Lincoln Highway, then walked to town and called a taxi cab."

"Did you get caught?"

"No." Miriam looked down for a moment. "I felt kinda bad about it, though."

"Trust me. You'll probably feel bad about this too, but I can see that you're determined to go." Shelby leaned over the side of the bed and reached into her purse. "Here." She pushed her cell phone and cord toward Miriam. "Plug it in somewhere when you get to the restaurant. Even thirty minutes will give you a little bit of a charge, and at least you'll have it on your way home, just in case you get into any trouble. I'm going to write in my journal some more for a while. I'll leave the window open so maybe I can hear the phone ringing in the barn if you need to call for something."

Miriam latched onto the phone, then took a deep breath. She had on her best green dress and black apron, and she smelled like orchids. Tonight was going to be the best night of her life.

It was nine o'clock when Shelby watched Miriam from the window. Her cousin seemed to be right. It appeared she was going to make a clean getaway. She waited until she saw Miriam maneuver the buggy onto the street before she climbed into bed. As she kicked back the quilt and tucked herself beneath the sheet, she felt an overwhelming urge. She leaned back against her pillow, then closed her eyes.

God, are You there?

She waited, not expecting an answer but not sure whether to go on.

I was wondering if maybe You could keep an eye on my cousin tonight. She's rather naive, and I don't want to see her get into any trouble. I think Saul is probably a good person, but sneaking around is never a good thing and can lead to other trouble. I should know.

Shelby opened her eyes and stared upward at the twinkling lights from the lantern, the smell of perfume still lingering in the air. She closed her eyes again.

I wish I knew why I'm being punished.

She paused.

Never mind. I know why. For the bad stuff I did. When will my penance be over? When will I feel happy again? Please, Lord. Please . . .

As she figured, no guidance came drifting into her mind, and her glimmer of hope was quickly replaced by anger. When she thought about the fellowship she used to feel when she went to church with her parents and the one-on-one connection with God she once had, her bitterness only escalated. Her parents had ruined her life in every way. Not only did they stop loving each other, but they'd stopped going to church. Shelby knew she was a grown woman, and she certainly could have gone to church on her own, but what was the point? God didn't care what happened to her, and all those years of praying and trying to live the right way hadn't served her well.

She recalled all the times she disobeyed her parents during the divorce, and she knew that drugs and alcohol hadn't served her well either, but God must still be punishing her for her bad choices. Otherwise He'd help her find some kind of peace in her heart. Especially at night, loneliness seemed to overtake her as recollections of better times haunted her. She reached for her journal, unlocked it, and then stared at the page. For the first time in a long while, she didn't have anything to write. She'd already voiced her thoughts . . . to God.

And He clearly wasn't hearing her.

Rebecca tossed and turned, just like she had the night before. She fought the anger building inside her about what happened yesterday. How could a guest in their home steal from them like that? She thought about the time and effort that had gone into making the quilts, and they were going to feel the loss of income for the next couple of months.

She rolled onto her side, tried to ignore Aaron's snoring, and then asked God to free her heart of anger . . . and worry. And as wrong as it was, she worried about Miriam's interest in Saul. She didn't know the boy well, but what she did know was that he'd been in trouble several times, even reprimanded by the bishop. But most troubling were the rumors that he might not get baptized and would leave the community. If that was true, where did that leave Miriam if she and Saul grew close? Miriam was eighteen, but in so many ways she was still a child, and Rebecca feared Miriam wouldn't be able to cope with a broken heart.

After another fifteen minutes of thrashing around because of her frustrating thoughts, she pushed back the sheet, reached for the lantern, then eased out of bed. Quietly she fumbled in the bedside drawer for a match. As she headed downstairs, the aroma of chocolate chip cookies still lingered in the air, and she smiled as she thought about John eating six of the warm treats earlier, straight from the oven. Her youngest boy had a sweet tooth for sure.

Rebecca poured herself a glass of milk, then peeled back the foil covering the cookies. She put the lantern on the counter and savored the moist cookie in her mouth, thinking that she could probably eat six cookies too, if she allowed herself. She rinsed it down with her milk, then slowly made her way back upstairs, hoping sleep would come soon and thankful she could sleep in a bit tomorrow since there was no church service.

Shelby would be glad she could sleep in. Poor girl just couldn't seem to get up in the morning. As she passed by the girls' room, she paused, then slowly turned the doorknob. Before she pushed the door wide, she lowered the flame on the lantern so as not to wake them. She smiled at Shelby, her head buried beneath the covers, wondering how she could sleep like that when it was so warm. Then she held the light a little higher toward the far bed, but Miriam was nowhere to be seen. Her heart thudded in her chest.

She stepped out of the bedroom and padded down the hallway to the bathroom. After shining the light into the small, empty room, she hurried back to the girls' bedroom. Gently she pulled the covers from Shelby's head and whispered, "Shelby, wake up, dear."

After a groan, Shelby cupped a hand above her eyes to block the light. "What is it, Rebecca?"

"Where's Miriam?"

Shelby bolted upright in the bed and cleared tangles from her face. "Huh?"

Rebecca's heart rate picked up. "Shelby, where is she?" She turned the flame up on the lantern. "Is she outside? Maybe on the porch? Did she go to the barn for some reason? Maybe she couldn't sleep." Rebecca walked to the window, but there wasn't a light coming from the barn. She spun around and edged closer to Shelby. "Did she tell you where she was going?"

Shelby rubbed sleep from her eyes, then blinked several times. "She isn't here right now."

Rebecca held the lantern higher and thrust her other hand on her hip. "I can see that. Where is she?"

"I'm not sure exactly."

"Shelby . . ." Rebecca took a deep breath, afraid her anger was going to boil over.

For nearly two hours, Miriam and Saul sat at Yoder's Pantry after they'd decided it was too late to go to a movie. It took awhile for Saul to seem comfortable, but once he started talking, Miriam hung on his every word. He loved to talk about cooking and recipes, especially about cooking for his family. Miriam could tell that it was Saul's way of loving and nurturing them, and it endeared him to her even more. Her Saul had an independent spirit, something she loved, and he was kindhearted.

As much fun as she was having with Saul, Shelby had been right about sneaking out. Guilt kept a steady hold on Miriam. She had to admit that regret about her choice was putting a damper on her time with Saul. She glanced at the clock again. Eleven thirty.

"This has been great," she said to Saul as he finished his second piece of pie, following the full meal they'd had earlier. "But I guess I need to go."

Saul chewed, then quickly swallowed. "*Ya,* this has been fun." He smiled, and momentarily Miriam forgot about everyone else but him. The dreamy way he'd been looking at her all night had caused her heart to flip several times. "And I have some new recipes to try out on *Daed* and the boys."

Miriam took a sip of her coffee, then stifled a yawn. But there was something else weighing on her mind, and even though she knew it was late, the question had been lurking on the tip of her tongue all night. "Saul, I've heard a couple of people say that you might not be baptized come the fall. That's not true, is it?"

Any hint of a dreamy look on Saul's face

vanished instantly, and his eyes averted hers. "Where'd you hear that?"

Miriam shrugged, disappointed since that was not the outright denial she'd hoped for. "Just rumors, I guess."

Saul reached for his coffee, spilling a bit over the side before he took a sip. Then he reached for his hat on the seat beside him. "I guess we better get you home before your parents don't let you out of the *haus* again." Miriam could tell his smile was forced and something had changed. Saul stood up and waited for Miriam to do the same.

A few minutes later Saul opened the door of her buggy. "I'm going to follow you home. It's too late for you to be on the road."

Alarms went off in Miriam's head. If she got caught coming home, it would be even worse if Saul was following her. "No, no. You don't have to do that. The storm they predicted just moved around us. I'll be fine going home." Even though she'd forgotten to charge it, she pulled Shelby's cell phone from her apron. "See, I have a phone."

To her surprise, Saul reached for it, then flipped it open. "I thought about getting one of these, but . . ." He stopped mid-sentence as his forehead creased. "The battery is dead. The light doesn't even come on."

"*Ach, ya.* I was supposed to charge it inside somewhere." Miriam hung her head, knowing that she wasn't being completely truthful with anyone tonight.

He handed the phone back to her. "I'm following you home." His tone was firm and protective, and Miriam smiled at him. Her parents never got up during the night, and she'd just be quiet going into the house. They'd never see Saul. She refocused her thoughts on whether or not he would kiss her tonight. He closed the door, then promised to stay right behind her.

Ten minutes later, as she was pulling up her driveway with Saul right behind her, she gasped at the light on in the den downstairs. Maybe Shelby was up. Or one of her brothers, which wouldn't be good. Her brothers would tattle on her.

She slowed the buggy, jumped out as soon as it stopped, then ran to Saul's buggy. "*Danki* for supper. I have to go!" She turned to run toward the house, then he called her name. She turned around, her heart pounding in her chest. "I'm sorry. I have to go." She looked over her shoulder toward the house, then back at Saul.

"Do you want to do something again?"

Miriam wanted to stay in the moment and talk to him more, especially since Saul had clearly avoided her question about being baptized. But the longer she stayed outside talking to Saul, the worse things were going to be when she went inside. "I'll call you from our barn phone tomorrow at" — she thought for a moment, remembering that it was an off-Sunday for church service — "at ten in the morning."

"Okay."

Saul sounded confused, but Miriam ran toward the house, knowing she'd been caught. She waited until Saul rounded the corner before she reached for the screen door, glad that the wooden door was closed. Maybe her parents hadn't seen Saul. She pulled the screen door toward her and was just about to turn the knob on the main door when she heard the sound of car tires on their driveway. She pulled her hand back, turned around, and waited to see who it was. Her stomach knotted inside her at the thought of what faced her on the other side of the door, but she couldn't imagine who would be visiting them at midnight.

She waited. The car wasn't even parked before another car turned into their driveway. Miriam held her hand up to block the headlights from both vehicles. She turned around when she heard the front door open. Her mother stepped onto the front porch, supported by her father, and she was sobbing uncontrollably. They were followed by her brothers, who were also crying. Shelby appeared behind them, and Miriam wasn't sure, but it looked like Shelby had been crying too.

"*Mamm!* What is it?" Miriam clutched her mother's arm when it appeared she might fall. Her father lifted his wife into his arms and held her close as a tear ran down his face. "*Daed,* what's wrong? Someone tell me."

Her mother pulled herself from *Daed's* arms, then stumbled down the porch steps. She fell into her brother Noah's arms. *Mamm's* sister Mary Ellen stepped out of the other car and ran to her mother and Noah. Miriam watched the scene unfolding and began to cry herself. She didn't know what had happened, but it was bad, and it clearly didn't have anything to do with her sneaking out to meet Saul.

8

Miriam tried to calm her breathing and her crying as they moved into the house. She couldn't believe it — her Uncle Ivan was dead. She'd just seen him at the market on Friday. Shelby kept her arm around Miriam as they moved into the house. Noah's wife, Carley, was doing her best to comfort Miriam's brothers, but all three boys couldn't stop crying.

It was bad enough that Uncle Ivan was in a car accident that killed him, but their loss felt even worse because he had been shunned recently, banned by his family for his recent choices. No one knew why her uncle was in a car so late at night.

Once Miriam was settled on the couch next to her aunts, Mary Ellen and Carley, Shelby offered to go make everyone some tea, but no one took her up on it. Shelby didn't even know Ivan, had only met him that one time, but yet she cried along with the rest of them.

"The policeman said he went quickly." Noah choked out the words as he ran a hand through his hair. "Never suffered. The other car hit the car Ivan was riding in head-on." Noah paused. "The driver of that car was also killed instantly, but the person who hit them survived. He's at Lancaster General in a coma."

"Oh no." *Mamm* wailed from the rocker across the room. Miriam's father leaned down beside the chair and clutched her hand, then *Mamm* said, "Poor Katie Ann . . . and their baby. Oh no, Aaron. As far as I know, Ivan still didn't know about the baby." *Mamm* dropped her head into her hands and sobbed.

They all knew Katie Ann was pregnant, but her aunt had chosen to keep her pregnancy a secret from Uncle Ivan, fearful he would return to Katie Ann out of obligation. Miriam's family had promised Katie Ann that they wouldn't mention anything to Ivan — at least for a while. Now he would never know, and Miriam wondered if they had done the right thing.

Mamm raised her head and continued, "Someone will have to call Katie Ann." *Mamm* dabbed at her eyes. "And we will need to call Samuel and Lillian."

Miriam tried to make sense of everything as she counted the other Stoltzfus siblings in her head. There was her mother, Samuel, Noah, and Mary Ellen. Everyone lived here in Lancaster County except for her Uncle Samuel, his wife, Lillian, and Ivan's wife, Katie Ann. Miriam missed her aunts and uncles, and she'd hoped to see them soon — but not like this.

"It's late, Rebecca." Her father squeezed *Mamm's* hand. "We'll call them at daylight."

Mamm nodded, and then Miriam's eyes met with her father's. His scowl caused Miriam to look away from him. She felt as low as a serpent slithering on the ground. She wanted to run across the room and comfort her mother, but her father's eyes kept her planted on the couch.

After about an hour, the group began to part ways, following more hugs and tears. Miriam couldn't stop thinking about her uncle, all the times she'd spent with him over the years, and how she'd been praying for him to come back to the church.

Once everyone was gone, Miriam cautiously eased toward her mother. "What would you like for me to do, *Mamm?*"

Her mother dabbed at her eyes, then glared at Miriam. "What would I like for you to do, Miriam?" She paused as her eyes narrowed with anger. "I would like for you not to sneak out of our home to go and meet a boy." She put both hands to her forehead and wept. "I can't talk about this right now." She turned to go up the stairs but turned around. "I don't want you seeing that boy."

"Let's go upstairs, Rebecca." Miriam's father coaxed her up the stairs, leaving the rest of them in the den. Shelby reached for John's hand and offered to take him back up to bed, but Miriam's eight-year-old brother wiped his eyes and said he didn't need her to. Ben and Elam eased past them, and Ben motioned for little John to follow them. Miriam stood in the middle of the den with Shelby, watching her family go upstairs. Then she cupped her face in her hands and cried. She felt Shelby's arms go around her, and she buried her face in her cousin's shoulder and wept.

Saul held the piece of plywood against the barn wall and nailed it firmly in place. It wasn't the best repair job, but it would keep things dry until he could fix it permanently. He released the breath he was holding, only to have his nostrils take in a full load of stench. Their mule, Gus, had kicked the siding in her stall yesterday after she got spooked by a skunk, which caused the skunk to spray everything in the stall. Saul pinched his nose and thought about how he was going to get the smell out of the barn — and off of Gus.

He glanced at the phone on *Daed's* workbench and figured it to be close to ten o'clock. Miriam would be calling soon, and thoughts about her had kept him up last night. *Daed* and James were working in the fields, and Ruben went to town for supplies they needed. Saul was glad to be alone with his thoughts this morning.

His father topped the list, and Saul fought to keep the worries from his heart. He knew that everything was the will of God, but he prayed constantly that God would see fit to cure his father of his drinking. It was like living with two different people — the man he admired and loved, and a strange being he didn't recognize when he drank. Once, in a drunken fit, his father had folded onto the floor like a small child and said that *Mamm's* and Hannah's deaths had left his soul without a spirit. It was a strange thing to say, but for some reason it stuck in Saul's mind. His father had never gotten over their deaths. *Daed* tried hard to stay focused for Saul and his brothers, but the alcohol seemed to just intensify his loss and turn him into a crazy man.

Saul fretted about Ruben and James. And his father. If he continued to see Miriam Raber, he'd only be adding her to his list of worries, and all this anxiety would drag a man down.

He picked up some tools that Ruben had left out on the workbench and began putting them in the proper storage bins. Then he glanced at the clock again.

Rebecca looked in the mirror hanging on a small chain in their bedroom. Even though they'd agreed to sleep late this morning, her eyes were puffy and red. She took a deep breath, then finished dressing. The thought of cooking breakfast made her feel sick to her stomach, but everyone had to eat.

"I shouldn't have been so hard on Miriam last night," she said to Aaron when he walked into their bedroom already dressed in a dark-blue shirt and black slacks. Rebecca had chosen a dark-brown dress and black apron to wear to the funeral home.

"Miriam shouldn't have snuck out to see the Fisher boy." Aaron pulled a pair of suspenders from the chest of drawers. "We will talk to Miriam about this after we've made Ivan's arrangements."

Rebecca sat down on the bed and pulled

on a pair of black socks. "Ivan was Miriam's *onkel,* though, and I spoke cruelly to her even though I knew she was hurting." She reached for her black shoes and pulled them closer. With one shoe in her hand, she rose up and looked at Aaron. "It wasn't even Miriam's fault, I'm sure."

"What do you mean?"

"Miriam would never disobey us, and Shelby has a history of being disobedient." She leaned down and pulled her shoe on. "I'm sure Shelby convinced her to go against our wishes. Miriam would never do that."

"You don't know that, Rebecca." Aaron raked a hand through his dark hair. "It ain't fair to blame Miriam's choices on Shelby."

Rebecca stood up, but she didn't say anything.

"Shelby seems like a *gut* girl. She tried to help last night when we found out about Ivan, and she shed tears along with the rest of us, even though she didn't know him."

"I'm not sure she should be here, Ivan. I'm not sure she's a *gut* influence on Miriam . . . or the boys. Maybe we shouldn't have agreed to let her stay here for the summer."

Aaron put his hands on Rebecca's shoulders. "I think we have enough to worry about this morning without adding this to the list."

Rebecca leaned her forehead against her husband's chest. "You're right." A tear trickled down her cheek. "I can't believe Ivan's gone."

"I will call Samuel later if you want me to. It will be best if Samuel tells Katie Ann in person, I think. Katie Ann will take the news hard."

She nodded as she pulled back and lifted her eyes to her husband's. "Samuel will take the news of our *bruder's* death hard too."

"*Ya.* I know."

Rebecca dreaded going to the funeral home, but Mr. Roberts handled the Amish funerals in their area, and he would tell them how to proceed. He'd agreed to meet them there on a Sunday. "I guess I better go get breakfast started."

"Breakfast is already cooked and out on the table."

Rebecca put a hand on her chest. "What?"

"Miriam and Shelby were finishing up when I went downstairs earlier."

"They shouldn't have done that." Rebecca hung her head as another tear rolled down her cheek. "Those girls are bound to be tired, and there was no need for them to get up so early to finish before I even got downstairs."

Aaron offered her a comforting smile. "They're *gut* girls, Rebecca. Both of them." He kissed her on the forehead. "Now, come downstairs and eat a little. I know you're going to say you're not hungry, but it's gonna be a long day, and you're going to need your strength."

She nodded, then followed Aaron down the stairs toward the scent of frying bacon.

Ben, Elam, and John were already sitting at the table when Rebecca and Aaron walked into the room, and Miriam and Shelby were scurrying around the kitchen.

"*Danki,* girls, for making breakfast." Rebecca attempted a smile and knew she should apologize to Miriam for the way she'd spoken to her the night before, but Miriam *had* snuck out of the house . . . Fear of her only daughter taking up with Saul Fisher kept her silent.

"Here, Rebecca, sit down." Shelby pulled out Rebecca's chair for her, and although it was a sweet gesture, Rebecca knew that from now on, she wouldn't be able to let her guard down around the girl.

Miriam placed a cup of coffee in front of Rebecca. Her daughter's eyes were swollen and red also. She wanted to stand up, pull

Miriam into her arms, and not only tell her that she was sorry for her harsh words the night before, but also vow to protect her from anything and anyone who threatened harm to her way of life. *"Danki,"* she said softly instead.

By the time eleven o'clock rolled around, Saul was sure that Miriam had changed her mind about wanting to spend time with him since she never called. Just as well. He had plenty to do around here and enough to worry about. But he couldn't deny that not hearing from her disappointed him. He squirted vinegar water on the inside of Gus's stall, hoping to rid the area of some of the smell.

"You still ain't got that skunk smell out of here?" Ruben walked into the barn carrying a plastic bag, his nose crinkling the closer he got to Saul. "Here's the plumbing parts you asked me to get in town, to fix the commode."

Saul took the bag and peeked inside. *"Danki."* He handed the bag back to Ruben. "I think you can handle fixing the toilet." He grinned. "Unless you wanna stay out here and try to get rid of the skunk smell."

Ruben snatched the bag from him. "I think I'll take care of the toilet. Have fun out here." His brother shuffled across the hay-covered floor and was almost out the door when he turned around. "Hey, did ya hear what happened last night? About the car accident?"

"No. What?"

"Ivan Stoltzfus was killed. He was ridin' in a car with another fella and was hit head-on by a truck last night around ten thirty."

Saul walked to his brother. "Are you sure?"

"*Ach, ya,* I'm sure." Ruben lifted his chin as he went on. "I heard some folks in town talkin' about it."

"That's Miriam's *onkel,*" Saul hung his head and whispered, mostly to himself.

"Ain't he the one who was shunned and living with the *Englisch* woman?"

Saul looked up at Ruben. "*Ya.* He was living with Lucy Turner." He rubbed his chin as he grew concerned for Miriam and her family. "Did anyone say when the funeral is?"

"I don't think they know yet."

"All right." He waved his hand. "Get on to fixin' that toilet."

Saul was going to get cleaned up. Then he was going to go find Miriam and see if there was anything he could do for her or her family.

Shelby chose not to go to the funeral home. She felt out of place, and Rebecca had seemed relieved that she wasn't going. So much had happened in the short time she'd been here that Shelby was grateful to have some quiet time. She couldn't stop crying last night or this morning when she saw everyone else crying. So much sadness. But this morning she was reevaluating her life. Perhaps death did that — made you rethink things.

She was pondering as she sat in the swing on the front porch. When the phone started ringing in the barn, she darted down the steps, swung the door wide, and reached the phone right before the answering machine picked up. "Hello."

"You sound out of breath."

Shelby sighed. "Hi, Mom."

"Did Rebecca tell you I called the other day? I tried you on your cell phone, but it was dead."

"They don't have electricity, Mother." Shelby rolled her eyes.

"Shelby, I miss you, and I was just wondering if you were enjoying your time there. I know you aren't happy with your father and me for making this decision, but —"

"Don't refer to you and Dad like you're a couple making decisions together. You're not a couple. You're divorced."

Silence for a moment. "Shelby, when it comes to you, we are working together to make the best decisions. You were not making good choices on your own."

"I don't need you to remind me, Mom. I know this. But sending me out here to the boonies isn't going to help." Shelby knew she was lying. It *was* helping for her to be away from everyone and everything in her past, and slowly she was getting to know her cousins. "Oh, and someone died last night. Rebecca's brother."

"Oh no. That's terrible. I should send something. A basket or something."

"I'm sure that will help a lot." Shelby figured her mother could detect the heavy sarcasm, but just to be sure, she also grunted as she shook her head. "Seriously, Mom . . . they are all about family around here. I'm sure they will be just fine without one of your *baskets.*"

"It's the thought, Shelby, at a time like this."

She carried the cordless phone to the window in the barn when she heard the *clippety-clop* of hooves coming up the driveway. "I have to go, Mom. Someone is here,

173

and I'm the only one home."

"Shelby, please call me back. I'm worried about you, and whether you believe it or not, your father and I love you, and even if we aren't together, we still —"

"I have to go, Mom. I'll call you later."

Shelby hung up, then left the barn. She walked toward the man tethering his horse, then saw it was Saul.

"Hi, Saul." She walked toward him and they met in the grass halfway between the barn and the house.

"How is everyone? Is Miriam okay?"

"They're all at the funeral home." Shelby shook her head and looked down for a moment. "It's terrible what happened." She thought about the man she'd met only briefly at the market. She'd been shocked to hear that Ivan's wife was pregnant, only making the situation even worse. She looked back up at Saul. "I'll tell them you came by, though."

Saul pushed back the rim of his hat. "I just wanted to tell them how sorry I am and see if there was anything me or my family can do."

Shelby twisted her mouth to one side, then crossed her arms across her chest. "I'm not sure you're on Rebecca and Aaron's happy list right now."

"What does that mean?" Saul frowned as he shifted his weight.

"No one's talking about it — in light of everything — but I don't think they're happy with Miriam for sneaking out of the house to see you. She'll probably get grounded or something when everything settles down."

"Sneaking out? What?"

Shelby squeezed her eyes closed for a moment, then opened them. "Oops. I assumed she told you."

Saul stood taller, shifting his weight from one foot to the other. "No, she didn't tell me." He paused, rubbing his chin. "And that ain't right. She shouldn't be sneaking around behind her parents' backs." He shook his head. "I wondered why they let her go out that late at night, but I just never asked her about it."

Shelby looked down and kicked the grass with her bare foot. She put her hands in the pockets of her blue jeans, then looked back up at him. "You know, she likes you a lot."

Saul looked toward the barn and didn't say anything for a moment. "I like her too," he said with a shrug.

Shelby leaned closer to him. "Don't be nonchalant, Saul."

"Huh?"

"She really likes you, but Jesse told me that you aren't going to be baptized here, and that you'll eventually leave this place. Is that true?"

Saul looped his thumbs beneath his suspenders, bit his lip, and looked toward the barn again. Shelby had her answer.

"Jesse needs to mind his own business." Saul finally faced Shelby. "I'll talk to Miriam."

"So it's true. You are leaving?"

"Ya." Saul turned toward his horse. "She'll probably end up with Jesse anyway."

"She doesn't want Jesse." Shelby followed Saul as he walked toward his buggy. She knew she was overstepping her bounds, but she was feeling unusually protective of Miriam — probably because Shelby knew what it was like to be abandoned by the man you loved. "She wants *you.*"

"I gotta go." Saul climbed into his buggy.

"I'm sure you do," Shelby mumbled as he pulled away. *Poor Miriam.*

Shelby waited until Saul was gone before she looked toward the sky. She closed her eyes to avoid the bright sun.

God, I thought that prayers for other people were answered before our own needs. I thought You'd help Miriam not to get hurt. Are You listening to me?

176

Shelby hung her head for a moment, then walked back to the house, dreading in her heart that she would have to tell Miriam that Saul was leaving here. But her cousin had a right to know before she got too involved with him.

Miriam sat quietly with her parents and brothers in a large room with empty caskets everywhere. Gold ones, blue ones, brown ones — all colors, and all very fancy. Her family was seated in the large room while Mr. Roberts went over the details of the funeral. As was custom, Uncle Ivan would be buried in a plain coffin with no ornament, then later laid to rest in a hand-dug grave in their community cemetery. The funeral home would take his body to her Aunt Mary Ellen's house tomorrow, where he would stay until the funeral two days later. Mary Ellen's home was the largest and would be best for receiving visitors. Uncle Noah wasn't Amish, so his wasn't an option. Miriam's Uncle Samuel, Aunt Lillian, cousin David, and Aunt Katie Ann were scheduled to arrive from Colorado tomorrow and would be staying with Mary Ellen.

Everyone in the room looked toward the door when it eased open. Lucy Turner walked in, her ivory skin streaked with tears, and Miriam didn't think she'd ever seen her look so plain. Barely any makeup, and she was wearing gray sweat pants and a gray T-shirt.

"I'm — I'm sorry to interrupt. I just didn't know what to do, or where to go, and — and I just wanted to make sure that everything — I'm sorry. I'm so sorry. I shouldn't have come."

She turned to leave, but it was Miriam's mother who spoke up. "Lucy, you may stay."

Lucy faced the group, dabbed at her eyes, and took a couple of steps forward, finally settling into a chair that was set apart from the rest of the group. Mr. Roberts waited, then finished things up by asking if anyone had any questions. When no one did, he excused himself. "I'll let you have some time alone," he said quietly.

It seemed strange for Lucy to be among the family. They'd all been fairly certain that Lucy had lured Ivan away from Katie Ann, even though *Mamm* had said repeatedly that Ivan was a grown man making his own choices. Even though Miriam knew it was wrong in the eyes of God, she didn't care for Lucy Turner. But seeing Lucy so upset made Miriam realize that — right or wrong — Lucy obviously cared about Uncle Ivan a lot. She felt sorry for Lucy's loss too.

9

Miriam wasn't home for ten minutes before Shelby pulled her upstairs. "Saul was here earlier," she said.

"I forgot to call him!" Miriam slapped herself on the forehead and sat down on the bed. "I better go try now, or at least leave a message for him."

"Miriam . . ."

"Ya?"

Shelby bit her bottom lip for a moment. "Saul's not planning to be baptized here, Miriam. He's going to leave this place." Shelby waved her arm around the room.

Miriam was sad and exhausted. This was the last thing she needed at the moment. She let out a heavy sigh. "Shelby, what would make you say that?"

"He told me."

Miriam wrapped her arms around herself, more despair weighing on her. She didn't say anything.

"I'm sorry, Miriam." Shelby leaned her head down into her hands for a moment, then looked back up. "I just thought you'd want to know."

"I guess that's why he avoided the question when I asked him about it." She blinked a few times and told herself that she'd cried enough today.

"Because men are jerks. That's why. That's what they do. They get close to you, then leave you." Shelby nodded strongly as she pinched her lips together.

"I can't think about this right now." Miriam shook her head, and despite how sad she was about her uncle's passing, she knew that she would be thinking about Saul too. "But . . . why did he come by earlier?"

"He said he came to check on you and to see if he could do anything for your family."

Miriam smiled. "That was nice of him."

"Be careful, Miriam. Now that you know he's leaving, guard your heart."

"I have to go downstairs and help *Mamm*."

"I'll come too."

Miriam walked out the door and down the stairs, Shelby following close behind. Everything was going to be all right. It saddened her that Saul was going to leave the community, but almost instantly her mind began to scramble with what-ifs. She'd always pictured her and Saul in the community — married and raising a family together. But what if only *part* of that picture became a reality?

Saul had no doubt that Shelby told Miriam that he would be leaving the community, and he knew in his head that it was for the best. He'd had the best time with Miriam last night, and he longed to spend even more time with her. It was as if years of silent infatuation had risen to the surface and overtaken them both, and it felt wonderful. He'd always loved Miriam from afar. She was the kind of woman he hoped to marry someday, but her life was here. And Saul had known since he was fourteen that his wasn't. The world had too much to offer, and he got his first glimpse when his father took him to an auction, an *Englisch* auction in Lancaster. *Daed* needed a new plow and some other farm equipment, and his father spent all day surveying what he planned to bid on, then did so at the auction. While his father was preoccupied, Saul met Ted Stark, a sixteen-year-old *Englisch* boy — with a car. Saul wasn't old enough to be in his *rumschpringe* yet, but it didn't stop him from seeing the world beyond his district with Ted for the next several months.

Saul's favorite part of his adventures — going to restaurants and critiquing the food. He'd worked part-time that summer, saved his money, and eaten at some mighty fine places. His favorite restaurant back then was one that used odd combinations of seasonings, and he could remember the taste long after he'd left.

One evening he'd worked up enough courage to speak to the chef, an *Englisch* fellow with no hair and a limp. After Saul questioned the man about a certain Italian dish, the chef — Claude — invited Saul to the back and actually showed him how to prepare the chestnut pasta with creamy porcini mushroom sauce. He decided that night that he would prepare fancy meals in a fancy restaurant if he was ever given the opportunity. Now, with a job offer in hand, it was time to act on his plans. *Best that Miriam knows now,* he supposed. And she'd surely not want to spend any more time with him.

Following family devotion, Saul noticed his father getting restless, pacing the room, and glancing out the window every few minutes.

"You waiting for someone?" Saul set down the Bible he was reading. Ruben and James were already upstairs, and Saul suspected

Ruben was locked in his room reading a magazine *Daed* probably wouldn't approve of. Ruben liked cars, and he took every opportunity to buy an automobile magazine and sneak it upstairs.

His father shook his head and blew it out slowly. "No, just stretching my legs."

Saul picked up the Bible and started reading again when he saw his father wipe sweat from his forehead, then reach for his hat on the rack.

"I'm going to go take a walk, get some fresh air."

Saul's stomach churned. He'd covered every square inch of the house, barn, and property looking for wine or other forms of alcohol, and he'd never found any — but when *Daed* went for a walk, he always came back drunk or with a bottle in his hand. It was hidden somewhere. Saul just didn't know where. His heart started to beat out of his chest as he put the book down again and stood up. "I'll go with you. I could use some fresh air too."

As he could have predicted, his father shook his head. "No, you stay to your studies. I'd like to just clear my mind with a *gut* walk." *Daed* pulled the door open and wasn't even over the threshold when Saul called to him.

"Ya?" He smiled, and Saul didn't think there was a person on the planet whose eyes were kinder than his father's. Saul just stared at him for a few moments. "What is it, *sohn?"*

"Daed." Saul slowly stood up as he bit his lip and walked toward his father. "Maybe tonight isn't really a *gut* night for a walk."

Daed lowered his head, a sad smile on his face when he looked up. "It's as good as any other night, Saul." And he left.

Tuesday morning Miriam gathered with the entire family at Mary Ellen's home for the funeral. Her Uncle Samuel, Aunt Lillian, and cousin David had flown in with Aunt Katie Ann, whose pregnant belly was easy to see. They'd arrived just last night from Colorado. Miriam had never flown in a plane, and she hoped she didn't ever have to. It was a last resort for travel and only in the case of emergencies.

She glanced around and her heart ached even more at seeing her Uncle Noah, Aunt Carley, and their daughter, Jenna; Aunt Mary Ellen and Uncle Abe and their children; Lillian's mother, Sarah Jane; close family friends Lizzie, Sadie, and Kade; their *Englisch* friend Barbie Beiler; and so many more. She figured there were close to two hundred people inside Mary Ellen's den, which was set up just like church service, backless benches for the men facing one way and more benches for the women facing toward the men.

Miriam was just taking her seat in between her mother and Shelby when she saw Saul walk in with his two brothers but without Zeb Fisher. Miriam wondered why Zeb wasn't there and hoped he wasn't ill. As she scanned the room, she saw Lucy Turner standing in the back, dressed in a knee-length black dress. When she located Aunt Katie Ann sitting three seats in front of Miriam, she wondered how it must feel for Katie Ann to know that Lucy was in the back of the room. She looked at Saul again and thought about what she would say to him later, when the time was appropriate.

Following the two-hour service, Miriam's heart was still heavy with sadness but soothed by prayer. Amish folks went by buggy to the cemetery, followed by a few cars. Bishop Ebersol spoke briefly at the burial site about admonition for the living, then closed in prayer. As Miriam followed her family to their buggy, Saul walked up beside her.

"I'm sorry, Miriam."

"Danki." Miriam glanced around to see

where her parents were. They were quite a ways in front of her with Shelby. "I'm sorry I didn't call. There was so much going on."

Saul brushed his hand against hers. "It's all right. I heard what happened, so I knew that's why you weren't able to call."

He started moving toward the buggies again, so Miriam did too, the two of them walking in silence for a few moments. They almost walked right into Miriam's mother and Shelby, who had turned around and seemed to be waiting on them.

Mamm raised her chin a bit as she sniffled. "Hello, Saul."

Saul removed his hat. "I'm sorry for your loss, Rebecca."

Miriam's mother nodded but quickly grabbed Miriam's hand. "Your *Aenti* Lillian is looking for you."

Saul nodded and didn't move as *Mamm* dragged her forward. She glanced over her shoulder and saw Saul's brothers walk up beside him, then they turned and walked the other way. She wondered if they would go to the meal at Mary Ellen's.

As soon as she arrived at her aunt and uncle's house, Miriam looked everywhere for Saul.

"I don't think he's here," Shelby said, standing in the yard and holding a glass of meadow tea. She took a sip of the drink. "I'm assuming you're looking for Saul?"

Miriam nodded, then Jesse walked up. "Miriam, I'm real sorry," he said as he removed his hat. "If there's anything me or my family can do, please let us know."

"*Danki,* Jesse."

Jesse turned to Shelby and gave a quick nod, then looked back at Miriam. "When you're feeling better, we should all go fishing at the Zook place again."

"Okay." Miriam wasn't much interested in going back to the Zook place unless Saul was going too.

"How about next Saturday? Do you think you'd be up to it then?" Jesse put his hat back on.

"I don't know if it will be too soon, or if I should —"

"I could stop by Saul's and see if he wants to go again too." Jesse smiled, and Miriam saw him glance at Shelby. Shelby said both Jesse and Saul liked her, but he seemed equally as focused on Shelby right now. Didn't Jesse realize that neither one of them was good for him? Miriam was in love with someone else, and Shelby wasn't Amish. But whatever his motives, his offer was too tempting.

"I guess by then we'd be able to go. We

could meet you out there. Maybe lunch-time? Me and Shelby could bring a picnic lunch."

Jesse smiled. "Sounds *gut*. I'll let Saul know."

After he walked away, Miriam looked at Shelby and watched her cousin's left brow rise a fraction. "Wonder what he's up to," Shelby said, smirking.

Miriam was glad for a distraction from the sadness that surrounded them. "I'm not sure he's up to anything. He just wants to go fishing." She was mildly concerned that Jesse might be interested in Shelby, and she had to question exactly why that would bother her so much. *Has Jesse always been my backup plan in case things didn't work with Saul?* She quickly tossed the selfish thought aside. Then she thought for a moment about Saul leaving and what that might mean for her life.

"Look." Shelby nodded her head to their left. "Isn't that your Aunt Katie Ann talking to Lucy?"

Miriam tried to be discreet as she glanced toward the two women. *"Ya,"* she whispered. She saw her aunt swipe at her eyes, then touch her expanded stomach. Lucy hung her head as she spoke.

Miriam watched Katie Ann press her lips

together, but her aunt eventually nodded. A few moments later the women parted ways.

"Katie Ann always wanted a baby. More than anyone I've ever known." Miriam sighed.

"I guess this is bittersweet, then."

"*Ya,* it is." She took a final look around for Saul, convinced that he and his brothers had gone home straight from the cemetery. At least she would see him next Saturday.

Miriam went to bed early Friday night, glad not to have any *Englisch* guests for supper for the second week in a row. *Mamm* had said earlier that even if she were not still mourning the death of her brother, she wouldn't have opted to host a supper tonight. Her mother couldn't seem to shake the fact that someone stole from her under her own roof. But Miriam knew her *mamm* had cried on and off most of the week following the funeral, saying that she would always regret that she didn't talk to Ivan before he died and, instead, had practiced the shunning to the fullest. Miriam recalled with regret how quickly she'd gotten away from her uncle while she and Shelby were in Bird-In-Hand. If she'd only known that it would be the last time she would see her uncle . . .

Surprisingly, Shelby was asleep before Miriam. She listened to her cousin snoring lightly, then reached for the lantern and darkened the room. Sleep wasn't going to come easy as her mind whirled with thoughts about Uncle Ivan. Then there was the fishing trip in the morning when she'd finally see Saul again.

Could Saul really the leave the community — and her? She kept asking herself what it was about Saul that made her so sure he was the one for her, even though they'd spent very little time together over the years. She was wise enough to know that mutual attraction was not enough. But something about Saul's personality had drawn her to him at an early age. He was edgy, adventuresome, but yet gentle and kind. He often bucked the traditional Amish ways, but always with the best of intentions. She thought again about how he defended her that day on the playground.

She rolled onto her side and stared out the window into a starlit night. She thought about everything outside of her small district, the only world she'd ever known. *Is it peaceful like it is here? Are folks good to each other?* Shelby had said it's a dangerous place.

She let her mind drift far away. She

pictured her and Saul out in the *Englisch* world together. She thought about being able to listen to music all the time, something she really enjoyed and something forbidden in her community. She thought about wearing *Englisch* clothes and traveling to other parts of the world. Would they do those things? Mostly she thought about just being with Saul, loving him. No matter their location, she knew that the basis of marriage was unconditional love and a union blessed by God. Her thoughts were unresolved when she finally drifted off to sleep.

When she opened her eyes Saturday morning, Shelby was buried beneath the covers as usual, so she quietly climbed out of bed, got dressed, and headed downstairs. In the kitchen, her mother was scurrying around the kitchen. *Mamm's* eyes were swollen, so she knew her mother's heart was going to hurt for a long time about Uncle Ivan. As soon as breakfast was over, she went outside and found her father alone in the barn, carrying a stack of old newspapers. He smiled at her when she walked into the barn.

"I don't know why your *mamm* insists on keeping these old copies of *The Budget*." He grinned as he shook his head. "She said it's like a scrapbook of everyone's birth announcements, obituaries, and news." He dropped the newspapers into a box in the corner. "I told her she didn't even know most of these folks from all over the United States, but you know how your *mamm* is. She doesn't really meet a stranger."

Miriam smiled as she moved closer to her father, and she pondered his statement. *Then why can't she accept Saul?*

Daed tipped back the rim of his hat. "What's on your mind, *dochder?*" He leaned against his workbench and looped his thumbs beneath his suspenders.

"Me and Shelby have a few chores to do this morning, then we were going to go fishing with Jesse and Saul . . . if that's okay." Miriam took a deep breath and waited.

Daed grinned. "So you came out here to ask me instead of asking your *mamm,* who's in the *haus?*"

Miriam hung her head as she kicked at the sandy floor of the barn with one foot.

"I guess it's all right, Miriam." *Daed* patted her on the shoulder as he moved past her toward the barn exit. "You *kinner* have fun."

Miriam lifted up on her toes. *"Danki, Daed!"* Then she ran to go find Shelby.

Rebecca marched to the barn to find Aaron.

"Hello, *mei lieb,*" her husband said casually as he carried a pile of hay to the horse's stall. "What brings you out to the barn this fine morning?"

Her husband's smile quickly faded when Rebecca drew closer. Aaron dropped the hay.

"What's wrong?"

Rebecca thrust her hands on her hips. "What's wrong?" she huffed. "Do you really have to ask me that? Our *dochder* just told me that you gave permission for her and Shelby to go fishing with Saul and Jesse. Why did you do that?"

Aaron took off his hat, dabbed at his forehead with a handkerchief, then put his hat back on. "We already talked to Miriam about sneaking out of the house, and both girls have worked extra hard." He put his own hands on his hips and faced off with her. "It's just fishing, Rebecca, and if Miriam wants to see that boy, she's going to. Wouldn't you rather it be during the daylight hours, instead of sneaking around? She's in her *rumschpringe,* and it's her time to figure out —"

193

"Oh shush, Aaron!" Rebecca waved her hand in the air, despite the scowl stretching across her husband's face. "That boy is not *gut* for Miriam. You should have just said no." She stomped her foot.

"Rebecca." Aaron sighed. "You barely know him. And I thought you'd be glad that Shelby and Jesse are going too."

"We saw how that worked out last time. Shelby and Jesse went home early and left Miriam and Saul alone."

Aaron grinned. "I seem to recall a certain girl in her *rumschpringe* who snuck out on more than one occasion to see the boy she liked." He paused, lifting one brow playfully. "And look how that turned out."

"It's not the same, Aaron." She walked closer to him. "Do you really want our *dochder* involved with a boy who's been in trouble? And it's not just that. There is much talk about him wanting to leave the community. Doesn't that scare you?"

Aaron gently put his hands on Rebecca's shoulders. "I hope that all our *kinner* make the choice to stay here, Rebecca, but this is what their running-around time is for. And Miriam is a smart girl, dedicated to her faith and her life here. She isn't going to leave here."

Rebecca let him pull her into his arms,

then she gently eased away. "Aaron, when we were courting . . . if you'd asked me to leave the community and go with you out into the *Englisch* world, I would have. I would have followed you anywhere. Young love is a dangerous thing."

Aaron smiled. "I didn't know that." He tipped the rim of his hat up a bit. "Not that I had any thoughts about leaving."

"I want you to talk to Saul. Find out what his intentions are."

"Rebecca, it's too soon for that. We don't even know if they are officially dating."

She blew out a breath of exasperation. "It's not too soon. It might already be too late!"

Shelby placed napkins in the picnic basket as she waited for Miriam to fill a thermos with tea. She had mixed emotions about the fishing trip. Even though there were four of them going, and she loved to fish, she still felt like the outsider — and not just because she wasn't Amish. Both men were vying for her cousin's attention, which did little for Shelby's fragile emotions. She was going to try to make the best of it anyway and enjoy the day outside fishing.

"Chicken salad sandwiches, potato chips, pickles, tea . . ." Miriam looked up at

Shelby. "What am I forgetting?"

"Pie?"

Miriam snapped her fingers. *"Ya!"* She cut four slices of apple pie, wrapped them individually in plastic wrap, and placed them on top of the other items.

Shelby closed the lid and picked up the basket. They were almost to the door when they bumped into Rebecca coming in.

"We won't be late, *Mamm,*" Miriam said meekly, avoiding her mother's eyes. Rebecca nodded, then scooted past them and into the den.

"Your mother is so unhappy," Shelby said as she placed the basket in the back of the spring buggy.

"I know. She's still real upset about *Onkel* Ivan." Miriam hung her head for a moment. "And she's still mad at me about sneaking out to see Saul, but I know it's more than that. She's afraid Saul will leave and that I'll go with him."

Shelby thought for a moment. "But you *know* Saul is leaving. I told you that."

Miriam grabbed the reins and backed up the horse. *"Ya.* I know."

"Are you going to say anything to him about it?"

"I don't know yet."

Shelby reached up and pulled her hair

tighter within her ponytail holder, then adjusted her black sunglasses. "Well, I'd sure say something if I were you."

Miriam chewed her bottom lip for a moment. "Maybe he'll change his mind."

"And maybe he won't. Then what?"

Her cousin was quiet as she maneuvered the topless buggy onto the road. "I don't know."

Shelby couldn't imagine Miriam leaving this place. *It's all she knows.* Which is why this situation had nothing but heartbreak written all over it.

Saul pulled up to the Zook farm at the same time as Jesse. He didn't really like Jesse being here, but Jesse was the one who'd come to his house and invited him. Maybe he was truly interested in Shelby. Saul selfishly hoped so.

His stomach churned thinking about how long it would take for Miriam to say that she heard he was leaving the community. Things at home had gotten even more complicated over the past week anyway, and Saul wasn't sure how he could leave in good conscience.

"Are you and Miriam officially dating?" Jesse glanced at Saul as both men tethered the horses to the fence.

Saul shrugged. "We've only been out once, plus these fishing trips."

Jesse stood taller and faced Saul. "Miriam is a *gut* girl. I hope you won't hurt her. Rumor has it you're leaving here."

Saul tensed as he took a deep breath, but he knew Jesse really did care for Miriam, and Jesse was right to be concerned. "I'm not going to hurt her."

"If you leave here, you will hurt her." Jesse eyed Saul with curiosity, but Saul had no intention of confiding in him. If one word of his father's drinking got out, it would be all over the community. He prayed every day that his father would stop so that Saul could pursue his plans to go work at the bistro, but his *daed's* drinking was getting more frequent — and worse.

They both turned at the sound of Miriam's buggy on the gravel driveway. After she pulled up, Jesse quickly offered her a hand down. Saul walked to the other side to help Shelby, but she'd already jumped down by the time he got there and was reaching for a picnic basket in the back.

"We brought lunch," she said, holding the basket and grinning. "Although . . . I can't take credit."

Saul took the basket and waited while Jesse pulled Miriam's fishing pole from the

198

back. They slowly made their way to the water's edge, and Miriam unfolded a red-and-white quilt to use as a big tablecloth. Once the food was spread out, everyone bowed their heads in prayer.

"Mmm. There's something different in this chicken salad." Saul wrapped his mouth around his sandwich and tried to figure out what Miriam's secret ingredient was. He swallowed, then smiled at her. "You gonna tell me?"

"Nope." She giggled. "But if you have a recipe you'd like to trade . . ."

Saul felt his face turning four shades of red.

"You cook, Saul?" Jesse grinned as he glanced at Shelby.

"He has to cook for his family, Jesse," Miriam said defensively, which warmed Saul's heart but also made him feel like a bit of a wimp.

"Sometimes," he added.

"Are we on for another competition?" Shelby asked as she helped Miriam gather up used paper plates and napkins.

"*Ya.* I'm in." Jesse stood up, then added, "But why don't we pair up differently? Probably ain't fair to have the girls against us, Saul."

Shelby laughed. "Why? Are you afraid

we'll win again?"

"You didn't win." Jesse looped his thumbs underneath his suspenders. "Me and Saul caught more fish."

"But . . . we caught the biggest one!" Shelby stood with her shoulders back, grinning.

Saul took a deep breath. He could see where this was going. Despite Jesse's earlier comments, he was going to haul Miriam off to the other side of the pond.

"I say Shelby and me against you two." Jesse pointed to Miriam and Saul.

Saul tried not to show his surprise and looked at Miriam, who was smiling broadly. "Okay," he said. "Miriam?"

"*Ya.* I'm pretty sure me and Saul can catch more fish than the two of you!"

Saul was glad to see Jesse grab Shelby's hand, then pull her toward the other end of the pond. "May the best couple win!"

Miriam wanted nothing more than to be alone with Saul, but there was an uncomfortable feeling that emerged inside of her when she saw Jesse and Shelby skipping off happily together. She wanted to be with Saul, so it seemed strange that she would feel this way. If it hadn't been for Shelby telling her that Saul was leaving, Miriam knew she never would have thought about life outside of their district. Now she kept thinking of all the possibilities that would be available to her if she did leave. She'd always wanted to be a teacher here, but her mother had said that she was more suited for marriage and family. In the *Englisch* world, maybe she could have both? She'd always thought there was plenty of time to get to know Saul better, but time was no longer on her side. One thing she knew for sure . . . she couldn't imagine her life here without him in it.

But what if Saul has no plans to ask me to leave with him? Then Jesse might already be with . . . Shelby? No. That doesn't make sense either. Shelby is Englisch.

Her uneasiness calmed when she felt Saul's hand on her back. "Here, I got your pole ready." He offered her the pole with a wiggling worm dangling from the hook, then held his other palm toward her. "And *ya* . . . I know you could have done it yourself, but I was just helping."

"*Danki,*" she said as she accepted the pole. She liked that he recognized her independence but also acted as a gentleman every time he was around her.

As the afternoon sun beat down on them, Miriam wondered if maybe they shouldn't have planned this so late in the day. She reached up and wiped beads of sweat from her forehead. Next thing she knew, she felt a breeze on her face along with a shower of ice cold water. "Wow!" She closed her eyes and enjoyed the sensation.

"I found these at the market in Bird-In-Hand when I was there this past week. I got one for you, since I knew we were going fishing."

Miriam accepted the battery-operated fan that, with the push of a button, also sprayed cold water. She turned it and pushed the button until the icy droplets were sprinkling Saul's face. "I like this," she said as she pulled it back her way. *"Danki."*

"I put some ice cubes in it before we came."

Miriam took her pole and her new fan and sat down on a stump near the edge of the water. Saul took a seat right next to her, causing her to jump. "This okay?" he asked.

She nodded, then tossed her line into the water.

"So what's in the chicken salad?" He grinned, and as Miriam turned to face him, their lips couldn't have been farther than six inches apart. She faced forward again.

"Uh, it's, uh —" She couldn't think.

"It almost tasted like lemon pepper?"

Miriam breathed a sigh of relief. "*Ya*. That's it." She didn't look at him but tried to stay focused on her line in the water. She picked up her fan, turned it on, and held down the button until cool water showered her face again.

"How 'bout a little of that this way?" Saul's leg brushed against hers as he shifted his weight to face her. Miriam pointed the fan toward his face. "Ah . . ."

She watched him close his eyes, enjoying the cool water. When he opened his eyes, he latched onto the fan, covering her hand, then turned it back toward her. After a few moments, he gently eased it down, then turned it off. Miriam tried not to look at him, but when his hand cupped her chin and he turned her toward him, she felt herself shaking. She'd never been kissed. And the moment was upon her. She'd always dreamed that Saul would be her first kiss. As his lips drew near hers, she watched him close his eyes, but her eyes seemed to have a mind of their own and remained wide open. With a jerk, she pulled away from him.

"Are you leaving here, Saul?"

Saul let out a heavy sigh, then scratched the back of his head. "I don't know."

"How can you not know? Shelby said you

told her that you were leaving."

"That was my plan, but now I'm not sure."

Miriam's insides warmed. *It's because of me that he's not leaving.* She felt a smile cross her lips. "Oh," she said.

"I have something to ask you too." Saul backed up a bit but was still facing her. "Did you sneak out to meet me Saturday night . . . without telling your folks?"

Miriam avoided his accusing eyes as she twisted her mouth from side to side. *"Ya."*

Saul shook his head. "Please don't do that again, Miriam. Your parents won't want me being around you if they think I'm getting you to do stuff like that. We'll see each other when it's okay with your parents."

Miriam nodded, glad there was a mention about seeing each other again but not sure it would really be okay with her parents.

"Why would you leave here, Saul?" She eased away from him a little and faced him, still sitting on the stump.

His eyes averted hers, and he sighed. Then he looked up grinning. "Promise you won't laugh?"

"No." Then she giggled as she raised her palm to him. *"Ya.* I promise. I won't laugh."

He pulled his hat off and scratched his forehead. "I have a job offer to work in a fancy restaurant in Pittsburgh." Saul paused when Miriam's eyes widened. "I'd be the apprentice chef." He looked hard into Miriam's eyes. "I answered an ad in the newspaper, and then I went and cooked some of my recipes for the owner." Saul shrugged. "It's a great opportunity for me, and I really want to go, but . . ." He sighed again.

Miriam smiled, her heart warm, yet frightened at the same time. She knew she'd go anywhere with Saul, especially now that he was willing to forgo leaving because of her. "Don't worry, Saul."

Tense lines formed across his forehead. "There is much to worry about," he said as he put his hat back on.

Miriam wanted to ease his pain. Even though there would be strife and upset in the community, she wanted him to know how she felt.

"I'll go with you, Saul. So please don't change your mind because . . . because of me." She looked toward the ground, stifling a smile.

Saul jumped up from the stump they were sitting on and looked down at her, his face drawn into a scowl. "What?" He put his hands on his hips. "*What?* If I go, you can't go with me, Miriam."

10

Saul chased after Miriam as she ran toward the buggies. He felt like a louse, but he'd be even more of a louse if he asked Miriam to leave her family and all that she's ever known behind.

"Miriam, wait!" He finally caught up with her and grabbed her arm so she'd stop. Tears spilled from her eyes, and with little thought, except that he couldn't stand to see her cry, he cupped her cheeks in his hands and kissed the tears on her face. "Please, Miriam. Please don't cry," he whispered. When his lips finally met with hers, he kissed her softly, and when she kissed him back, something inside of Saul made him want to beg her to go with him if he left, but nothing could be more selfish. He eased away from her. "I'm sorry I made you cry." He brushed away her tears with his thumbs, then pulled her into his arms.

"I am such a *dummkopp.*" Her body shook

as she choked out the words, her face buried in his chest. "I should have known that you didn't feel the same way I do."

He gently pushed her away. "Is that what you think, Miriam? I've liked you since we were *kinner.*" He kissed her again. "But I would never ask you to leave your family and your friends. Never."

She sniffled as she gazed into his eyes, and Saul wanted to drop to one knee right there in the old Zook front yard.

"I thought you had changed your mind about leaving our community because of *me,*" she squeaked out as she started to cry again. "And I wanted you to know that I would go with you, if that were the case." She stepped back from him and stomped her foot. "I'm such a *dummkopp!*" she repeated even louder this time.

Saul pulled his eyes from hers as he rubbed his forehead. He couldn't tell her the real reason he might not be able to go, but her willingness to follow him certainly gave him cause for speculation — *Would she really go with me?* He could envision a life with Miriam. But just as quickly the image faded. *Ruben and James.* He couldn't leave his brothers, not with their father like this. "You're not a *dummkopp,* Miriam. Please don't say that."

"I want to go home, Saul." She swiped at her eyes, and Saul saw Jesse and Shelby heading their way. "I'm embarrassed, and I want to go home."

"Miriam, you don't understand."

"*Ya.* I do." She moved toward her buggy. Saul followed her.

"I can't ask you to leave here."

She faced him, her cheeks stained with tears, and she spoke softly. "No. It appears you can't."

Jesse walked up on them, Shelby trailing behind. "What's going on?" Jesse nudged Saul out of the way and put his hand on Miriam's arm. "Miriam, what is it?"

"It's nothing, Jesse." She sniffled again, and Saul didn't think he could feel any lower.

Shelby charged ahead, pushing Jesse out of the way. "Miriam, what's wrong?" She didn't wait for an answer but instead balled her hands into fists at her sides, moving closer to Saul. He backed up. "What did you do to her?"

"Shelby, he didn't do anything." Miriam grabbed her cousin's arm. "Come on, we need to get home."

Saul opened his mouth to say something, but everyone was glaring at him. "I'm sorry." It was all he knew to say.

Saul pulled into his driveway, and his stomach began to ache the way it always did. Who would he come home to? Which father would greet him?

However, when he saw Ruben and James happily playing basketball, his fears subsided.

He parked the buggy, then hollered, "Can one of you put Rascal in the barn? I'll go get supper started." He paused as he wrapped the reins around the post. "Everything okay?"

Both boys nodded, and Ruben started to make his way toward the horse and buggy. Saul walked inside. His father was sitting in his chair, reading the Bible. *"Wie bischt, Daed?"*

His father took off his reading glasses. *"Gut, gut.* I finished the last of the planting, and . . ." *Daed* smiled. "I took off early."

Saul let out a huge sigh of relief. This was the man he knew and loved, not the monster trapped in a way that Saul couldn't understand. *"Gut* for you, *Daed.* You work hard and deserve to take off early." Saul hung his hat on the rack by the door. "I'll go get supper started."

"*Sohn,* can we talk?"

Saul held his breath for a moment. "Sure."

His father motioned for Saul to sit down on the couch across from him. "I've been doing some thinking, and I've made arrangements to have a hundred acres deeded to you. That way when you find a *fraa,* you'll already have the land to build on. How does that sound? It's the acreage on the north side of the house. There's plenty of room for your own planting, and a house would be perfect up on the hill out there."

Daed smiled, and Saul knew that this was his father's way of apologizing for recent events. Saul could see his dream slipping further and further away, and he was still confused about Miriam and her willingness to leave the community to be with him. *Does she care about me that much?*

"*Danki, Daed,*" Saul finally said as he forced a smile.

"Tomorrow we'll walk the land, see what you think, and where might be the best place for you to build a home. I still think you could put a nice *haus* right on top of the hill." *Daed* stood up and walked to where Saul was standing. He put his hand on Saul's shoulder. "Today is a new day. A day blessed by our Lord." He paused as his eyes grew sad. "Perhaps we could think of it as a new beginning."

Saul was never affectionate with his father — or his brothers. It wasn't their way. But he couldn't help but put his arms around his father. "I love you, *Daed*."

When his father squeezed him and whispered, "I love you too, *sohn*," Saul knew everything was going to somehow be okay. Even if he never did become a chef in a restaurant.

Shelby was the last one in the tub this evening. After she finished in the bathroom, she passed by Rebecca and Aaron's room on the way to her room, and she heard her name. Instinctively she paused, even though she knew she shouldn't be eavesdropping.

"I don't care, Aaron. I still think that Miriam would have never snuck out if Shelby hadn't put her up to it."

"I told you before, Rebecca . . . you don't know if Shelby encouraged Miriam to do that. You ain't being fair about it."

Shelby brought her hand to her mouth, her feet rooted to the floor, and she listened.

"There is much worry in my heart concerning Miriam. Not only is she being influenced by an *Englisch* outsider, but we also have Saul Fisher to worry about. What if he leaves and tries to take our Miriam with him?"

Shelby kept her hand over her mouth as she blinked back tears. *An outsider?* She was just starting to feel more at home here than she had in Fayetteville. And today had been wonderful — Jesse had been wonderful. But hearing Rebecca speak about her this way pushed a tear down her cheek. She forced her feet to move and hurried down the hallway. When she opened the door, Miriam was sitting on the side of her bed, her eyes red and swollen. She knew her cousin needed to talk, but she just couldn't tonight.

She walked to her bed, crawled underneath the covers, then glanced at Miriam, whose eyes widened as if she couldn't believe Shelby was going to go to sleep. "I don't feel well, Miriam. I'm so sorry. Can we talk tomorrow? I know you're upset about Saul and sad about your uncle, but I feel like I need to go to sleep."

Miriam hung her head a bit but then looked at Shelby and sniffled. "Sure. We can talk tomorrow. I probably need to sleep too."

Sleep was the last thing on Shelby's mind. Her life was a wreck, and now the family she thought she'd found didn't want her either. No one wanted her. Not her parents. Not Tommy. And now . . . not Rebecca. She covered her head with the sheet and buried her sobs in her pillow, hoping the sound of the fan would drown out her self-pity. Her cousin had enough worries, and Shelby couldn't even keep herself together enough to listen to the one person she'd come to trust and love. *Like a sister.*

God, if You're there, please, oh please, help me. I feel so lost and alone. I don't know who else to turn to.

Shelby realized right away that her plea sounded as though God was her last effort, her last hope. She could remember a time when she used to turn to God first. She took a deep breath.

Dear heavenly Father, lately I began to feel like I was part of a family again and that my life was on the mend. Now I'm confused and alone. Please, God, help me to find peace in my heart. Please . . . What is Your plan for me?

She buried her head into her pillow even farther, pulling the edges up over her ears, as if covering her ears would prevent her from hearing anything that she didn't want to hear. What did she expect to hear?

Please, God. Please . . .

She heard Miriam crawl underneath her covers and twist the knob on the lantern until the room went dark. All that could be heard was the steady spinning of the fan on the nightstand. She stifled her tears, pulled the sheet away from her head, then rolled onto her back. She stared at the ceiling, into darkness. *Please, God.*

She squeezed her eyes closed and mouthed the words over and over. *Please, God . . . Please, God . . .*

I am here for you, My child. I will never forsake you.

She held her breath, released it slowly, then felt a sense of calm . . . as if God had sent the Holy Spirit directly to her at that perfect moment, as only He could do. When she finally began to breathe, she slowly sat up in bed, hugged herself tightly, and began to sob.

"Shelby . . ."

She heard her cousin but didn't answer. The room seemed brighter somehow, and she wanted to bask in the knowledge that God was with her, that He would always be with her, even when she couldn't understand His plan for her.

"Dear Lord, I'm sorry. I'm sorry I doubted You." She cried harder until she felt Miriam's arms around her.

"I'm here, my sister. I'm here," Miriam said softly.

Shelby turned to Miriam, who was sitting on the edge of her bed. "God has not forsaken me."

"Of course He hasn't." Miriam rubbed her back as she spoke.

Shelby wept in Miriam's arms for a long time, knowing that the pains of her past were slowly being released into God's hands.

After a long while, Miriam turned the lantern up, then they sat like Indians and talked well into the night. Miriam told her everything that happened with Saul, and Shelby told Miriam about her parents' divorce, how her faith had slipped, and about the bad choices she'd made. It was painful to tell Miriam about the shoplifting and how she'd experimented with drinking and drugs, but her cousin never judged.

She didn't tell her what she overheard Rebecca saying. She knew Miriam well enough to know that she would go straight to her mother and tell the truth — that it was Miriam who insisted on sneaking out. And Shelby figured Miriam had enough troubles right now.

But her heart ached every time she heard Rebecca's voice, calling her the "*Englisch* outsider."

I want to belong somewhere.

But tonight, for the first time in a long while, she had faith that God would put her on the right path.

Rebecca's dreams continued to wake her up during the night and stayed with her throughout her days. She feared she would never get any sleep unless she had a heart-to-heart talk with Miriam. She could tell her daughter was reluctant to travel to town with her — just the two of them. Miriam had scoffed when Rebecca mentioned it, and then she'd shuffled across the yard toward the buggy like she was being punished.

"Why aren't we taking the spring buggy?" Miriam asked not long after they got on the road.

Rebecca enjoyed the topless buggy on a pretty day too, but today was a day for their covered buggy. "I need the room in the backseat for supplies, plus it's going to rain."

"It doesn't look like rain." Miriam's voice was bordering on snippy as she turned to face Rebecca.

Rebecca just smiled. "We'll see." She kept the buggy at a steady pace and waited until they had crossed Lincoln Highway before she brought up the subject that was causing her so much grief. She decided to ease into it slowly.

"I saw Zeb Fisher and the two younger

216

boys at church Sunday, but I didn't see Saul."

Miriam kept her eyes straight ahead as she spoke. "Ruben said that he was feeling poorly that morning." She shrugged, then faced out her buggy window. "I haven't seen or talked to Saul in four days."

Relief flooded over Rebecca even though she hated to hear her daughter sound so sad. Maybe her worries were unfounded after all. She tried to think of a casual way to talk more about Saul, but before her thoughts could get organized, Miriam spoke again.

"I know you don't like him."

Rebecca waited for a car to cross in front of them, then flicked the reins until the horse picked up speed. She turned to face Miriam briefly, shocked at the way her daughter's eyes cut into her, but she took a deep breath, determined to keep things pleasant between them. "Please understand, Miriam . . . I don't really know Saul well enough to form an opinion of him, but the things I've heard . . ." Rebecca shook her head before turning to Miriam again. "All this talk about him leaving frightens me. If the two of you are close . . ."

"You don't need to be frightened." Miriam looked out her window to the right

217

again. Rebecca couldn't see her expression, but she heard the sadness in her voice again. "He doesn't want me to go with him." Miriam dabbed at her eye, but Rebecca was having trouble getting past the fact that they had actually discussed such a thing. "Saul is probably leaving, but I won't be going with him." Miriam faced forward and raised her chin a bit. Rebecca watched as Miriam blinked back tears, but as much as her heart hurt for her daughter, relief was still her primary emotion.

Mamm sighed. "I'm sorry, Miriam."

"No, you're not."

Instinctively Rebecca opened her mouth to reprimand Miriam for her harsh tone, but she didn't. Instead, they rode quietly for a while. Finally, Rebecca spoke again.

"I'm sorry that you're hurting, Miriam. But the thought of you leaving here . . . I just can't . . ." Rebecca trailed off and shook her head, wondering when Miriam had gotten old enough for things to get so complicated between them.

Miriam twisted to face Rebecca, and while Rebecca kept her eyes on the road, she could feel her daughter's eyes blazing into her again. "*Mamm,* it's my choice. I choose whether or not to get baptized."

Rebecca took a deep breath and tried to

choose her words carefully, keeping in mind that Miriam was hurting, but also knowing that she knew what was best for Miriam. "I know that, Miriam. But your father and I can't help but worry that you'll be drawn to a world you know little about."

"Worry is a sin," her daughter responded flatly, in the same tone that was getting harder for Rebecca to ignore. She took another deep breath.

"*Ya,* it is. But I'm human, Miriam." She paused. "Look at Shelby. She had troubles in her hometown, and now she's bringing you troubles."

Miriam scowled. "How is Shelby bringing me troubles?"

"You snuck out of the *haus,* Miriam. That is something you would never have done before. I'm sure that was Shelby's idea."

Miriam chuckled.

"You think this is funny?" Rebecca slowed the buggy as they neared the market. She braved a quick glance at Miriam, not finding humor in any of this.

"*Ya.* I do. Especially since Shelby is the one who tried to talk me out of it." They were quiet again for a few moments. "And I think Shelby only shares her experiences with me as a way to help me not to make bad choices."

Rebecca heard what Miriam was saying, but it was taking time for her words to sink in. *Have I been wrong about Shelby?*

"I hear her crying a lot at night, after she thinks I'm asleep."

Rebecca parked the buggy, then hung her head for a moment as she questioned what kind of mother figure she'd been for Shelby in the absence of her own mother. "Do you think she's homesick?"

"I don't think so. She just seems . . . lonely. I think she's been angry about a lot of things. Her parents, her ex-boyfriend, her old friends, and . . . at God."

Rebecca questioned her priorities for a moment as she stared at her only daughter. "You're a *gut* girl, Miriam. Maybe you can help her to find her way."

"God will do that."

Rebecca nodded, then they both stepped out of the buggy. She tethered the horse at the pole outside of the market, then stared up at the dark clouds forming to her west.

I was right.

About the rain.

Shelby thought about the conversation she'd overhead between Rebecca and Aaron. On her hands and knees, she scrubbed the bathtub even harder. Ben, Elam, and John were with Aaron, and Shelby wanted to surprise Rebecca when she got home. She planned to have the entire upstairs scrubbed clean, and then she'd do as much as she could downstairs. Nothing was ever really dirty here. Rebecca saw to that. But with six of them in the house, the bathtub always needed a good scrubbing.

She wasn't sure why Rebecca's approval was so important to her. She'd be gone in another six weeks — back to her home, or what was left of it. To her surprise, Paradise had started to feel like home. She loved cooking in the evenings with Rebecca and Miriam, and was even starting to make it downstairs in time to help with breakfast. Gardening wasn't her favorite thing, nor the lack of air-conditioning, but the freedom to not wear makeup or be judged by others — most of the time — made up for some of the inconveniences, such as not having a cell phone, computer, or television.

Aaron was a storyteller and often told tales in the evenings after devotion time, and everyone laughed. Despite the recent death in the family, there was still laughter in this house, something she couldn't remember hearing at home — at least not in a long, long time. No one screamed at each other here, and for the most part, everyone did as they were told, worked hard, and didn't complain. It was a simpler way of life that had started out as a punishment but had wrapped around her like a safe cocoon.

She wrung out the sponge, put it underneath the sink in the bathroom, then stopped and stilled herself when she thought she heard a knock at the door. Realizing she was right, she dried her hands on a towel, then headed down the stairs. When she opened the door, Jesse was standing on the porch holding a fishing pole.

"Jesse, hi." She pushed the screen open. "Come on in."

Jesse glanced around the yard, then looked over her shoulder. "Is Miriam here?"

Shelby's heart dropped. She should have known Jesse was here to see Miriam. "No. I'm sorry. She went to town with Rebecca. I'll tell her you stopped by to see her."

Jesse repositioned his weight. "I, uh — I didn't come to see Miriam. I came to see you."

Shelby smiled. "Oh. Well, come on in."

He looked over her shoulder again, then scanned the yard. "Is anyone home?"

"No. Aaron and the boys are out there." She pointed to her left toward the back fields. "And Rebecca and Miriam went to town." She pushed the door open wider.

"Maybe you could just come out on the porch," Jesse said as he scrunched his handsome face up and nodded to his side.

"Oh." Shelby joined him on the porch. "Are we not supposed to be alone in the house together?"

Jesse stood taller. "It wouldn't be proper."

Shelby loved Jesse's manners and the formality of his speech. "Okay." She sat down in one of the rocking chairs on the front porch and motioned for Jesse to do the same.

"I bought this for you." Jesse pushed the fishing pole toward her. "You can't keep using everyone's hand-me-downs. You need your own pole."

Shelby struggled not to burst into tears. It was the nicest thing anyone had done for her in a long time, and coming from Jesse, it warmed her insides even more.

"Danki," she said in his dialect.

"Ach, you learnin' yourself the *Deitsch?"*

She laughed. "I'm picking up words and phrases here and there." She thought about hearing the young men at the market and their inappropriate comments in Pennsylvania *Deitsch.*

"Does Rebecca say *kumme esse? Mei mamm* always says that at supper time."

Shelby tapped her finger to her chin.

"Hmm . . . no. I don't remember hearing Rebecca say that. What does it mean?"

" 'Come eat.' Tonight, tell everyone *kumme esse,* and they'll think you're converting." He smiled, then stood up. "I best be gettin' on my way. I'm on lunch break from my job at the City Dump."

Shelby tried not to react, but her brows rose just the same.

Jesse grinned. "It's a furniture store in Ronks."

"Oh." Shelby brought her hand to her chest. "I thought you looked awfully clean to work at a dump." Then she squeezed her eyes closed and thought about how dumb that sounded.

"So when do you want to try out your new fishing pole? Saturday?" The beginning of a smile tipped the corner of his mouth, and Shelby felt like she was going to melt right there on the porch.

"Sure. Do you want Miriam to make us a lunch again? Maybe some chicken salad?"

Jesse looped his thumbs underneath his suspenders, and when he took a deep breath, it was hard for Shelby not to notice how well his broad shoulders filled out his blue shirt. "I — I was wondering if you wanted to go. I mean, just you. And me."

His mouth twitched as he waited for her to answer.

Shelby's heart pounded against her chest so hard that when she finally did answer, it was more like a squeak. "Sure."

Jesse smiled. "*Gut.* Then can I come for you at noon?"

"Sure. Okay." She fought the swooning effect that overtook her. "Do you want me to bring lunch?"

"No. It is my invitation, so I'll ask *mei mamm* to make lunch for us."

Shelby put her hands on her hips and grinned. "You're scared of my cooking, huh? Believe me, I can whoop up some sandwiches."

He laughed, then his expression stilled. "I ain't scared of your cooking, Shelby . . ." He paused. "But you do scare me." With a smile on his face, he winked, then turned and walked down the porch steps, waving when he got to his buggy.

She watched him maneuver the buggy down the driveway and onto the street. She couldn't wait to tell Miriam that she had a date. With Jesse Dienner.

11

Miriam waited with Shelby on the front porch Saturday. It was almost noon, and Jesse was due to pick up Shelby any minute. Miriam struggled to figure this out. For years she'd known that Jesse was smitten with her, and it gave her a strange sense of comfort. It was wrong, since she'd always wanted to be with Saul, but the feelings were there anyway.

"I offered to make lunch." Shelby ran her hands along a crisp white shirt that was tucked into a pair of dark blue jeans. "But Jesse said he would have his mother pack us a lunch."

"Why did you wear a white shirt to go fishing?"

Shelby glanced down at her blouse. "I don't know. I like this shirt." She cringed as she studied her choice further, as if seeing the bright white fabric for the first time. "I'm going to go change." She jumped up from the rocker she was sitting in. "I won't be long!"

Miriam slouched down into a rocker and tried to fight the self-pity that lingered around her. No Saul. And now no Jesse. Why was it that she'd never really noticed Jesse until he took an interest in Shelby? He was handsome. And there would never be a worry about Jesse leaving the community. Jesse would be a wonderful husband and father.

What are you doing? Miriam shook her head to clear her wicked thoughts. She knew she didn't want Jesse, but rationally he would be the best person for her. Then everyone would be happy — everyone but Miriam. And — now — possibly Shelby.

She watched him pull into the driveway, so she straightened her curved spine. She reminded herself that there was a bigger issue at hand. What if Jesse really likes Shelby? Her cousin would be leaving, and Jesse could end up hurt. She briefly wondered if Jesse would consider leaving the community. What if he fell for Shelby? Would he so willingly follow her, like Miriam had been so ready to follow Saul — if he'd wanted her to?

"*Wie bischt,* Miriam?" Jesse strolled up wearing a light-blue shirt, black trousers, and a smile. Miriam was sure he'd never looked better in his life. She sighed.

"I'm *gut.* Shelby will be here in a minute."

Jesse smiled. "I bet it wonders you that I would be going out with an *Englisch* woman."

Miriam wondered briefly if Jesse was trying to make her jealous, but when the screen door slammed and Jesse's eyes darted to Shelby — it became obvious to Miriam where Jesse's interest lay. His eyes twinkled as a full smile spread across his face.

With no time to respond, Miriam said, "Well, you two kids have fun," then crossed her legs and plastered on a grin — just like her mother would. She wasn't sure why she said it, and both Shelby and Jesse gave her strange looks.

Once they were gone, Miriam slithered back down in the chair again, knowing her mother would reprimand her for such pitiful posture. But she didn't much care at the moment.

Little John strolled onto the porch holding a large piece of watermelon. He walked up to where she was sloped down in the chair.

"Want some?" Red juice dripped down his chin.

Miriam shook her head. "No. *Danki,*

though."

Her youngest brother sat down on the porch and dangled his legs off the side. Miriam smiled when she saw watermelon juice on the tops of his bare feet. She could remember being eight years old, when there wasn't anything a piece of watermelon couldn't cure on a hot day. Brushing back a strand of hair that had fallen in front of her face, she decided that she could either sit here and feel sorry for herself or do something productive. She'd already weeded the garden and picked the tomatoes, strawberries, rhubarb, and cabbage that were ready. Housecleaning was done, and her parents allowed her Saturday afternoon to do anything she wanted. She wanted to go fishing. With Saul.

Scowling, she pulled herself up and headed into the house. When she walked into the den, she heard sniffling. Her mother quickly faced the window to the backyard, but Miriam saw her dab her eyes. Guilt flooded over her when she thought about how self-absorbed she'd been. Uncle Ivan had died just two weeks ago. Katie Ann and the rest of her family from Colorado had left two days after the funeral.

"*Mamm,* can I get you anything or do anything for you?"

Her mother slowly turned around, sniffled once. "No. *Danki,* Miriam. I'm all right." She walked to the couch, sat down, and picked up a book. Miriam sat down in the rocker across from her and kicked it into motion. She waited awhile, in case *Mamm* wanted to talk, but her mother kept her head buried in a book.

"*Mamm* . . . do you care if I take the spring buggy for a drive?"

"It's not hitched up, and your *daed,* Ben, and Elam are at your *Aenti* Mary Ellen's *haus* helping your *Onkel* Abe put up a new fence."

Miriam thought briefly about going to see if her cousin Linda wanted to go running around, but she really didn't feel like conversation. "I can hitch the buggy up."

Mamm looked up from the book. "I guess it would be all right."

Miriam stood up and shuffled across the wooden floor toward the front door.

"Miriam?"

"Ya?"

Mamm crossed one leg over the other and folded her hands atop the book in her lap. "Tell me about this — this outing with Shelby and Jesse."

"What do you want to know? They went fishing."

Mamm's forehead creased as she narrowed her eyes at Miriam. "You know what I mean. You don't think Jesse would be silly enough to date an *Englisch* girl, do you? I mean, Shelby will be leaving next month."

Miriam was dreading that day. She would miss Shelby. She wasn't sure that her cousin had completely opened up to her, but Shelby didn't write in that journal every night anymore, and Miriam thought that might be a good thing. She was hoping her cousin would seek the Lord for guidance and help with all that ailed her. Although . . . when she darted away with Jesse Dienner, she'd seemed just fine.

Finally, she shrugged. "I don't know, *Mamm.* I think they're just friends."

"Jesse will make a fine husband for a lucky *maedel* someday." She smiled all-knowingly at Miriam.

"I guess." She pulled the screen open. *But not for me.*

Saul regretted the way things ended the last time he saw Miriam, but he decided to leave well enough alone. Miriam was better off without him, and he didn't know how long he'd have the strength to tell her that she couldn't go with him when he left. He still couldn't believe what she'd said. It was like a dream — the thought of him and Miriam sharing a life together. But it was a dream that was out of reach. Leaving here was his dream, not hers. He could never let her do that.

He tried to stay focused on the positive, first and foremost his father, who hadn't had a drinking episode since he and Saul last talked. Soon Saul would need to tell him about his job offer. He needed to do it before *Daed* deeded over the property to him. But for the first time since he'd found out about his job, he felt a void in his life. Miriam never should have told him that she'd go with him. Now all he could do was think about the possibilities of a life with her.

He crawled into his buggy and headed toward the creek. He'd left Ruben and James an unfair amount of chores to do, but he'd make it up to them next weekend. Today he needed to be around friends, and he knew they would be gathered at Pequea Creek, like they always were on Saturday afternoons.

He'd barely turned onto Blackhorse Road when he saw Miriam drive by going the other direction. She waved but didn't even look his way. *Don't turn around. Keep going.* He gritted his teeth and managed to keep going for about a hundred yards before he grunted to himself and turned the buggy around. He picked up the pace until he was close to catching up with her. She eventually slowed to a stop, and he pulled up beside her.

"Are you following me?" She turned her head to face him, without even the hint of a smile on her face.

"*Ya*. I am. We need to talk, Miriam. Where are you off to?"

She raised her chin. "Nowhere. I'm just riding around. It's a nice day."

"Let's take your buggy back to your house, then you can ride with me to the creek. We can talk on the way." Saul waited a moment, then added, "Please."

She shifted in her seat and faced him from her buggy. "I don't know what we have to talk about, Saul. I misunderstood something, and now I feel . . . embarrassed."

Saul wanted to get out and go to her, but he didn't have anywhere to tie up his horse. "I don't think you really misunderstood. It's complicated, Miriam."

"It doesn't have to be," she said in the sweetest voice Saul had ever heard.

"Then, please, let's talk. I have some things I want to say to you." He knew she couldn't go with him. They'd barely started seeing each other. Then why did it seem like he'd been with Miriam his entire life? In some ways, he figured he had. His heart had belonged to her since they were young. In addition to his attraction to her, he also found that her goodness offset the trouble he often found himself in, and she made him want to be a better person. His thoughts conflicted, he wasn't sure what he would say to her, but he couldn't stand to have her mad at him or not understand how he felt about her.

"Okay," she finally said.

She turned her horse around, and Saul followed her back to her house.

Rebecca hung little John's bedsheets out to dry. Her youngest still wet the bed every now and then, despite her many attempts to curb his late-night liquids and make sure he went to the bathroom before bedtime. She jumped when Aaron wrapped his arms around her from behind and nuzzled her neck.

"Aaron, what are you doing?" She pinned up the corner of the white sheet, squinting from the sun's glare. "I thought you were at Abe's putting up a fence?"

"That's what I have *sohns* for," he teased as he kissed her on the neck.

"You smell of work, so you must have been busy doing something." She clipped the last of the sheet on the line, then spun around to face her husband.

"We finished the fence, so the boys stayed to play volleyball, and I decided to come home and spend some alone time with *mei fraa.*" He pulled her close. "I know Shelby is gone. Is Miriam here?" Frowning, he glanced around.

"No. She took the spring buggy and went for a drive. It's just us, Aaron." She pushed him away. "But I have chores to do."

Aaron grabbed her shoulders and drew her to him again. "I think we best seize this moment, Rebecca." He looked up at the sky and squinted. "It's the middle of the day, and no one is at home." He smiled broadly.

"Shame on you, Aaron Raber. Such thoughts from a man your age in the middle of the afternoon."

Her husband of twenty years leaned in and kissed her with the same passion as when they were teenagers, and taking a nap didn't sound like such a bad idea. Next thing she knew, Aaron scooped her into his arms and started walking toward the house. "Why, Aaron . . ." She batted her eyes at him.

"Nap time, *mei leib.*"

"Don't drop me going up these porch steps."

Aaron didn't get up the first step when they heard the *clippety-clop* of hooves on the driveway. "Goodness! Put me down before someone sees!"

"It's Miriam." Aaron set her on the ground.

"She just left. I wonder what she's doing home so early." Rebecca held her hand to her forehead and strained to see. "Someone's behind her. I hope nothing's wrong." She moved across the yard until the second buggy came into view. "Oh no." She sighed. "It's Saul Fisher," she whispered to Aaron.

"*Ach,* Rebecca . . ." Aaron shook his head.

"Don't '*ach,* Rebecca' me." She stood tall. "This won't be *gut.* I'm sure of it." She folded her arms across her chest and waited. Miriam tied the horse to the stump by the fence, then she waited for Saul to follow her into the yard.

"*Mamm, Daed,* I'm going to go with Saul to the creek, if that's all right." Miriam's eyes pleaded with hers, but Rebecca knew this was a terrible dilemma. She'd allowed her to go on a drive, and she could have just as easily met Saul at the creek, so how could she deny this request? Her mind worked doubly hard to think of a way.

236

"I don't know, Miriam. I mean —"

"Of course you can go, *mei dochder.* You go and have a *gut* time." Aaron stroked his beard, and Rebecca could have punched him.

Saul walked forward and nodded to Rebecca, then extended his hand to Aaron. "*Danki,* sir. I'll have her home well before the supper hour."

A smiled tipped the corner of Aaron's mouth as he glanced at Rebecca, then back at Saul. "That sounds mighty fine, Saul."

"*Danki, Daed.* I just have to go put the horse in the barn." Miriam turned to go back to the buggy.

"You *kinner* run along. I'll take care of that." Aaron waved his arm for them to go.

"*Danki,*" Saul said as he and Miriam made their way to Saul's buggy.

Aaron waited until they had turned the corner before he attempted to scoop Rebecca back into his arms. Kicking, she fell out of his arms, almost all the way to the ground. "What are you doing?" she demanded.

"Taking up where we left off." He winked. "Nap time, remember?"

"I am no longer tired!"

She marched into the house and slammed the door.

"Did you see the look on your *mamm's* face?" Saul said as he got his horse into a steady trot. He shook his head. "I don't think she cares for you spending time with me."

Miriam was quite sure her mother didn't approve of her seeing Saul. "*Mamm's* heard the rumors that you might be leaving the community."

Saul turned at the next gravel side road.

"This isn't the way to the creek."

"I know." He pulled the buggy to the side of the road, no houses visible, only a few cows grazing to their left. "We can talk here."

Miriam's heart started to pound. She wasn't sure she wanted to hear what he had to say. He twisted in his seat to face her, drew in a deep breath, and then let it out slowly.

"Like I told you, I got this job offer, and I wasn't going to get baptized this fall. I'd made up my mind about that, but I started to change my mind because — because of Ruben and James. I wasn't sure if I should leave them."

Miriam could feel her face turning pinker

by the moment. "Saul, we really don't need to talk about this. I understand."

"No. I don't think you do." He reached for her hand, and visions of him kissing her flashed through her mind. He intertwined their fingers, locking his eyes with hers. "I think I've always been *in lieb* with you, Miriam . . . since we were young *kinner.* That may sound crazy, but it's true."

Doesn't sound crazy to me. She held her breath as her heart danced.

"But, Miriam, every man in this community wants to be with you, and I never once considered that you might feel the way I always have."

Miriam held up one finger. "That's not true, Saul. We've watched each other and flirted for years. You had to have known I felt something too."

"*Ya, ya.* I thought you liked me well enough, but I never felt like I was *gut* enough for you, Miriam. And I can't give you what you want — a life here. I feel pulled to go do something else, and I want this job and the freedom to explore the world outside of our community. But since you told me you'd go with me, I can't stop picturing us together now." He pulled his eyes from her and sighed. "And I can't let you leave here."

Miriam was still reeling over the fact that he'd said he'd loved her for a long time. But now that the reality was set before her, it frightened her. She didn't know anything about the world outside of their district. In her fantasies, this was the time when she would tell him how much she loved him and vow to follow him anywhere. Instead, she sat speechless.

"Anyway, I didn't want you to think that I didn't care about you, or think about you going with me, because it's keeping me up at night now." Saul looked up and stared deeply into her eyes. "I love you, Miriam. I always have."

Miriam bit her lip as she blinked back tears. No matter their future, she couldn't let him not know how she felt too. "I love you too, Saul."

He let go of her hand, then pulled her into his arms. "It would be so unfair to ask you to come with me," he whispered.

Miriam felt like she couldn't breathe. *Why does he keep saying that?* Was he waiting for her to offer to go with him again? Being with Saul was all she'd dreamed about, but visions of her family kept popping into her mind. Could she really leave them and become part of a world that was foreign to her? Or could she stay here around all that was familiar — and not have Saul?

He eased away from her, cupped her cheek, then kissed her in a way that solidified her decision.

"I want to go with you, Saul. I'll go anywhere with you."

He smiled. "I can't *ask* you to do that, but I won't insist you stay. Are you sure? Is it really what you want, Miriam, to be with me as much as I want to be with you?"

Miriam felt herself trembling, unsure how much of it was from his kiss, the feel of his arms around her, or the fear of speaking the words she'd always dreamed about. She tried to calm her beating heart and prayed she was doing the right thing.

"*Ya.* I want to go with you."

12

Miriam sat at the creek's edge with Leah and Hannah and watched as Saul edged onto the diving rock and prepared to jump. She heard Saul's friends cheering him to jump, and his eyes met with hers right before he hit the water, like they'd done so many times before. But after their talk on the way to the creek, she knew things were different now. She felt a wave of excitement and confusion rush through her as she watched his head pop out of the water, searching until he found her.

"How are you doing, Miriam?" Leah asked. "We haven't seen you since your *onkel's* funeral."

"I'm fine." She hung her head for a moment but quickly looked back up.

"I like your cousin Shelby. I was sorry to meet her at such a sad time," Hannah said. "She seems sweet, though."

"She is," Miriam said, then for reasons

she couldn't explain, she envisioned Shelby and Jesse alone together fishing at the Zook farm. *Am I doing the right thing by leaving with Saul?* It was all she'd ever wanted, to be with Saul. What would she do in the outside world? Would she work at a job outside the home? How often would she see her family? Would they join a church in the city?

Why haven't I thought of these things before?

"So tell us, Miriam . . . Last time we were here, you went to go talk to Saul. How did that go?" Leah nudged Hannah. "It must have gone *gut,* since he brought you here today."

Miriam smiled as she thought about the way Saul kissed her, and momentarily her worries drifted to the back of her mind where she hoped they would stay. "*Ya,* we're dating."

Hannah pressed her lips firmly together for a moment. "Be careful, Miriam. I don't think Saul is the settling-down type, and I still keep hearing that he might not be baptized in the fall. Some say he won't stay here."

"He's the settling-down type," Miriam said smugly.

Leah leaned across Hannah again. "I

don't know." She giggled. "But he sure is handsome, and I sure do like watching him jump."

Miriam knew jealousy was a sin, but it reared its ugly head just the same. "He asked me to leave here with him."

"Who?" Hannah asked.

"Saul."

Hannah's mouth fell open, then she exchanged looks with Leah. When she turned back to Miriam, her forehead was creased with concern. "Of course you told him no, right?"

Miriam drew in a calming breath as she sat up taller. "I'm going with him. He has a job offer at a restaurant in Pittsburgh."

Leah was now practically in Hannah's lap as she leaned inward to hear Miriam.

"How did he propose? Tell us the details." Hannah nudged Leah out of her lap. "This happened so fast. I can't believe you'll be leaving here. What did your parents say?"

As the questions slammed into Miriam faster and harder, she tried to gather her thoughts. And the first realization that hit her was — *He asked me to go with him, but he didn't ask me to marry him. What does that mean?*

Then she pondered some more. No, he didn't *ask* her to go with him. She volunteered. "I haven't told *Mamm* and *Daed* yet."

Hannah brought her hand to her mouth to stifle a gasp, and Leah's eyes got round as saucers.

"I'm going to tell them soon."

"Will you be married here before you go?"

"I — I don't know." Miriam stood up. "I have to go." She didn't look back as she hurried toward Saul's buggy, even though she heard Hannah call her name. Choking back tears, she squatted next to the buggy, out of view of everyone. She was breathing much too hard, and her hands were trembling.

"Miriam?" Saul squatted down beside her in the grass a few moments later. She didn't hear him walk up, and she felt ridiculous. He put his hand on her shoulder. "What's wrong?"

She forced herself to stand up. "I'm sorry to cut your time short with your friends, but I'm not feeling well."

"No problem." He helped her into the buggy, then went around to the other side. Within a few minutes he had them back on the road toward home. "Maybe you got too hot. Do you want me to stop at that little store when we get into town and get you something cold to drink?"

She shook her head. "No, I'll be okay."

They rode quietly for a while, and Miriam

knew she wouldn't sleep tonight unless she asked Saul a few questions. "Do you think I'll have a job in Pittsburgh?"

"Do you want to work?"

She shrugged. "Maybe." They were quiet again, then she asked, "How often do you think we will see our families?"

"Pittsburgh isn't that far." He paused. "You're having second thoughts, aren't you?" Saul slowed the buggy to cross Lincoln Highway, then picked up speed when they turned onto Black Horse Road.

"Saul, I — I . . . Can you stop the buggy?"

Instantly Saul pulled back on the reins, then pulled off on the first gravel road he could. He turned to face her. "You haven't really thought this through, have you?" He searched her eyes. "I love you, Miriam. And I can picture our life together. But I would never, ever push you into leaving here. You have to be sure, Miriam."

"When would we go?"

"The end of August."

"That's only a month away." She heard the alarm in her voice. Saul reached up and touched her cheek.

"Sweet Miriam." He blinked a few times. "I think this is happening too fast for you." He pulled her into his arms and cupped the nape of her neck, and she rested her head against his chest. His heart was beating fast, and she wondered if he was having second thoughts. "I want you to be happy, whatever that is for you. I won't deny that I want you to make this journey with me, but you have to be sure." He lifted her face and kissed her gently on the lips. "I love you."

"How do you know that, Saul? We've barely spent any time together." It seemed odd to be asking him the question when she didn't have any doubts about how she felt about him. Only fears about this life-changing situation.

Saul was quiet for a few moments, then said, "Maybe I should be asking you the same thing." Before she could respond, he continued, "Do you remember the day at the creek when Lizzie Petersheim brought her sister, Annie?"

Miriam thought back. Little Annie had Down syndrome, but she'd died last year. "That was a few years ago, but *ya,* I remember. Why?"

"Everyone was occupied, even Lizzie, that day. Annie kept coughing, and she had all kinds of . . . *stuff* . . . dripping from her nose. I watched you that day. You cleaned Annie up, and you kept her by your side the rest of the time."

Miriam barely remembered that day.

"Saul, anyone would have done that."

"Barbie Beiler fell and broke her leg. Remember that?"

"*Ya.*"

"You went over there every day and helped her run her bed-and-breakfast."

Miriam shook her head. "Saul, these are things anyone in our community would have done."

"But they didn't, Miriam. You did. And depending on how much time you've got, I can give you a dozen more reasons why I've grown to love you over the years." He shifted his eyes away from her. "You make me want to be a better person."

"Saul . . ." She reached up and touched his cheek until he turned to face her. "I think you're a wonderful person, and sometimes the way you help others is a bit different, perhaps more adventuresome than our ways . . . but I've watched you for years too. And your zestful spirit is one of the things that I love."

Saul leaned in and kissed her gently. "I want to spend the rest of my life getting to know everything about you. And I know this is happening fast, but I'm sure that I love you, and I'm sure that I want to be with you always. I know that we would have to throw a wedding together really fast, and —"

Miriam's eyes widened as she put some distance between them. "A wedding?"

"You didn't think we'd move to Pittsburgh together without being married, did you? But only if you're sure, Miriam."

"I'm sure!" She threw her arms around his neck, knowing that this was the piece of the puzzle she needed the most. Everything else would come together. Just knowing that Saul wanted to spend the rest of his life with her would ease the worry that was sure to come in the following weeks — she couldn't imagine how she would tell her parents.

Saul eased away from her, stepped out of the buggy, then walked around to her side. As he dropped to one knee, Miriam covered her mouth with her hand.

"I'm sorry I didn't do this properly." He reached for her hand. "Miriam Raber, I've loved you since I saw you in the first grade, and I love you more now than I thought possible. I'm a plain man making a plain proposal, but I will love you forever and always take care of you if you'll agree to marry me and become *mei fraa*."

Miriam jumped from the buggy and into his arms. "Oh, Saul! I will!"

Shelby couldn't believe how much time had passed. It was nearly four o'clock. She wouldn't be home in time to help with supper preparation, and she'd been trying so hard lately to impress Rebecca. But she couldn't recall having as much fun as she'd had today in a long time.

She watched Jesse loading the fishing poles into the back of his topless buggy, and she wished this time with him could go on forever. They'd laughed, talked, and he'd shared Amish customs that she'd never heard of before. Her favorite was when he explained how a barn raising was done. When a young couple is starting out and needs a barn — or in the event of a fire — a new barn is erected in one day. Jesse told her that the entire community would arrive early in the morning to construct the barn. It was a family affair and a welcomed opportunity for fellowship in the community.

She reached into her purse sitting on the front seat of the buggy and glanced at her cell phone. She'd charged it earlier in the week in town, and she saw that she now had two missed calls from her mother and four from her father. *Suddenly they care about me?* She tossed it back into her purse.

"Missing your friends back home?" Jesse cradled her elbow and helped her into the buggy. He made her feel like a princess.

"No. I really don't."

He climbed into the buggy on the other side, flicked the reins, and backed the horse and buggy up. Shelby was hot, sweating like she couldn't recall sweating before, had no makeup on, no perfume, no jewelry, and she'd never felt better — or more appreciated for the person she was — than at this moment. Jesse had listened to her all afternoon, and she found herself telling him things she hadn't even told Miriam. Maybe it was an unintentional test to see if he would judge her for the mistakes she'd made. If so, Jesse had passed the test. He made her feel . . . worthy, like a person who deserved to be happy — and forgiven.

Thank You, Lord, for this beautiful day.

"So, Shelby. Tell me. What is the thing you like most about your visit here?"

Shelby leaned her head back, closed her eyes, and enjoyed the wind in her face while she thought about his question. "Family," she finally said as she turned to face him. "Not just Miriam's family, but the way the whole community is like one big family.

Everyone helps each other, loves each other."

Jesse smiled. "And what do you like the least?"

Shelby laughed. "Would it be wrong of me to say the lack of air-conditioning?"

"I take every opportunity to go into town and walk the air-conditioned shops this time of year. We all do." He smiled, then whistled for his horse to pick up the pace. "I wonder what it would be like to leave here sometimes."

Shelby was shocked. From everything that Miriam had told her about Jesse, she didn't think Jesse would consider the idea. She blurted the first thing that popped into her head. "You don't want to leave here, Jesse."

"What makes you so sure? I think about it sometimes."

"Because — because there's a sense of peace here that's hard to find out there." She turned to look at him when she felt his eyes on her.

"That peace is in your heart, Shelby. You can have that anywhere." He smiled. "You just happen to be finding it here. It sounds like you're working through things, healing from a bad time. But the peacefulness in your heart only comes from a true relationship with God. When you can let your cares go and trust that all things are of God's will, then there's no worry or fear, things that block the voice of God."

"Don't you worry about things?" Shelby often chewed her nails to the quick with worry, and she thought about how freeing it must be to just turn everything over to God. She was working on that.

"Of course. I'm Amish, but I'm still human. I struggle with it all the time. Right now my aunt is sick. I'm worried she'll die. It would be God's will for her to go to her heavenly home, but I still worry. I would miss her."

They rode along quietly for a while. Soon Jesse would be dropping her off at home.

Home. That's what her cousins' farm had become over the past couple of months. Only one thing bothered her about being here, and that was Rebecca, who still seemed guarded with her, as if her presence was a threat to their family somehow. If Rebecca only knew how much Shelby treasured what Rebecca's family had, she wouldn't be so fearful.

When Jesse pulled up the driveway, Shelby turned to him. "Thank you so much for today, Jesse. I had a wonderful time." She giggled. "Even though we didn't catch a single fish."

"I had a *gut* time too, Shelby. We will have to do it again."

When?

She waited until Jesse brought the buggy to a complete stop, then she picked up her purse and stepped out. She'd already asked him to hold on to her new fishing pole, hoping for another invite. "Thanks again." As she was walking away, he called her name.

"Yeah?" She turned to face him.

"I have my lunch hour at the City Dump from noon until one o'clock." He smiled. "Remember, that's the name of the place where I work."

Shelby nodded, guessing what he was about to ask her.

"Anytime you're in town, I'd be glad to buy you lunch. Maybe Miriam can bring you sometime."

"That would be great. I'll see you soon."

Jesse smiled. "I hope so."

Shelby wasn't sure she'd ever really felt butterflies in her stomach before today.

It was routine now for Miriam and Shelby to stay up late talking, later than they should considering that the day started at four o'clock in the morning. They were expected to help with breakfast no matter how late they'd stayed up the night before. But there was much to cover this evening. Miriam let Shelby go first, and her cousin told her about her day with Jesse. In light of Saul's proposal, any thoughts of Jesse as her "safe person" had vanished.

She was glad to see Shelby so happy, but she was worried for both her and for Jesse. Until, that is, Shelby told her what Jesse said.

"You mean he actually said he thinks about leaving sometimes?" Miriam was shocked.

Shelby's expression grew solemn. "Why would anyone want to leave here?"

Miriam laughed. "Usually the *Englisch* want to know why anyone would want to *stay* here."

Shelby ran her brush the length of her hair, and Miriam couldn't help but think about her wedding night when Saul would see her hair in its entirety. Then she cringed when she thought about having to tell her parents that she would be leaving the community with Saul, but she tried to stay focused on the life she knew they would have.

"I could live here."

Miriam sat perfectly still and stared at Shelby. "Really?" Then she folded her arms across her chest and stared at Shelby.

"Shelby, you can't choose to live here just because you might be falling for Jesse. That's not right. That's not our way."

Shelby's eyes teared up, and Miriam regretted what she'd said. "I'm sorry."

"No, it's okay. I guess it must seem that way." Shelby hung her head. "I just like you — and your family. I like being here."

Miriam didn't say anything. Suddenly she wasn't sure that this was the best time to share her news with Shelby. But if not Shelby, then who? She was about to burst, needing to share with someone. That someone couldn't be her mother, which saddened her. She recalled a time when she used to tell her mother everything.

"Although . . ." Shelby stopped brushing her hair and frowned. "I think your mother is ready for me to go."

"Why would you say that?"

Shelby sighed as she stuffed her brush back into the drawer. "I overheard your mother saying that she thinks I'm a bad influence on you. More or less, that's what she said."

"Are you talking about me sneaking out to meet Saul? Because if so . . . I already cleared that up with *Mamm*."

"You did?" Shelby straightened. "Was she mad at you?"

"Not as mad as she's going to be."

"What do you mean?"

Miriam crossed her legs beneath her and folded her hands in her lap. "You can't tell anyone what I'm about to tell you. Not until I'm able to tell my parents."

Shelby's eyes widened. "I won't. I won't. What is it, Miriam?"

"I'm leaving here. With Saul. In one month."

13

Rebecca pulled a rhubarb pie from the oven and placed it on top of the stove to cool. She was alone in the house, so she sat down at the kitchen table and picked up a copy of *The Budget.* Before she started reading, she glanced around the room. It seemed almost sinful to just sit and do nothing. But Aaron and the boys were working outdoors, and Miriam and Shelby finished their chores in record time this morning, so Rebecca said they could take the buggy to town. Every day they charged through their chores so they could go to town at lunchtime. Those girls were up to something, but she wasn't sure what it was.

She opened the newspaper and began to scan the happenings in Amish and Mennonite communities in the United States. A warm breeze blew through the opened windows in the kitchen, and the smell of freshly baked rhubarb wafted through the air. As she began to relax and not feel guilty for allowing herself idle time, she heard a buggy coming up the driveway. She closed the newspaper and walked to the front door where she saw Marie King and her daughter, Leah, step down from their buggy.

"Marie, Leah. How nice to see you." She kept the door open while the women made their way up the porch steps. "I just pulled a rhubarb pie from the oven, and I was looking for an excuse to have a piece. Can I get you both some pie?"

"No. *Danki,* Rebecca." Marie didn't seem her usual bubbly self, and Leah kept her head hung low and avoided looking at Rebecca.

"Marie, is everything all right?" Rebecca motioned with her hand for both women to take a seat at the kitchen table. "Here, sit. No one is at home, and this is the perfect time to talk. Can I get either of you some *kaffi?*"

Marie shook her head, a solemn look on her face, and Leah still wouldn't look up.

"Rebecca . . ." Marie took a deep breath. "Leah told her father and me some — some upsetting news." She paused as a frown set into her features. "News that I don't think you are aware of, and I have much concern about it."

Rebecca's pulse picked up. "Marie, you're scaring me. What's wrong?"

"It's about Miriam." Marie reached across the table and put her hand on Rebecca's. "Leah tells us that Miriam is leaving the community, and maybe she's already told you, but —"

Rebecca pulled her hand away and brought it to her chest. "What?"

"Oh dear." Marie sighed. "I was afraid she hadn't told you, and maybe it's not our place, but it worries me so, this situation."

Rebecca stared hard at Leah as she tried to calm her beating heart. "Leah, what did Miriam tell you?" *Oh dear Lord, don't let it be true.*

Leah blinked back tears. "I shouldn't have said anything. I should have waited to tell *Mamm* until I was sure that Miriam told you."

"No, Leah. You did the right thing," Rebecca said as she fought her own tears. "What exactly did Miriam tell you?"

"She — she said that . . ." Leah turned to her mother. "Miriam is never going to forgive me for this."

"Leah, please," Rebecca prodded. "If I need to get Bishop Ebersol involved in whatever is going on, I need to know."

"She's going to marry Saul Fisher, and

they are leaving the community." A tear rolled down Leah's cheek.

Rebecca stood from the table, turned, and faced the window, then covered her mouth with her hand. *This can't be happening.* She spun around and faced Marie and Leah. "Miriam told you this? When?"

"Saturday at the creek."

Marie stood up and walked to Rebecca. She put her hand on her shoulder. "I just thought you should know, that maybe there might be time to talk Miriam out of this."

Oh, I will talk her out of it. "Danki, Marie." She glanced at Leah. "And you did the right thing, Leah. We will surely have a talk with Miriam." She shook her head as she spoke. "Miriam has always been committed to live her life here." *I'm sure Saul has been pushing her to do this.*

Marie folded her arms across her chest. "They are evidently planning to get married and leave here the end of August."

"What?" Rebecca shrieked. "That's barely a month away."

Marie pulled Rebecca into a hug. "I know, dear. I'm so sorry. I can imagine how I would feel if it was Leah doing this. Please let me know if there's anything I can do."

"*Ya*, I will." Rebecca eased away from Marie. "Please don't tell anyone about this just yet. I want to have time to talk to Bishop Ebersol, and of course, I need to talk to Aaron. And Miriam."

"Hannah knows too," Leah said softly.

Rebecca drew in a deep breath. Hannah's mother, Eve, couldn't be quieted when it came to gossip. "All right. *Danki* for stopping by."

After they were gone, Rebecca sat back down at the kitchen table, covered her face with her hands, and cried.

Miriam dropped off Shelby at the City Dump at noon, then went to meet Saul at his place. When she pulled up in her buggy, Saul was leading two horses to the barn. She waved at his father and two brothers as she passed them on her right working in the fields.

"I brought turkey sandwiches." She stepped out of the buggy. "I would have brought enough for your *daed* and brothers too, but you said not to."

"Plenty of leftover meat loaf for them inside." He took the picnic basket from her. "I know it's hot, but do you care if we eat outside, by ourselves? I have some stuff to show you."

"Okay."

Saul led her to a picnic table nestled

beneath a grove of oak trees. Miriam started laying out the food.

"You look so pretty," he said when she looked up and saw him staring at her.

"*Danki.* I'm happy."

"Me too." He glanced around to see if anyone was watching, then leaned over and kissed her. "Wait 'til you see what I have to show you. I went to the library yesterday, and the lady who works there helped me print some stuff."

Saul waited until after they ate to go into his house. When he came back, he was carrying a stack of papers. "These are places that we can rent, and they're close to my new job. I have enough saved for a year's rent."

Miriam looked through the pictures of small apartments not much bigger than their basement. She looked up at the man she was going to marry. "Saul, what will I do while you're at work?"

"I've thought about that, Miriam. What do you want to do? Do you want to try to go to school, or get a job, or stay at home and take care of our house?" He smiled. "And someday, our *kinner.*"

Miriam felt her cheeks reddening. "I think that I should probably get a job and work, don't you? We'll need to save our money so we can buy our own home someday. What do you think?"

The flow of Saul's smile warmed her. "I just want you to be happy. I'll make a *gut* life for you, Miriam." He paused, as if far away for a moment. "I can picture me as a chef in a fancy restaurant. And just think how *gut* we'll eat at home."

Miriam smiled as she thought about Saul cooking for her in their own home. She couldn't imagine her father or brothers ever cooking a meal. "Here comes your *daed*," she said when she saw Zeb Fisher walking toward them. She stood up to greet him.

"Keep your seat, Miriam. Nice to see you." Zeb smiled as he walked past them and toward the house.

"Have you told your *daed* yet?"

Saul shifted his weight on the bench. "No. What about you? You tell your folks?" He shook his head. "Your parents are gonna be real upset. Do you want me to be with you when you tell them?"

"You'd do that?" Miriam's insides warmed as she sat back down across from him.

"Of course I would." He reached over and squeezed her hand. "I'll do anything for you."

Maybe it was the way he was looking at her, so solemn and serious, or maybe it was his soft, raspy, level tone of voice, but no matter what . . . she believed him. Saul was the kind of man she wanted to live the rest of her life with.

"I love you, Saul."

"I love you too, Miriam."

Miriam and Shelby talked and laughed all the way home. Miriam was still worried about what was happening between Shelby and Jesse, but it was good to see her cousin so happy. Turns out, Shelby used to be a big reader, and Jesse read a lot too. They'd read some of the same Christian books, and Shelby said they'd spent their entire lunch hour talking about books.

When Miriam pulled to a stop at home, she saw her parents sitting on the front porch in the rocking chairs, and they didn't look happy at all. *Mamm's* arms were folded across her chest, her legs were crossed, and she was kicking that rocker so hard it looked like it might lift off the ground at any moment. *Daed* was scowling in a way that made Miriam want to turn the buggy around and leave.

"Uh-oh," Shelby whispered. "Something's up."

They walked cautiously toward the porch. "Miriam, we need to speak with you," her father said in a voice that sounded frightfully unfamiliar.

"Ya, Daed." Miriam didn't look at her parents as she padded up the steps to the porch. Shelby followed but passed by Miriam and went inside.

Daed stood up and started to pace. "Sit down, Miriam."

Miriam did as she was told. She glanced at her mother, and Miriam could tell she'd been crying. She was pretty sure she knew what this was about. *I should have never told Hannah and Leah about me and Saul.* Miriam was hoping that her mother would take over the conversation, like she usually did. She wasn't sure that anything her mother could say would be nearly as scary as the way her father was looking at her, his mouth pinched together in a frown and his eyes squinted.

Daed took a few deep breaths, then stroked his beard several times before he glared at Miriam. "Do you have any idea how upsetting it was for your *mamm* today when Marie and Leah King came over to tell her about your plans? Did you not think that your parents should be the first to know that you are planning to marry Saul Fisher?" He walked closer and bent at the waist. "And that you are planning to leave the community? Do you not think us worthy of this news before it is spread around the community like sinful gossip? So tell me, Miriam, that this news is not true."

"I — I . . ." She sought help from her mother with her eyes, but *Mamm* just looked down at her feet and kicked the rocker even harder with her bare feet. "I love him, *Daed*. I love Saul." Her voice cracked as she spoke, but a tear rolled down her cheek when her father grunted. "I've always loved him," she added as she put her face to her hands.

"Look at me, *maedel*."

It wasn't a plea, it was a demand, and Miriam did as she was told. She met eyes with her father and waited.

"I've always known you liked Saul. But this rushed courtship so that you can move with him is disgraceful." Her father pulled his eyes from Miriam, and he stared out into the pasture. "Are you — are you in a family way?"

Miriam started to cry harder. "No, *Daed*. No. Never." She looked to her mother, but *Mamm* refused to look at her.

Her father turned around, then moved toward her. *Daed* had never laid a hand on her except as a young child who needed a spanking, but he was shaking so much that Miriam feared he might. But he squatted down beside her, and when he did, Miriam saw tears in his eyes.

"Then why, *mei maedel,* do you need to marry so quickly and leave us? Why not bring this boy around, let us get to know him better? And why do you both choose to leave your families?"

Miriam tried to breathe, to control her sobs. "Saul has a job in Pittsburgh working as a chef in a new restaurant. It starts in September."

Daed stood up and rubbed his eyes. "And he can support you doing this *job?*"

Miriam had thought of this too, despite the fact that Saul said he had some money saved. "I will work too, if I need to."

"A woman's place is in the home." *Mamm* finally spoke up. "Taking care of her husband, their *haus,* and their *kinner.* Working in the *Englisch* world in Pittsburgh is no place for you, Miriam."

Miriam knew that she needed to remind her parents that she was in her *rumschpringe,* and that according to the *Ordnung,* she had a right not to get baptized and to seek out a life among the *Englisch.* Fear kept her from doing just that. Everything her parents said only magnified her anxiety about going. She needed her family's support. She needed their blessing.

"I can still have a nice home and *kinner,*" she said in a whisper between sobs.

"No." Her father crossed his arms across his chest. "You will not leave with Saul."

Miriam hung her head and cried. She needed Saul, but she needed her parents too.

Rebecca pulled back the covers and got into bed. She snuggled up against Aaron who had his head buried in a book. She'd prayed a lot since their conversation with Miriam, and the guidance she felt she was receiving from God surprised her. She felt called to share her feelings with Aaron.

"Aaron . . ."

"*Ya?*" He didn't take his eyes from his reading.

"We cannot keep her here against her will." She eased away from him, fluffed her pillow behind her, then crossed her ankles beneath the covers. "Besides, I thought you said you saw this coming, her seeing Saul."

Aaron closed the book. "*Ya,* I did. I've known for years those two were smitten with each other. One only has to watch them for a few minutes when they are in the same room to know that." Aaron looked at her for a moment, a hurt expression clouding his face. "But I never thought Saul would drag our only *dochder* away from the only place she's known." He paused, then scratched his head. "And to go be a cook. What kind of man goes to be a cook?"

Rebecca stifled a grin, although not one thing about this situation was funny.

"You told me to be firm, Rebecca. So I was."

She rubbed his arm. "*Ya,* you were." Rebecca's heart hurt for Miriam. But how could her daughter be in love? Surely she wasn't old enough. She sighed, recalling how she was the same age when she fell in love with Aaron. "But, *mei lieb,* we cannot stop her."

Aaron twisted to face her. "Why are you soft about this now? You don't want her to leave." He gave his head a taut nod. "We will stop her."

"She has free will, Aaron. We have to trust God to guide her."

"Is this the same woman who told me to make sure our *dochder* didn't leave the community?"

"I'm scared, Aaron. And I know you're scared too. Because usually where Miriam is concerned, you are a big ol' softie." She put her head on his shoulder. "But if she ends up leaving, we cannot shun her. It wouldn't be right."

"You sound like you've already given up. I will not give up."

"I'm not giving up either, Aaron. But . . ." She gazed into her husband's eyes. "Can you bear to see your only *dochder* with a broken heart?"

"If it means keeping her in the community, then *ya* . . . I can."

"*Ach,* Aaron. You don't mean that."

"If she chooses to leave with that boy, she will get no help from me. I'm not surprised that Saul Fisher is her choice for a spouse, but I always thought that boy would stay here." He shook his head. "How wrong I was."

Rebecca leaned up and kissed her husband. "We are both forgetting everything that we know and believe in, *mei lieb.* Everything is God's will. It's in His hands. We will have to trust that everything will work out."

Aaron sighed. "When you put it that way, I know you're right." He pulled Rebecca close. "But it scares me, the thought of our baby girl leaving."

Rebecca put her hand on her heart. "Me too." *And I plan to pay a visit to Saul Fisher as soon as possible.*

Shelby wasn't sure what to say to Miriam.

Her cousin had been crying on and off all afternoon since her talk with her parents. No one said much at supper, and after helping clean up the kitchen, both Miriam and Shelby headed upstairs.

"I don't understand, though. I thought you got to choose if you wanted to stay or not." Shelby reached into her purse and pulled out her diary.

Miriam sniffled, then frowned. "You haven't written in that in a long time. Why are you writing in it?"

Shelby pulled the cap off of her pen. "I just feel like it. Maybe because I haven't written in it in a long time."

"I thought — I thought that you were happier now, and — and talking to God instead of that book."

Shelby briefly wondered if Miriam had looked at her diary. "It's not the same. Sometimes I just like to voice my thoughts to . . ." She paused, thought for a moment, then closed the diary, realizing that she *had* been voicing her thoughts — to God. "Maybe you're right." She dropped it back in her purse, then sighed. "So what are you going to do about you and Saul? Are you still going to go?"

"I love him. I'm going wherever he wants to go."

Shelby thought for a moment. "Is it really fair of him to ask you to leave here, though?"

"He didn't ask. He said he would never ask me. I offered."

"Hmm . . ." Shelby crossed her legs beneath her and faced Miriam on the other bed. "Will you be shunned by your family, like your Uncle Ivan was?"

Miriam sat taller as she dabbed at her eyes. "Well, I shouldn't be, that's for sure. I'm not baptized. Neither is Saul. We should both have the freedom to choose." She started to cry again. "*Mei daed* has never spoken to me like that."

"You'd be leaving in less than a month. It doesn't sound like your parents are going to help you get married, either." Shelby cringed when Miriam started to cry harder. "I'm sorry. I guess I shouldn't have said that."

"I'm scared. And I need my family's blessing. I don't know how I can leave without it. But I don't know how I can live without Saul in my life, either."

They were quiet for a few moments.

"Are you sure you can be happy away from here, Miriam? The *Englisch* world, as you call it, can be a scary place." She uncrossed her legs and dangled them over the side of the bed. "Hey, would Saul reconsider and stay here?"

"I'm not asking him to give up his dream."

"What about your dreams, Miriam?"

She smiled. "I just want to be with Saul. We will build dreams together."

Shelby thought about the time she'd been spending with Jesse and what good friends they were becoming. He wasn't like the guys back home. Jesse was polite, never pushy, and seemed interested in what she had to say. And more than once he'd said he wondered what it would be like to live away from here.

Was he just making conversation or would he really consider leaving this peaceful place? Shelby was starting to feel like her heart was back in a dangerous place. Maybe it would be best to stop spending so much time with Jesse — for both their sakes.

14

It took several more days before Rebecca found the right time to go see Saul. It was later in the evening but well before dark, and everyone was occupied after supper. Aaron and the boys were milking the cows and taking care of things in the barn. Miriam and Shelby were doing whatever they did up in that bedroom for hours each evening after their chores were done.

Rebecca couldn't help but worry about what sort of plans might be in the works. Was Miriam secretly planning a wedding, perhaps even somewhere far away? Rebecca's heart broke at the thought of not seeing Miriam get married, and she was equally as upset for Miriam, who moped around the house, barely speaking to anyone — except Shelby.

She thought about her first phone call with Shelby's mother. There was an urgency in the woman's voice, as if Shelby would never mend unless she was sent far away from friends who were causing her to make bad choices.

One thing that bothered her a lot was the lack of communication between Shelby and her parents. She'd asked Shelby about it, but the girl just shrugged and looked away, commenting that she had talked to each of her parents a few times.

Rebecca shook her head. She couldn't imagine Miriam being away from her for one day, much less two months — with barely any conversation. Divorce must affect people in strange ways, Rebecca assumed, but to put oneself first over the well-being of one's children — well, it just seemed wrong.

She pulled into the Fisher driveway, surprised not to see anyone outside. This was Rebecca's family's favorite time of night. As soon as Aaron and the boys got through with the cows and secured things up for the night, they'd often sit on the porch and watch the sun set, or sometimes Aaron would even join the boys for a game of basketball. Miriam used to join in for those activities often as well, and Rebecca loved to sit and watch her family enjoying some fun after a hard day's work.

After parking the buggy, she tethered the

horse to a pole by the fence. She hadn't taken two steps when Saul's two brothers came tearing across the yard from the barn. Breathless, the boys wound around her and stopped, almost blocking her way.

"Hello, Ruben. Hello, James." She waited while the boys caught their breath, and as she looked at them, she realized that she hadn't been here since Sarah and Hannah had died. Zeb and the boys didn't have any other family, and Rebecca had assumed that the bishop must not push Zeb to hold church service at his house. Rebecca silently reprimanded herself for not coming to check on Zeb and the boys over the years. Surely they would have enjoyed a home-cooked meal. Then she remembered Saul's job offer, and she doubted Zeb or the boys missed any meals. "I need to talk to Saul. Is he home?"

She hadn't planned out what she would say, but hopefully God would give her the right words to convince Saul not to take her baby girl away from the only life she'd ever known.

Rebecca looked on as Ruben and James both stuttered, looking back and forth at each other. "He's busy right now. Can we give him a message?" the older boy, Ruben, finally said.

"There is no message. I need to talk to him. Do you know when he'll be home?" Rebecca glanced to her right and saw three buggies. Surely the Fisher family didn't own more than three buggies. "Or is he home and just busy?"

"*Ya*. He's busy," James said. Rebecca knew him to be about thirteen now. Handsome boys, both of them. Saul was a nice-looking fellow too, so Rebecca could see Miriam's attraction, but hadn't she taught her daughter to look past just charm and looks?

"I would like to wait for him, please." Rebecca knew she was being rude, but this was an urgent matter that needed to be handled as soon as possible. She'd already waited too long to make this visit.

Both boys stood their ground, not moving. Rebecca folded her arms across her chest. "Perhaps I could wait on the porch for him. Can you please let him know that I am waiting to speak to him? It's important."

Ruben bit his bottom lip, glanced at James, then said, "Sure. Please have a seat on the porch, and I'll let Saul know you're here." He turned back to James. "Can you get Rebecca some tea?"

"No bother. I don't need any tea. *Danki*, though." She scooted past the boys, walked up the porch steps, then took a seat in the porch swing.

Ruben and James both went into the house, closing the screen and wooden door behind them. Rebecca could hear movement inside, but all the doors and windows were shut, which seemed ridiculous in this heat. She patted the sweat on her cheeks with her hands, then dabbed at her forehead. *Maybe they secretly have air-conditioning inside.*

Less than a minute later she heard a loud crash inside the house, followed by loud voices, though she couldn't understand what was being said. She rose from the swing, eased her way to the front door, then leaned her ear against it.

"I can't get him up. He's out cold!"

"What do we do? And by the way, Miriam's mother is on the porch."

Rebecca listened, unsure what to do. The voices grew softer for a few moments, then she heard James say, "Saul, maybe Miriam's mother can help us! We need some help! We need someone to tell us what to do!"

"No!"

Rebecca recognized Saul's voice as the one who'd denied his brother's request.

What in the world is going on in there? She took a deep breath, eased the screen away from the door, and grabbed the doorknob. In one quick motion, she turned the knob and pushed the door open. She stepped inside before anyone could say anything.

Bringing her hand to her mouth to stifle a gasp, she wished she could turn around and go back outside. She eyed the scene before her, and Saul was the first one to speak.

"Rebecca, please go home." Saul's eyes were wet with tears, and Rebecca started to do as he asked until she saw blood on Zeb Fisher's face. All three boys were squatting down around their father, and the rank smell of red wine filled the room. Rebecca moved toward them, squatted down between Saul and James, then spoke directly to Ruben as she leaned over Zeb.

"This isn't bad, boys. Ruben, go get me a wet rag, and see if you can find some ointment. We'll have your father fixed up in no time."

"Sarah, is that you?" Zeb could barely open his eyes as he spoke.

"No, Zeb. It's Rebecca Raber. You've got a nasty cut on your face, but we're going to doctor it for you. You'll be just fine."

"Hannah, *mei dochder?*" Zeb's lids flitted open for only a couple of seconds before they closed again.

Ruben returned with a wet rag and some

ointment, and Rebecca dabbed at Zeb's chin. He could probably use a couple of stitches, but taking him to the hospital right now would cause scandal for this family.

Rebecca glanced around at the boys as sweat poured down everyone's faces. "Saul, why don't you open some windows?"

"But someone might come by or —"

Rebecca raised her brows. "Someone already did. *Me.* Now open those windows before everyone suffocates in here."

Saul did as she asked, and a breeze quickly filled the den. Once she'd tended to Zeb as best she could, she told the boys to just put him on the couch. "He'll wake up in the morning with a nasty headache, but he will be all right."

"We know," James said as he swiped at his eyes.

"Hush, James." Saul frowned at his brother as he reached underneath Zeb's shoulders. James and Ruben each grabbed a leg, and the boys lifted Zeb onto the couch.

Rebecca glanced around at the boys as she realized that they had done this more than once. *How many times?*

"Boys, has this happened before?" Rebecca directed the question to James, since he seemed the most willing to talk.

"All the time," James said as he shook his head.

Saul quickly grabbed both his brothers by the arm. "Go finish your chores. I'll take it from here."

Ruben and James moved toward the door. James turned around and faced Rebecca, his eyes somehow pleading with hers, and Rebecca's heart hurt for this family. The boys were barely out the door when Saul spoke.

"Please don't tell anyone, Rebecca. Please." Saul's eyes melded with hers in a way that left Rebecca speechless. "Please. I'm begging you."

"Saul . . ." she finally said. "Why don't we step into the kitchen?"

Saul pointed to his right. Rebecca walked ahead of him, and she was surprised how clean and fresh the kitchen was, especially for four men living alone. White counter-tops were shiny and clean, and nothing looked out of place. Rebecca sat down in one of six chairs around an oak table in the middle of the room.

"Do you want something to drink?" Saul didn't sit down.

Rebecca pulled the chair out next to her. "No, I'm fine. Sit down, Saul."

He sighed but did as she asked. "Are you

going to tell anyone about this?"

Rebecca rubbed her forehead for a moment, then looked up at him. "Saul, if this goes on all the time, like James said, then you boys need —"

"It ain't that often." Saul leaned back in the chair and looped his thumbs beneath his suspenders. She noticed the blood on Saul's shirt and quickly glanced over him to see if he might be hurt. He didn't appear to be.

"Your father needs some help, Saul. You all do."

Saul pushed the chair from the table and stood up. His eyes blazed as he spoke to Rebecca. "*Mei daed* is the best man I've ever known. He is a loving man. He loves his family. He loves us!"

Rebecca stood up, slowly putting her hand on Saul's shoulder. "Of course he does, Saul."

Saul jerked away from her. "He would never do anything to hurt us." The boy blinked as fast as he could, but a tear still rolled down his cheek, and he quickly wiped it away.

"Saul . . ." She paused as their eyes locked. "How long has this been going on?"

He pulled his eyes from hers, folded his

arms across his chest, and stared past Rebecca.

"Since your *mamm* and Hannah died?"

Saul bit his bottom lip and wouldn't look at her.

A knot was building in Rebecca's throat, but now was not the time to cry, even though her heart was breaking for Saul and his brothers. "Saul, you need some help."

"Why did you come here, Rebecca?" Saul leaned against the kitchen counter, his arms still folded across his chest. "Is it about me and Miriam?"

She cautiously took a step toward him. "*Ya,* but, Saul, I think right now we need to talk about what is happening here, and —"

"If you're worried about me taking Miriam away from here, don't worry about it anymore." He swiped at his eyes again. "I can't leave Ruben and James. They ain't old enough to take care of everything around here."

Rebecca was quiet for a moment. *You're only eighteen, dear child. You're not old enough either.*

"Is this why you are so anxious to leave our community, Saul?"

"No." He wouldn't look at her.

"I can understand. You've been raising your brothers, cooking, cleaning, taking care of your father, and —"

"*Mei daed's* drinking is not the reason why I want to leave. I'm not running away from everything."

Rebecca ignored Saul's sharp tone and softened her own. "Then why, Saul? Why do you want to take my baby girl and leave here?"

Saul uncrossed his arms, then rubbed his forehead for a moment. "I told you. I can't leave now anyway."

"Maybe in a few years when you are both older, you can rethink this, and —"

Saul shook his head, then locked eyes with Rebecca. "My job offer is only good for September." He paused, then stood taller. "I love Miriam. I would have made a *gut* home for her, taken care of her, and always made sure she was happy."

"Why cooking?" Rebecca eased herself back into a kitchen chair.

"What?"

Rebecca twisted her mouth to one side. "Why does cooking interest you so, and why do you think you need to leave here to go cook?"

Saul's blue eyes brightened for a moment as if he was about to tell her exciting news, then he looked away as his expression fell. "It ain't acceptable for a man to cook here.

It's women's work."

Rebecca thought for a moment. "True. But I'm sure Miriam would let you do some of the cooking." Miriam marrying Saul might not be ideal, but if Rebecca could keep them both in the community — well, it seemed the lesser of the two evils.

Saul shuffled to a chair across from her, sat down, then leaned forward a bit. His eyes brightened again. "Do you know how many different recipes there are for rhubarb?"

Rebecca sighed, feeling they were getting off topic.

"There's rhubarb compote and all kinds of rhubarb sauces for fish, chicken, and beef." He shook his head. "It's not just for pies and jam." After he paused, he grinned. "And I have a great recipe for rhubarb soup with mint in it."

Rebecca opened her mouth to try to redirect the conversation, but Saul kept going. "And do you know how many different things you can make with eggs? Breakfast frittatas, crepes, quiches . . ." He shook his head. "It'll make you never want to scramble another egg for breakfast."

I enjoy scrambled eggs. Rebecca scowled a bit, realizing Saul knew more at his young age about cooking than she'd probably know in her lifetime.

"And the gadgets, electric gadgets that are available to help with the cooking . . . it's amazing." Saul let out a heavy sigh, then stood up from the table. "It was just a dream." He glanced around the corner into the den where his father was sleeping on the couch, and a big wave of reality brought them back to the subject at hand. Saul spun around and faced her. "Are you going to tell anyone about this?" He swallowed hard.

Rebecca stood up and took a deep breath. "Saul, don't you feel that you and your brothers could use some help, and that maybe —"

"No. Please." Saul took a step toward her. "I won't take Miriam away from here, but please don't tell."

Rebecca rubbed her forehead as she thought about how miserable Miriam had been. Was she really being fair to Miriam — and Saul? She'd tried to rule out the possibility of true love between the two of them. *They're so young.* But just as soon as she saw fit to, she thought about her and Aaron. Their love was as real and true then as it was now. *Do Miriam and Saul have that kind of love?*

Miriam and Saul's whirlwind romance gave cause for speculation. Like her husband, Rebecca had known that Miriam admired Saul from afar. And yes, they'd grown up together. But true love was more than attraction, and Rebecca wondered if Miriam and Saul shared the kind of everlasting love blessed by God. Saul was standing at the counter, writing something on a piece of paper. He walked toward Rebecca and handed her the note.

Rebecca pulled the piece of paper closer, struggling to read it without her glasses. "A recipe for rhubarb mint soup." She scowled. "Saul, you can't bribe me with a recipe."

"It's not a bribe." Saul lifted one shoulder. "More of an offering of peace."

Rebecca tucked the recipe into her apron pocket. "I need to go." She left the kitchen and eased through the den, past Zeb on the couch, and toward the door. Saul followed. She'd won this round. Miriam wouldn't be leaving here. But as she glanced at Zeb on the couch, she didn't feel victorious at all.

"Good-bye, Saul."

It was two days later when Saul finally caught up with Miriam. He'd managed to get a message to Jesse, who gave it to Shelby for Miriam — for her to meet him at the covered bridge in Ronks on Thursday at six in the evening. Saul worried that Rebecca had told Miriam everything, and he wondered what she would be thinking — about him, his father, and their family. Miriam didn't seem one to judge, and it wasn't their way, but he was still fearful.

Today he would tell her that he planned to stay in the community. Marrying Miriam would be wonderful, but he couldn't help but feel that the dream he'd had for years was just out of reach, and that he'd never have this opportunity again. They'd both be baptized, and there'd be no need to rush a wedding. Plenty of time. Since he wouldn't be going anywhere.

He greeted Miriam with a kiss when he walked up to her. She was standing under the bridge, her buggy parked off the side of the road. "Do your folks know where you are?" He couldn't stand the thought of Miriam lying to her parents to sneak off and see him. It shouldn't be like that.

"I told them I was going for a ride."

"How is everything at home?"

"Tense. No one is saying much." She leaned closer to him. "But it doesn't matter, Saul. I love my family, but you are going to be my husband, and I'll go anywhere with you. Your dreams are my dreams."

Saul pulled her into a hug and held her tight for a few moments before he eased her away, feeling relieved that Rebecca hadn't shared anything. "Miriam, I've decided not to take the job in Pittsburgh."

She stepped back from him. "Why? Why not? Saul, please don't do this because of me. I've thought a lot about it, and I want to go out into the world. I want to experience things I've never been able to." She reached into the pocket of her black apron. "Look! I found this in a magazine. It's a person who helps you find houses — a realtor. And look at this." She pulled another piece of paper from her pocket. "This is a list of things to do in Pittsburgh" She smiled. "Look, there's museums and beautiful churches. All kinds of things for us to see and learn about." He watched her take a deep breath, then her face brightened even more. "And . . . I'm so excited about this! There is a job for a preschool teacher right near where you work. Oh, Saul. I've always wanted to work with children. And this is a class for what they call special needs children, *kinner* who need lots of extra love and care."

"That all sounds great, Miriam." Saul tried to share her enthusiasm, and there was nothing he wanted more than to take her with him to Pittsburgh, if she truly wanted to go. "I just don't think I can leave Ruben and James right now." Miriam actually hung her head, and it saddened him to see that she was genuinely disappointed. "I — I thought you'd be happy about this. Now we can stay in the community, raise a family here."

"But it's your dream. I want to be a part of your dreams, Saul. What made you decide you can't leave Ruben and James? Is your father ill? Does the farm need help? If so, maybe someone in the community can pitch in."

Saul avoided her eyes, knowing he was going to give her a partial version of the truth. "Maybe when they're older," he said, careful not to get locked into her gaze.

"But what about your job?" Her forehead creased as she spoke.

"I'm gonna write a letter to the owner of the restaurant and turn it down. There will be others." Although he knew there wouldn't.

"Saul, if we get baptized into the community, then we can't ever leave here without being shunned." She put her hand to her chest. "My family won't be happy if I leave here with you, but I won't be shunned."

Saul felt the life being zapped out of him. Too much was happening at once, and worry filled his heart. "I love you, Miriam. I want to marry you and be with you wherever we are."

She cut her eyes at him, then put her hands on her hips. "Saul, I love you too. And maybe I should feel happy about staying in our community, but . . ." She took a deep breath. "It's your *dream.*"

"I'll build new dreams with you."

Miriam studied him for a few moments. Something was different about him, as if his spirit ran dry. His eyes drooped with sadness, and the smile that normally filled his face when he saw her seemed forced. "Did you talk with your *daed?* What did he say? Did he disapprove of you leaving? Is that why you don't want to leave? Because James and Ruben seem fine."

He shook his head, then leaned back against the inside of the bridge. "Miriam, you'll be happier here with your family. We'll have a *gut* life."

If that were true, then why did he look like he'd just settled for second best?

Saul shifted his weight, then pulled off his straw hat and wiped his brow. "I just changed my mind."

Miriam folded her arms across her chest. This didn't make sense. And she had a hunch who was behind this. Her parents.

"Did *mei mamm* or *daed* talk to you?"

Saul scuffed one foot against the road and avoided her eyes. "Your *mamm* came for a visit, but —"

"I knew it!" Miriam stomped her foot. "I am eighteen years old and in my *rum-schpringe.* She shouldn't be doing this. I have a right to make my own choices."

Saul gently grabbed both her shoulders and gazed into her eyes. "Miriam, you wouldn't have made a choice to leave this place if it weren't for me. I know that."

"And you wouldn't have made a choice to stay if it weren't for — for my mother." She pulled away from him. "You are letting *mei mamm* take away your dreams, and that's not right." She shook her head. "I'm not letting her do that. We are going to get married, go to Pittsburgh, and you are going to be a great chef in that new restaurant."

Saul pulled her into a hug. "No, Miriam," he whispered. "I'm not going."

Such sadness in his voice. *This is not right.* Miriam wanted her mother to undo whatever she'd done to change Saul's mind.

15

For two days, Rebecca had pondered what, if anything, she should do about Saul and his family. It didn't seem right for those three boys to be taking care of Zeb, then — understandably — hiding it from the community. They were too young to carry such burdens. Even Saul.

"Just stay out of it, Rebecca," Aaron said after Rebecca voiced her concerns. He raised his eyes above his Bible. "Be glad that Miriam will be staying here in the district. That's the most important thing."

"Keep your voice down. Miriam and Shelby are on the porch in the rockers." She spoke in a whisper, then tapped her finger to her chin as she thought about what her husband said. Keeping Miriam in the community should be Rebecca's only concern, but she couldn't ignore the little voice in her head pushing her to listen to her heart. And her heart hurt for everyone involved.

She leaned her head back against the couch while Aaron sat across the room in the rocking chair reading. Closing her eyes, she prayed to do right by all concerned. The boys were upstairs. The house was so quiet. She didn't mean to eavesdrop, but she couldn't stop herself when she clearly heard her daughter's voice.

"Saul is so sad, Shelby. It's like his spirit has withered. I want to be with the Saul I'm in love with, the one with hopes and dreams. He's adventuresome, and it's one of the things I love about him."

Rebecca opened her eyes and leaned one ear closer to the window, her heart heavy as she listened.

"Are you going to talk to your mom?"

"*Ya.* I am. I cannot believe that she would ruin Saul's life like this. And mine. Whatever she said to him, now he is refusing to go to Pittsburgh and follow his dreams. It's not right. In the *Ordnung,* it's clear that we get to experience the outside world and decide for ourselves if we want to leave."

Rebecca brought her hand to her mouth and held her breath, not wanting to miss what Miriam said, but with each word, her heart ached.

"Miriam, I probably sound like a broken record, but . . it's a rough world out there, and there are so many things that you don't know anything about. It's dangerous. There are bad people everywhere. I just don't understand why you would want to leave here. It's so safe, and everyone is so loving and kind. It's all about family, and I love that."

Rebecca heard Aaron grunt, and she looked at him.

"Guess you were wrong about Shelby, no?"

"Shh, Aaron." She narrowed her eyes at her husband, who could evidently hear the girls talking even though he was across the room. She listened as Miriam responded to Shelby's remarks.

"I could've been happy here, Shelby. But I can be happy in Pittsburgh too. I'm a Daughter of the Promise, and if I take those beliefs with me and live by them, it doesn't matter where I live."

Rebecca glanced at Aaron and whispered, "I don't want her to go, Aaron, but you must admit, we raised her right." Aaron scowled, but together they kept listening.

"What's a Daughter of the Promise?"

"It's a spiritual journey that a woman takes when she finds true meaning to the words *faith, hope,* and *love.* I have a strong faith, hope for my future, and I love God with all my heart." After a pause, Miriam added, "And Saul."

"I think you're lucky, Miriam. I would have loved to have grown up in a place like this, especially with your family. I love your family." She giggled. "Even your mom. I wish my mom cared about me even half as much as your mom cares about you."

Rebecca brushed away a tear.

"Let's go to bed, Rebecca. We've intruded on those girls enough." Aaron spoke in a whisper as he stood up and reached for her hand.

"I've been so wrong about Shelby."

"*Ya*. You have." Aaron put his arm around her as they moved toward the stairs, then he let her edge in front of him. She took a few steps, then turned around to face him.

"We got what we wanted today, Aaron. Saul isn't leaving, and Miriam isn't going anywhere with him." She looked down at her husband. "Why do I feel so bad?"

"I don't feel so *gut* either, *mei leib*. I don't like to see Miriam hurting. And my heart hurts for Zeb and those boys." He paused. "But I can't bear the thought of Miriam leaving."

Rebecca turned and started back up the stairs again, wondering if sleep would come tonight.

■ ■ ■ ■

Miriam was nervous to face off with her parents, but by Friday, she'd made up her mind. *Mamm* still wasn't hosting suppers, and Miriam knew that it was partly because she was still mourning Uncle Ivan's death, but also because of the money that was stolen during the last meal she hosted.

After supper Shelby coaxed Miriam's brothers outside, challenging them to a game of basketball, so that Miriam could speak privately with her parents. She wished she could talk only to her mother, tell her how wrong she'd been to convince Saul to stay here, but the decisions about her life affected her father too. Normally *Daed* was more easygoing than her mother, but when it came to her leaving, *Daed's* behavior went from calm to crazy. She wasn't looking forward to talking to either of them, but if there was any chance that they might see her side and convince Saul to accept his job offer, then it was worth a try.

"This is about Saul, no?" Her father eased into one of the rockers. *Mamm* sat in the other one while Miriam took a seat on the couch across from them.

"*Ya.*" Miriam folded her hands in her lap,

then took a deep breath. She looked from one parent to the other. "*Mamm, Daed* . . . I love Saul. I've always loved him. I want to marry him. And his dream is to live in Pittsburgh and be a chef in a nice restaurant. Without that dream, he'll never be completely happy. He's carried that dream for a long time. I don't know what you said to him, *Mamm,* but now he's not going. Saul said he wants us to get baptized, married, and live our lives here. But I know that's not what he really wants. I don't think it's fair that —"

"Fair?" Her father scowled as he spoke. "It's not fair for Saul to take you away from here."

"*Daed,* he didn't talk me into this. And don't you think I'm scared and nervous?" Miriam felt the lump forming in her throat. She swallowed hard, then hung her head. "I need the blessing of my family."

"Miriam, what if you both get to Pittsburgh and you don't like it?" *Mamm* rubbed her eyes and shook her head. "Then what?"

"Then we come back. Or we do something else. We won't be shunned." Miriam wondered if there would be some type of private shunning if she left. "Will we? Because I don't think I could stand that." A tear rolled down her cheek. "I need you both. I need

299

your blessing."

Mamm blinked back tears but didn't say anything. Her father abruptly stood up from his chair. "You will not have my blessing if you choose to leave here."

"Daed!" Miriam cried. "Please." She covered her face with her hands until she felt her mother's arm come around her. When she looked up, her father was gone.

"I will talk to your father, Miriam." *Mamm* patted her shoulder.

"The way you talked to Saul?" She pulled away from her mother. "The only reason you're saying you'll talk to *Daed* is because you know Saul isn't planning for us to leave now. You talked him out of going. He was ready for us to go start our lives. Now he isn't the same, *Mamm*. He is so sad. And both of us were so excited. *Ya*, I was nervous and scared, but still excited." She gazed into her mother's eyes. "You've raised me *gut*, *Mamm*. I'll carry my love for God wherever I go. I'm sorry you can't see that."

Tears flowed as she raced up the stairs.

"Why didn't you tell her the truth?" Aaron sat down on the edge of the bed, still in his work clothes. Rebecca sat down beside him and sighed. She leaned down and stepped out of her shoes.

"I think Saul should tell her."

"And in the meantime, you have to listen to her blame you?" Aaron stood up, looked down at her, and put his hands on his hips. "I do not want that boy taking Miriam away from us."

"I know you don't. I don't either." Rebecca stood up. She pulled Aaron into a hug and kissed him on the cheek before she burrowed her head against his chest. "But we are going to have to let her make this decision."

He eased her away. "It sounds like the decision is made. Saul isn't going to leave his brothers with Zeb. So they will just get baptized, married, and live here in Paradise."

Rebecca rubbed her forehead. "And what about Saul's brothers, Ruben and James? They're only young teenagers. They shouldn't have to be handling this at their age. And what about Zeb? I think his drinking probably started after Sarah and Hannah were killed. But it doesn't give him the right to raise those boys that way. Zeb needs some help, Aaron."

"*Ach,* Rebecca." Aaron sat down on the bed again and put his head in his hands. "I wish we could just leave it alone, let the *kinner* get married and stay here."

She sat down on the bed and put her arm around her husband, then rested her head on his shoulder. "I know, Aaron. It would scare me to death for Miriam to venture out into the *Englisch* world." She paused, kissed him again on the cheek. "But it scares me even more that we might be trying to manipulate God's plans for them."

"We ain't doing that. Saul made the decision not to go so he could stay and tend to his *bruders* and *daed.*"

Rebecca sighed. "I know." She paused. "It certainly says something about the type of person Saul is, no? He would give up his dreams for family. Isn't that the kind of person we want our daughter marrying, Aaron? Wherever they choose to live."

Her husband sighed. "I guess so. But still . . ."

"You know that a small percentage of our young people will venture out into the *Englisch* world."

Aaron slipped his suspenders off his shoulders and let them hang at his side. "I know. I just don't want Miriam in that percentage."

Rebecca couldn't agree more, but she also didn't want to be responsible for ruining her daughter's life, as Miriam had put it.

■ ■ ■ ■

Shelby walked to the barn after everyone was in bed. She knew her mother would still be awake and probably worried since they hadn't spoken in a couple of weeks. Shelby's cell phone had been dead for a while. She put the lantern on the workbench, then lifted herself up to sit between it and the phone. As she picked up the cordless phone from the base, her stomach churned. She loved her parents, but she dreaded going home in a couple of weeks. She couldn't believe her stay here was almost over.

"Shelby! Thank goodness! Why haven't you called?"

"Why haven't *you* called?" Shelby's voice was flat as she spoke.

"I've tried several times. Your cell phone must be dead."

"Yes. But you have the number to their phone in the barn, the phone I'm calling you from."

"Well, we're talking now. Tell me what you've been doing."

"We stay busy, and like I told you before, we get up early, but I —"

"Honey, hold on a sec. I have another call."

Shelby sighed as her mother put her on hold. She waited.

"Okay. Sorry about that. It was Richard, telling me he's running late. We're going to Joe's Place tonight for dinner. I bet you miss the food at Joe's."

Shelby thought about the mouthwatering steaks she used to enjoy at her favorite restaurant back home. "I like the food here too. Rebecca is a great cook. Miriam is a good cook too. I help prepare the meals, so I'm learning to make a lot of different things."

"That's good. You'll have to try out some new recipes for me and Richard when you get home."

Shelby's heart leaped in her chest. "Mom? How often is Richard there?"

The line was silent for long enough that Shelby knew the answer.

"I was going to talk to you about that, Shelby. I know you don't know Richard all that well, but he's become so important to me, and we've been spending a lot of time together while you've been away. You'll love him as much as I do."

"Mom! Is he *living* there?"

"I know I always said I didn't believe in living together, but it's different because I'm older, Shelby, and I've already been married to your father."

"Lead by example, Mother." Shelby shook her head.

"Shelby, try to understand — Hang on, honey. Let me tell Richard I'll call him back."

Shelby stood still, the phone at her ear, for about ten seconds, then slammed it back into the carrier. She jerked around to grab the lantern but knocked it with her elbow. It rolled about two feet away and rested against a hay bale. Within seconds the hay swelled to a glowing orange ball, and Shelby froze.

Water. She ran out of the barn, turned on the faucet, and pulled a garden hose into the barn. By the time she got to the bale, the fire had spread to the workbench and the east wall. Chickens were cackling, the horses were reared up and kicking the stalls, and Shelby's heart was pounding out of her chest. She was unsure whether to run for help or to keep spraying the stream of water on the fire.

Please, God. Help me. What do I do?

Instinctively she ran to the horse stalls and flipped the latches, and the animals ran free to safety. She opened the chicken coop, hoping the chickens would follow her as she ran out of the barn to get help. Aaron met her in the yard.

"Shelby! Are you all right? Are you hurt?"

She shook her head but couldn't speak. Ben, Elam, and John ran past her, followed by Miriam. But Aaron sent them back. "It's too late! Go back! Wet the yard in the front of the *haus* with the other hose — try to keep the fire from spreading to the house."

Why didn't I call 911? Shelby looked on as the rest of the family tried to control the spreading fire and made sure animals were a safe distance away. Even little John was coaxing the chickens toward the backyard. *What have I done?*

"Shelby! Are you all right?" Rebecca threw her arms around her. "Are you hurt?"

"I — I . . ." She couldn't talk.

Rebecca eased her away and cupped Shelby's cheeks in her hands, and even in the moonlight, Shelby could see the concern on Rebecca's face. "Nod if you're okay."

Shelby did.

"That's all that counts."

Rebecca kissed Shelby on the forehead, then went to help secure the animals. Shelby heard sirens, so she knew the fire wouldn't spread to the house. She stood alone in the middle of the yard and buried her face in her hands, sobbing.

16

Miriam watched members of the community clearing the rubble from the fire the next day. Even though the barn had been leveled, the animals survived and the fire never got near the house. Luckily, a neighbor down the road spotted the smoke from his place.

She smiled at Saul as he walked by her carrying a load of debris. Several areas still smoldered, and Saul's father and brothers were busy keeping the hot spots wet. Her own brothers were busy building temporary housing for the chickens and pigs, and her Uncle Noah, Uncle Abe, and friend Kade Saunders helped her father drag the larger pieces of burnt lumber to the far side of the house. Miriam counted more than sixty people helping out on this hot Saturday morning. The following Saturday most of those same people, plus some, would be back for the barn raising.

She blew a loose strand of hair from her face and accepted a tray of glasses of iced tea from Sadie Saunders before passing them out herself. It didn't matter that her mother was trying to ruin Saul's life; his entire family was still here helping. That was the way things were done, and Miriam briefly wondered how folks would be out in the *Englisch* world during a crisis. She still hadn't given up hope that she and Saul would be leaving for Pittsburgh in a couple of weeks. She had to figure out a way to convince him to go.

"Do you know where Shelby is?"

Miriam turned at the sound of her mother's voice, sloshing tea from one of the glasses onto the tray. "She's upstairs."

Mamm frowned. "I'm worried about her. Poor thing was in shock last night and pale as a ghost before she went to bed. She didn't say much."

Miriam tried to put her own hurt and resentment toward her mother aside. "I thought I heard her crying during the night. And before she went to sleep, she just kept saying how sorry she was, over and over again."

Mamm shook her head. "It was an accident, and God saw fit to spare us any harm. I'll go check on her."

Rebecca knocked on the bedroom door, then pushed it open before Shelby had time to answer. "Shelby?" She stepped into the room, and her heart dropped. "What are you doing?" Rebecca eyed Shelby's packed suitcases. Her young cousin was sitting on the edge of the bed, her eyes swollen and red. Rebecca sat down beside her. "Shelby?"

Shelby sniffled as she kept her head hung. "I figured you would be ready for me to leave. I know I still have a couple of weeks, but after what happened —" She started to cry.

Rebecca put a hand on her shoulder. "Shelby. The fire in the barn was an accident. We are thanking the Lord that you are safe. That everyone is safe. Child, we hold no ill will toward you."

Shelby still didn't look at her. "I'm so sorry, Rebecca."

Rebecca twisted to face her. "Shelby, look at me." When Shelby finally did, Rebecca cupped her cheek in her hand. "Sweet Shelby, please don't leave yet."

A tear rolled down Shelby's cheek. "I would be leaving soon anyway. And I know you don't like me here, and —"

"That's not true." Rebecca lowered her hand and gazed into Shelby's eyes, realizing they'd never really had a heart-to-heart conversation. "I — I was worried when you arrived, Shelby. We're not used to having *Englisch* living in our home, and I admit . . ." Shame fell over Rebecca as she thought about the blame she'd mistakenly placed on Shelby in the past. "I was fearful." She lifted Shelby's chin, then smiled. "But you are part of this family. And I know that you have been a *gut* influence on our Miriam." Rebecca frowned. "Even if we've questioned her choices."

Shelby turned on the bed, bent one leg underneath her, then stared hard at Rebecca. "I think Saul loves Miriam very much. But I can understand why you wouldn't want her to leave here." Shelby looked away, stared at the wall for a moment as if remembering something, then said, "It's a scary place out there."

They were both quiet for a few moments. Rebecca finally stood up and folded her arms across her chest. "Young lady, you get busy unpacking those bags." Shelby looked up at her. "Because you haven't lived until you've experienced an Amish barn raising." She grinned. "Do you really want to miss that?"

Shelby's eyes teared up again. "You don't want to send me away? Seems like every time I did something bad, my parents were ready to ship me off. This wasn't the first time. When I was thirteen, I got sent to my aunt's to live because I failed two classes." Shelby paused, swiping at her eyes. "There were other times."

Rebecca sighed as she lowered her hands to her sides. "No, my dear. No one is shipping you anywhere, except perhaps outside to help serve tea to the neighbors helping us."

A grin tipped the corner of Shelby's mouth. "Yes, ma'am."

Rebecca folded her hands in front of her and stood taller. "Now, get these bags unpacked, and I'll see you downstairs." She winked at Shelby, then headed out the door.

Once downstairs Rebecca grabbed a pitcher of tea from the kitchen table and headed out the back door — just in time to see Bishop Ebersol pulling up. She'd prayed about this situation with Zeb and the boys, and now she knew that she must talk to the bishop. She took a deep breath and walked outside.

Saul stopped dead in his tracks with a handful of burnt wood when he saw Rebecca at the side of the house talking with Bishop Ebersol, and twice the bishop glanced toward Saul's father. There was no doubt in Saul's mind that Rebecca was telling the bishop about his *daed*. It would only be a matter of time before the entire community found out. How could she do this after Saul promised to stay here in the community? Clearly Rebecca's ultimate goal was to make sure that Saul didn't marry Miriam, here or anywhere else.

And I'm here helping your family while you go destroying mine?

He dropped the wood on the pile of debris and turned again toward the bishop, locking eyes with him briefly until he saw Miriam walk up beside him.

"I wonder what *Mamm* is talking to Bishop Ebersol about." Miriam handed Saul a glass of iced tea.

Saul accepted the tea, took a long drink, then shrugged. First, his dreams of going to Pittsburgh had been shattered, and now he couldn't help but worry that Miriam would change her mind about him once she found out about his father.

"Saul, no matter what, I still think we should go to Pittsburgh, like we planned."

"I told you. We can't. Because of Ruben and James." Saul didn't mean his words to sound so harsh, but it was hard to watch everything falling apart right before his eyes.

"I — I don't understand that. Your father will take care of Ruben and James, and —"

"I can't talk about this right now." Saul walked away, thinking it was only a matter of time before Miriam didn't want anything to do with him or his family. He couldn't look back.

Miriam stood completely still as she watched Saul walk away. Maybe he'd decided against marrying her after all. Maybe he couldn't deal with her meddlesome mother. She turned toward Bishop Ebersol and *Mamm* and watched them for a moment. Bishop Ebersol was stroking his long gray beard as her mother did most of the talking. She didn't see her father walk up beside her.

"I can't stand to see you leave here, *mei dochder.*" *Daed* frowned as he spoke. "But I can't stand to see you unhappy either."

Miriam didn't say anything.

"You love that boy?"

She turned to face him. "With all my heart, *Daed.*"

Her father shook his head and stared at the ground. "You don't know anything about the *Englisch* world, *dochder.*"

Miriam kept her eyes on her mother and the bishop. "And apparently I'm not going to."

"What would be so terrible about you and Saul staying here, raising a family here?"

She turned to face her father. "Because Saul has a dream, *Daed.* A dream he's had for a long time. I would be the same person, *Daed,* whether I'm here or in Pittsburgh. I love God. I can love Him from anywhere." She lifted one shoulder, then dropped it. "But Saul is so unhappy right now, I don't even know if he still wants to marry me."

"If he loves you, he should want to marry you no matter where you live."

Miriam's mouth dropped for a moment. "You and *Mamm* should love me no matter where I live too."

Daed put one hand on his hip as he rubbed his forehead with the other, then he sighed. "Of course we will always love you, Miriam." He gazed at her with soft eyes and a gentle smile, and Miriam felt like a little girl all of a sudden.

"Then what is it, *Daed?* Why can't you stand the thought of me leaving with Saul?" She moved closer to him. "My faith will go with me wherever I go. Don't you believe that, *Daed?* You've raised me *gut.*" She touched his arm. "Please, *Daed.* Have faith in me."

"I do."

Miriam kept her eyes locked with his and waited for him to go on.

"I would just — just miss you. So very much." He covered his eyes with one hand, and Miriam realized she'd never seen her father cry. Until now.

Miriam put her arms around him and cried with him for a moment.

I would miss all of you too.

Rebecca finished her conversation with Bishop Ebersol, then headed toward the house. Before going inside, she stopped and lowered her head to pray that she'd done the right thing. When she looked up, Aaron was standing right in front of her.

"This could all backfire on you, especially when Zeb finds out."

She lifted her head. "I have to believe I did the right thing, Aaron. I've prayed about this, and it's just not right — what's goin' on over there."

Her husband shook his head, then glanced around until he saw Zeb carrying a stack of wood, a smile on his face. "I know we don't know Zeb and the boys as well as we should, but it wonders me if it's right to interfere in a man's life like that, even if we're trying to do *gut* for everyone involved." He edged closer and stroked his beard. "He's here helping our family, and you're telling his family secrets."

"Secrets that can cause harm to his children." Rebecca's voice cracked as she began to second-guess what she'd just done.

"I hope it doesn't bring shame to Zeb's family. That's all I'm saying."

Rebecca bit her bottom lip for a moment, then eased closer to her husband. "You know that's not why I'm doing this."

"I know, Rebecca. But what you are doing is going to cost us something very precious."

Rebecca realized that there would be a cost for what she'd done, but in her heart she believed it was the right thing for everyone. She could only hope and pray that she'd helped the Fishers, even if they never saw it that way. Just the same, her own actions frightened her, and she blinked back tears.

"Don't cry, Rebecca. Please don't cry." Aaron discreetly reached for her hand and squeezed. "We will pray extra hard about this." He paused when Shelby walked by them toward the barn. He waited until she was out of earshot before he asked Rebecca, "Where's she been?"

"She was upstairs packing. She thought we were going to send her home early because of what happened." Rebecca shook her head.

"She didn't mean to burn down the barn. It was an accident."

"That's what I told her." Rebecca watched Shelby join Miriam and take two glasses of tea from a tray, then pass them out to the fellows nearby. "I worry about her. I think divorce must cause all kinds of problems when there are *kinner* involved, no?"

"I don't know, Rebecca. Divorce or not — it seems odd to me that her folks don't call or check on her more often."

Rebecca couldn't agree more.

Shelby wound her way around the crowd, careful to avoid Jesse. She'd stopped going to lunch with him and hadn't made an effort to get in touch with him. She was leaving in two weeks, and they'd already become much too close. Saying good-bye was going to be hard enough.

She missed their lunches and talks about books, but she knew Miriam was right. If she were to get close to Jesse, it wouldn't be fair to either one of them, even if Jesse had hinted that he had a curiosity about the world outside of this safe community. He belonged here, and although she didn't want their friendship to come to a halt, she'd rekindled another relationship. Her time with the Lord brought her a sense of peace that she hadn't had in a long time. She credited Miriam and her family for reconnecting her with God, but Shelby knew that through prayer, He was changing her life.

She'd replaced writing in her diary with prayer, and instead of regret about her choices in the past, her parents' choices, and the life she'd led — now she was working on not carrying the burdens of the past, hers or her parents. Causing the barn fire could have been a setback and destroyed all that she'd been working toward — feelings and recognition that she hoped to take from here when she had to leave. But after talking with Rebecca, she found their forgiveness amazing. She wondered briefly how either of her parents would have reacted to such an accident. She recalled the time she accidentally broke her mother's favorite crystal vase. Not quite tall enough to smell the flowers at nine years old, she tipped the vase toward her and spilled the water. She knocked it off the table when she was wiping up the water. First there was yelling, then she was sent to her room for the afternoon. *But it was an accident.*

Lost in thought, she didn't see Jesse walk up beside her. "Got an extra one of those?"

Sweat ran the length of Jesse's face as he eyed the two glasses of iced tea Shelby was holding. "Sure." She eased one in his direction.

Jesse gulped the cold drink for several seconds, and Shelby started to walk away but stopped when she heard her name. She slowly turned around.

Jesse had one hand on his hip as his eyes narrowed. "Did I do something to upset you, Shelby?"

She avoided his intense green eyes as she nervously moistened her dry lips, then finally looked up at him, realizing how much she'd missed him. "No. Everything's fine."

He tipped back his straw hat and scratched his forehead for a few moments. "It sure don't seem fine. We were having lunch, talking . . . then you just didn't want to spend any more time with me." He paused, his lips pressed together for a moment. "I figure I must have done something."

She shook her head. "No, Jesse. You didn't do anything. It's just — I'll be leaving soon, and I just . . ." She bit her bottom lip, unsure how much to say.

Jesse eased closer to her, folding his arms

across his chest. "Didn't want to break my heart?"

Shelby's eyes grew big as saucers, and she was sure her face was four shades of red. "What?"

"I like you, Shelby." His tight expression relaxed into a smile. "And I'm pretty sure you like me too."

She smiled tentatively, but her heart was racing. "Is that so?"

"*Ya*. And I figure you didn't want us to get too close, since you're leaving and all."

Just the thought of leaving caused her smile to fade. To agree with him would make it that much harder in two weeks. "I've just been busy, Jesse." She glanced around at everyone working, then hung her head. "And I feel terrible about what happened."

Jesse leaned down until Shelby was forced to lock eyes with him, eyes filled with tenderness. "Do you know how many barn fires we have each year from lanterns or propane heaters?" He waved his arm around the yard. "And you see how we handle it, no? And by the end of the day next Saturday, your cousins will have a brand-new barn." He chuckled, then whispered, "Theirs was old anyway."

She stifled a smile. "Thanks for saying that."

"So how about going for a ride with me Tuesday after work? I get off early that day." He winked at her. "We could go fishing at the Zook place."

Shelby took a deep breath, then lifted her chin a bit. "I can't, Jesse. I'm sorry." She handed him the full glass of tea she was holding and took his empty glass. "I have to go."

She didn't turn around as she headed back to the house. But she couldn't help but wonder if she was making a mistake. As she walked up the porch steps, she wondered if they would keep in touch or write letters.

Saul watched his father across the yard saying good-bye to Rebecca and Aaron. He heard Miriam's parents both thank *Daed* as they smiled. Saul cringed at the sight. From this moment forward, he would be watching out of the window, waiting for Bishop Ebersol to show up, and he would be praying it was on one of *Daed's* good nights. He had Rebecca Raber to thank for that.

He picked up his tool belt from where he'd left it earlier, then strapped it around his waist. He glanced up at his father a couple of times. The best man he'd ever known. And no matter his shortcomings, his father didn't deserve to be shamed by the community, as would surely happen when word of his drinking got out.

Saul had never seen his father drink a drop of alcohol until a few days after his mother and Hannah were buried. It seemed harmless enough at the time. Lots of folks in the district partook of wine, some even whiskey and beer. But for *Daed,* it slowly began to take him to a faraway place, somewhere free from the pain of *Mamm's* and Hannah's deaths. But it seemed like the more he drank, the more he began to change — into someone Saul didn't recognize anymore. But no matter what, Saul knew the man his father really was, the man buried beneath grief so thick he couldn't dig his way through it.

He headed toward his buggy as moments of his childhood flashed before his face. He recalled the time he'd begged his father for a sled one Christmas following a bad harvest. Money was tight, and the sled was on display at a fancy store in town. Saul didn't understand until he was much older why his father had taken on a job in the evenings. Saul and both his brothers each got brand-new fancy sleds that year, different than the kind they could have made themselves. These were faster and slicker, and Saul and his brothers had many a race down the hill behind the house that year.

More memories of his father breezed through his mind, and Saul fought not to question the Lord's will, why his mother and Hannah were taken away from them all. How different their lives might have been. He watched his father walking toward him, a smile stretched across his face.

"*Gut* people, Rebecca and Aaron. I regret that we haven't spent more time with them." His father's kind gray eyes brightened. "But I guess we will now that you and Miriam are getting married." He put his hand on Saul's shoulder. "She seems like a good choice for a *fraa, sohn.*" *Daed* pulled his arm back, then started unhitching the horse. "Your *bruders* said that they will get a ride home later." He walked around to the passenger side of the buggy, Saul's cue to drive. "Have you thought about the *haus* you will build on the property I'm deeding to you? Many bedrooms for many *kinner,* no?"

Saul stared at his father, blinked a few times, and forced the images of his father on the living room floor out of his mind. *How can this be the same man?* He managed a weak smile and nodded as he climbed into the driver's seat of the buggy. His father took a seat beside him, and Saul eased away, realizing he hadn't even said good-bye to Miriam. He knew she wasn't to blame for her parents' actions, but right now it seemed to be the Fishers against the Rabers. Rebecca Raber had seen fit to tell the bishop his family's secrets, even though he'd promised to stay here with Miriam and get married in the district.

It would serve Rebecca right if Saul swept Miriam away from here.

But what about Ruben and James?

Saul wondered if he was placing blame on the right person. He glanced at his father, then took a deep breath.

17

Miriam walked into the kitchen on Wednesday, surprised that Shelby was up before her and already helping *Mamm.* It was the second time this week.

"Shelby scrambled some special eggs this morning," *Mamm* said, smiling. "They have onions, tomatoes, peppers, cheese, and . . ."

Mamm rattled off some more ingredients, but Miriam wasn't listening. She didn't feel like smiling this morning, and with each day that passed since Saturday, her mood had grown worse. Saul hadn't said goodbye after helping clean the fire debris, and she hadn't talked to him since. She wasn't sure who she blamed more — her mother for meddling, or Saul for letting her mother affect their relationship.

"I'm calling them *mei Englisch* special eggs." Shelby glanced at Miriam's mother, who chuckled.

"Even learning some *Dietsch* while you're

325

here." *Mamm* placed a jar of rhubarb jam on the table.

"Mind if I call everyone to *kumme esse?*" Shelby said with a bright smile.

Mamm laughed again. "I think those hungry boys are already on their way, but I'm impressed, Shelby."

Miriam rolled her eyes as she pulled the orange juice from the refrigerator. *Must be nice that* Mamm *can be so cheerful.* She wanted to ask her mother what she'd talked to Bishop Ebersol about on Saturday, but most likely *Mamm* would say it was a private matter. Besides, her father and brothers were making their way into the kitchen.

Following prayer, they began to eat, and everyone loved Shelby's eggs. Miriam had to admit they were good. She savored the taste as she thought about how much Shelby had become a part of the family. Shelby and her mother had been interacting a lot more, especially since the barn fire, which Miriam didn't mind, especially right now, when Miriam had little to say to *Mamm.* Besides, it didn't sound like Shelby had nearly as good a mother as Miriam and her brothers.

Miriam reached for a piece of bacon and pondered her thought. Yes, she was angry with her mother, but she also knew her mother was a good person. And she loved her very much. She glanced around the table at her family. John stuffed his mouth with a biscuit, his hair unintentionally spiked on top as if he'd slept in the same position all night. His bright blue eyes shone with innocence, and Miriam felt like crying all of a sudden.

He's only eight years old. I'll miss seeing him grow up if I leave with Saul. Maybe pushing for this move with Saul, to fulfill his dreams, is a mistake.

What are my *dreams?*

Saul watched from the front yard as Miriam pulled into the driveway. He suspected she was angry with him for leaving Saturday without saying good-bye. He was angry at himself. Glancing at the sun, he figured it was nearing the supper hour, and he planned to make asparagus soup, a recipe of his mother's that he'd added some spices to, giving it a zestier flavor. He couldn't wait until he could cook for Miriam in their own home — even if it wouldn't be in Pittsburgh. He sighed as he thought about the times he'd fantasized about cooking at one of the fancy *Englisch* restaurants.

"I've missed you," he said as he approached her side of the spring buggy, and as her face lit with a smile, he didn't think he'd meant anything more in his life. He extended his hand to help her down. "I'm sorry I didn't say bye on Saturday."

"It's all right." She kept her hand in his as they stood facing each other. "You seemed upset that *mei mamm* was talking to Bishop Ebersol. I was wondering if she was talking about us."

"Maybe. Maybe about our wedding. We should choose a date, then publish it." He squeezed her hand.

Miriam's blue eyes sparkled. "*Mamm* made some rhubarb soup the other day, and she put mint in it. It was her third time to try to make the soup." Miriam crinkled her nose. "It was terrible — for the third time. She mumbled your name and gave it to the dog." She brought a hand to her mouth, stifling a grin. "Know anything about that?"

Saul laughed. "I gave her that recipe when she was here."

Miriam giggled, but then her smile faded. She looked down for a moment, then turned to him and asked, "What did she say to you that day, Saul?"

When he didn't answer, she said, "I can't wait to be your *fraa*, Saul, but are you sure you can be happy here? I still don't understand why you've given up going to Pittsburgh, and I think *mei mamm* had something to do with it."

Saul knew Rebecca wasn't to blame for his decision. She might have destroyed his family's reputation by talking to Bishop Ebersol, but Saul was making the best choices for his family. It just wasn't God's plan for him to leave here and pursue a life in the *Englisch* world. No matter how much he'd wanted it and prayed about it, there were just too many obstacles in his path. He remembered his mother saying once that if things are meant to be and part of God's plan, then they come easily and without forced effort. So instead of praying for a new life outside of his community, Saul had been praying that he would accept God's will for both him and Miriam, whatever that might be.

"No, Miriam. Your *mamm* didn't convince me to stay here. I just ain't ready to leave Ruben and James yet." He clutched her hand with both of his.

Miriam squared her shoulders and stood taller. "Maybe we shouldn't get baptized, then. Maybe we should wait and see if you decide to go to Pittsburgh later, in a few years."

"You would do that for me? Wait?"

"*Ya.* I would."

Saul heard her say she would wait for him,

but her tone was reluctant, and he knew right then that he could never do that to her. He didn't feel worthy of all the sacrifices she was willing to make for him, especially since she didn't know the real reason why he couldn't go to Pittsburgh. Now was the time to be completely honest with her.

He touched her chin, quickly glanced around the yard, then kissed her lightly on the lips, grateful that his father and brothers were already inside. "I love you, Miriam. I don't want to wait to get married. We're going to get baptized in October, then marry in November. Nothing would make me a happier man." He smiled at her, then took a deep breath. "But there's something I want to tell you."

They both turned when they heard horse hooves clicking against the driveway.

"Bishop Ebersol," Saul said and hung his head. "This is what I wanted to talk to you about."

"About Bishop Ebersol? Why is he here?" The look of concern in her eyes made Saul's heart ache.

"*Ya.* He's probably here to talk to my father . . ."

"What? What are you talking about, Saul?" Miriam's hand was on his arm.

Bishop Ebersol pulled in beside Miriam's buggy before Saul had time to answer. He wasn't sure what to tell her anyway. Miriam dropped her hand to her side, and Saul's heart thudded in his chest as he watched the older man step down from his covered buggy, aided by a long black cane in one hand. Saul could feel his world getting ready to crash down around him.

Once everyone found out, his family would be avoided, shamed in the community. It wasn't their way to judge, but Saul knew there would be plenty who would practice their own private form of shunning. He locked eyes with Miriam and wondered how she would be affected by it. *Will you still want to marry me?*

"Hello, Saul. *Wie bischt?*" Bishop Ebersol extended his hand to Saul, then he turned to Miriam and nodded. "Hello, Miriam." He stroked his long gray beard that ran the length of his chest. "I need to see your father, Saul. Is he inside?"

Saul was sure Bishop Ebersol could see his heart beating beneath his dark-blue shirt. He took a deep breath. "*Ya.* He is inside with *mei bruders.*" Saul gestured toward the house, then turned to Miriam.

"I should go. *Mamm* will be waiting for me to help with supper." Miriam backed up a step and offered a weak smile. "Bye, Saul. Good-bye, Bishop Ebersol."

"See you Saturday at the barn raising, Miriam." Saul gave her a quick wave of his hand, and Bishop Ebersol again nodded at her. They waited a few moments until Miriam was heading down the driveway, then the bishop said, "I know it is near the supper hour, but it's important that I speak with your father. I've not been well the past few days, or I would have come sooner."

Saul knew there was no way to avoid the crisis at hand, but he didn't want James and Ruben around when his father was humiliated. "I'll go let *Daed* know you're here, and I'll ask James and Ruben to help me in the barn so that you can talk."

"That will be *gut.*"

Saul's steps were heavy as he walked into the house. *Daed* was reading but still in his work clothes, and James and Ruben were nowhere in sight.

"Where's James and Ruben?" Saul asked when he entered the den.

His father eased his reading glasses off and smiled. "We all worked hard today, so I told them to go ahead and bathe. I'll milk the cows later after supper. They deserve a break." His father chuckled. "I'd give you a break too, *mei sohn,* and cook us some supper, but I'm not much *gut* in the kitchen."

You're a gut *man. And now the bishop is here to humiliate you.*

"Bishop Ebersol is here to talk to you. Privately, I think."

Daed's eyes clouded as his expression soured. "I wonder why." Then he stood up. "The bishop is always welcome, of course."

"I'll go see if James and Ruben want to play basketball before I start supper, so you and the bishop can talk."

His father nodded. Saul darted up the stairs and summoned James and Ruben, who were always happy when Saul challenged them to play a game.

But a few minutes later, as Saul aimed the ball for his first shot, he watched his father opening the door for Bishop Ebersol. He threw, but the ball didn't go anywhere near the basket. *This is it.*

He saw Ruben toss the ball out of the corner of his eye, but he felt like his breath was being sucked out of him as he bent over and leaned his hands on his knees, wondering how this night would change all their lives.

A car coming up the driveway pulled his attention from the game. He waited and was surprised to see Noah Stoltzfus step out. Noah was Rebecca's brother who ran a clinic for both *Englisch* and Amish in the area. He'd been shunned years ago for leaving the Order to become a doctor, but his contributions to the community had earned him respect, and over time hardly anyone recognized the shunning. This was bad timing, though, and he couldn't imagine what Noah was doing here. He couldn't recall Noah visiting before.

"Hi, boys." Noah waved as he crossed the yard, hurrying across the grass and up the porch steps.

"Wait!" Saul called out to Noah as he ran toward him, dropping the basketball. "*Daed's* got company. Bishop Ebersol is here."

Noah spun around. "I know. I'm here to meet with them." He offered a brief smile, then quickly turned, pounded up the stairs, and was inside the house before Saul could say a word.

"Why's Noah here?" James asked as he ran to Saul's side.

Ruben joined them within seconds. "And why is the bishop here?"

They are all here to destroy our lives.

Friday morning Miriam, Shelby, and *Mamm* were busy preparing food to be served at the barn raising the next day. Miriam had been thinking about what had happened at Saul's. She didn't understand what Saul wanted to tell her or why Bishop Ebersol was at his house, but she suspected her mother knew something. She'd tried to catch her mother alone several times, but *Mamm* had been busy preparing for the barn raising. She'd also been teaching Shelby more Pennsylvania *Deitsch.* Her cousin seemed to enjoy learning new words and phrases, although Miriam wasn't sure why. Miriam had noticed the two of them growing even closer, and they hardly noticed Miriam was in the room that morning, which was fine by Miriam. She was glad to see her cousin happy.

Shelby's parents were due to arrive in a week, and Miriam was going to miss Shelby terribly, especially their late-night chats. It really was like having a sister.

Even with all of the windows and doors open in the house, the kitchen was still sweltering as they worked. Miriam could feel the sweat dripping down her back beneath her dress. *Mamm* wanted to get the cooking done early before it got too hot, but in August, it was hot all the time. She wiped her forehead with the back of her hand as she leaned down to pull a lemon sponge pie from the oven.

"Someone's here." Shelby walked to the opened door in the kitchen and peered through the screen. "In a car."

Mamm joined Shelby by the door. "I don't recognize that car."

Miriam put the pie on a cooling rack, then went to peer over Shelby's and *Mamm's* shoulders. "Uh-oh."

Shelby twisted her neck to face Miriam. "What?"

They watched the blond-haired woman balancing on heeled sandals as she made her way across the yard.

"What is Lucy Turner doing here?" *Mamm* asked in a whisper.

Lucy clicked up the stairs and stopped on the other side of the screen. "Hello, Rebecca. Can I talk to you for a moment?" She clasped her hands and held them against her sleeveless red blouse. "It's important."

"Of course." *Mamm* pushed the screen door open, and Miriam and Shelby backed up so Lucy could come into the kitchen. "Let's go into the den." *Mamm* motioned with her hand for Lucy to follow her. Miriam knew *Mamm* preferred folks to enter through the den, but with two doors on the porch, it was hard to direct people to the actual front door. Plus, Miriam was sure

Lucy saw them staring at her through the screen door in the kitchen.

"I can see that you're in the middle of supper preparation, so I won't take up much of your time."

Miriam and Shelby didn't move. Miriam held her breath as she strained to hear what Lucy had to say.

Shelby leaned close. "I think the shoofly pie is probably ready," she whispered in Miriam's ear.

Miriam put her first finger to her mouth and kept it there until Shelby shrugged. She leaned her ear toward the entryway from the kitchen to the den, straining to hear Lucy.

"I need to know how I can reach Katie Ann. I know this must seem awkward, but it's important that I speak with her. So I was hoping that you could give me her address and phone number in Colorado."

Miriam blinked as she turned to Shelby and whispered, "Why would she want Katie Ann's address and phone number?"

"How should I know?"

Miriam put her finger back to her lip and leaned in again. It was her mother's voice she heard next.

"Lucy, I'm not sure what to do about this matter, but our Katie Ann is still grieving,

I'm sure. It might be best not to call her right now."

"I understand, but what I have to tell Katie Ann, I would like to do in person. I'm planning to travel to Canaan to do so. I know from Ivan that's where they lived, but I think it would be less shocking for Katie Ann if she knew I was coming as opposed to my just showing up on her doorstep."

"I see."

It was quiet for a few moments, and Miriam wondered if her mother was going to hand over Katie Ann's phone number and address. She fumbled with the string on her prayer covering while she and Shelby waited, but when she heard footsteps moving in the opposite direction, Miriam knew that *Mamm* was ushering her to the door in the den that led to the front of the house.

Miriam heard their voices, but she could no longer make out what was being said. She heard Lucy's car on the driveway before her mother returned to the kitchen. Shelby was busy pulling the almost-burnt shoofly pie from the oven as Miriam asked, "Did you give her *Aenti* Katie Ann's address and phone number?"

Mamm drew her brows into a frown. "*Mei maedel,* were you eavesdropping?"

"It's hard not to hear when you're so close

by." Miriam paused. "What do you think Lucy wants? Poor *Aenti* Katie Ann. I bet she doesn't think fondly of Lucy or want to talk to her." Miriam let out a small gasp. "I think it would be awful if Lucy just showed up on Katie Ann's doorstep, though, without Katie Ann being warned."

Mamm put her hands on her hips, pressed her lips together, then watched through the screen door as Lucy drove away in her car. "I did write down the phone number and address for her." *Mamm* turned slowly around and faced Miriam. "If Lucy is determined to go see Katie Ann, she will. It will be best if she calls her first to warn her." *Mamm* tapped her fingers on her crossed arms. "Maybe I'll call Katie Ann tomorrow to let her know that Lucy has her number and address and might pay her a visit. It sure wonders me why Lucy feels the need to travel all the way to Colorado to talk to Katie Ann, though."

They were all quiet for a minute, then Shelby changed the subject.

"I know I'm leaving here soon, but I sure hope I can come back for Miriam's wedding in November."

"You have to come back!" Miriam bounced on her toes as she wiped her hands on her black apron. She couldn't imagine

339

getting married without Shelby nearby. Then she turned to her mother. "*Mamm,* you know, we need to start planning since that's only three months away. I'll need a new dress, and —"

"Plenty of time for all that," *Mamm* said abruptly, then walked across the den toward the mudroom. When she returned, she was toting a broom and dustpan. "Little John spilled his plate this morning, and I think I missed some of the crumbs." She began to sweep rapidly as if the conversation about Miriam's wedding was not up for discussion.

"*Mamm . . .*" Miriam edged closer to where her mother was sweeping. "Saul and I are going to be baptized in October. Don't you think we need to be planning my wedding?"

"Miriam, I'm busy right now. I told you that we have plenty of time."

Miriam recalled when her friend Anna Kauffman published her wedding announcement. They only had six months to plan the event, and everyone was panicking. Why was her mother acting so unconcerned? "I'm going to marry him, *Mamm,* even if you don't like it," Miriam grumbled.

"I'm sure you are," *Mamm* said as she scooped the tiny amount of crumbs into the dustpan.

Miriam folded her arms across her chest and knew the Lord would not be happy with her actions. Her tone with her mother was unacceptable, but her mother was refusing to accept Saul.

Miriam dried a few dishes, then paused as she closed her eyes and bowed her head, facing away from her mother and Shelby.

Dear Lord, please guide me and Saul onto the path You have planned for us — whether it's here or in Pittsburgh.

She opened one eye and glanced around the room at the only life she'd ever known, then closed her eyes again.

And please help Mamm to love Saul — or at least accept that I love him.

18

By two o'clock on Saturday, the barn was almost framed in, and a sense of fellowship had spread among the hundred or so folks present. But Saul felt lost as he mechanically worked alongside his father and wondered what he'd say to Miriam. He'd asked his father about the bishop and Noah's visit, but his father only said, "Always *gut* to have company." But there was a sadness in his father's eyes, so Saul knew there was more to it. He felt the need to stay close to his father, although watching Miriam throughout the day brought a longing to be near her as well.

Ruben and James knew something was going on, and they had asked Saul about their visitors several times. Saul told them he didn't know. It was the truth. But he felt a dark cloud looming over his family, and he kept waiting for the bottom to fall out.

"*Sohn,* I think we'll be done here soon."

His father pounded a nail into a board high above them while Saul held it in place. "You and me need to talk privately when we get home."

His *daed* didn't look at him, but Saul couldn't take his eyes off his father, a complicated man with years of pain mapped across his face, his long dark beard speckled with gray and his tall frame thinner than in his younger years. "*Ya,* okay," he said softly.

Twice he'd seen Rebecca talking to the bishop again, and once he caught her in deep conversation with his father. What were they all plotting? Maybe they were planning to shun his father. Saul didn't know how he, Ruben, and James could keep the farm going by themselves. Despite *Daed's* shortcomings, his father could work circles around all three of them.

Rebecca walked by and gave him a hesitant smile. He glared at her, then hammered in another nail with strength he didn't know he possessed. He was beginning to think that Rebecca would do anything to keep him from marrying Miriam. His family would be shamed when the news leaked out, as it surely would, and even though Saul believed that Miriam loved him, could she hold up to the gossip that festered even among a community that preached against such a sin?

He took a deep breath and tried to calm his racing heart, wishing he didn't need to have that conversation with his father when he got home.

Rebecca knew that Bishop Ebersol had talked to Zeb, and she'd spoken to Zeb earlier in the afternoon, although it was one of the most awkward conversations she'd ever had. But she'd prayed hard about the situation, and she had to believe that God had guided her to busy herself in someone else's private life for the good of everyone involved, including her daughter.

She thought about Miriam, wondering how her daughter would take the events soon to unfold around her, and briefly worried that she should have talked to Miriam before she took matters into her own hands. There was no mistaking the way Saul had looked at her earlier, such anger in his eyes.

Lord, please continue to guide me. I pray I'm doing the right thing.

She waved as the last buggy left around four that afternoon with plans to finish out the inside of the barn the following Saturday. She felt Aaron's arm come around her waist.

"It's a fine barn, no?"

"*Ya.* Not as big as our other barn, but much sturdier." Rebecca crossed one arm on her chest and brought her other hand to her chin. "We needed a new barn."

"*Mei daadi* built that barn."

They both stood quietly in the yard as the August sun shone down on them from a cloudless sky. Rebecca dripped with sweat. Everyone had worked hard today, and there was nothing like seeing a new barn following a day of hard work and fellowship. But Rebecca couldn't fully enjoy their efforts. Saul and Miriam weighed heavily on her mind.

"Zeb said he is going to talk to Saul tonight." She turned to face Aaron. "Are we doing the right thing?"

"We?" Aaron smiled. "There is no 'we,' *mei fraa.* I told you I wasn't sure about any of this. You believe you are doing the right thing. I am praying you are."

"Do you think that we will lose our *dochder* once this unfolds?" She blinked back tears as she searched her husband's eyes.

"I don't know, Rebecca." He shook his head. "It fears me, keeps me up at night."

"Me too." She turned to face him, looked up into his hazel eyes. "But I believe I am doing the right thing, for everyone."

Aaron smiled, kissed her lightly on the

lips. "I hope so."

Saul didn't think his stomach could churn any faster or harder. No one said much during supper, and with Ruben and James out milking the cows, Saul quickly finished cleaning up the kitchen dishes, then joined his father in the den. His father was sitting on the couch, leaning forward with his elbows on his knees and his hands folded under his chin. He looked up at Saul, then nodded for Saul to take a seat in the rocker across from him.

Daed was pale, and his hand was trembling. He'd seen his father's hands shake before, which happened when he hadn't had any alcohol for a while. Saul copied his father's posture and leaned forward, his elbows also on his knees. Outside, he heard crickets chirping and the cows mooing, and the evening sun shone through the window in the den. A normal night. But Saul knew things were far from normal.

His father stroked his beard and avoided making eye contact. "Saul, I have a drinking problem."

Saul didn't move or breathe. Even though he knew his father's drinking would be at the core of the conversation, he didn't expect his father to blurt it out. He waited for him to go on, keeping his eyes on his father's face.

Daed looked up, blinked a few times, and said, "I need to go away for a while, *sohn.*" He fixed his eyes on Saul as if searching for a reaction. "Bishop Ebersol and me both agree that this is something I need to do. Noah Stoltzfus is helping us make the arrangements." His father leaned back against the couch and sighed. "I'm sorry for everything that I've put you and your *bruders* through."

Saul felt his eyes watering up, but he was determined not to cry. He stared hard into his *daed's* weathered face, the evidence of hard work, a nurturing father. "*Daed,* you've been a *gut* father." Saul blinked back tears as he sat up in his chair. "When *Mamm* and Hannah died, I know it was hard, and" — Saul took a deep breath — "and you've always taken care of us."

His father stirred uneasily on the couch as he shook his head. "No, Saul. I have failed in the Lord's eyes, and I must right my ways." He choked out the words as if just talking caused pain in his throat. "I want to be a better father, and to do that, I need to go away for a while."

"No, *Daed.* Miriam and I are getting baptized in October, then married in November." Saul couldn't imagine his father not being at those two important events in his life. "You have to be here."

"I will be at your wedding, Saul."

Saul leaned forward again and laid his forehead in his hands for a moment, relieved that if his father left, he wouldn't be gone long. He looked back up after a few moments when his *daed* started to speak again.

"Bishop Ebersol and Noah are *gut* men. I have an illness, Saul. And that is what the bishop will tell our community if anyone asks, but we know that sometimes rumors and gossip can start, and I hope —"

"This is all Rebecca Raber's fault!" Saul bolted from the rocker and took two steps toward his father, feeling the heat in his face. "She told the bishop about your — your problem. She only did this because she doesn't want me to marry Miriam! And now you're going to be sent away! How am I going to run the farm with just Ruben and James? Miriam probably won't even want to marry me once this gets out, and —" Saul closed his mouth and took a deep breath when he saw the pain in his father's eyes. "I'm sorry, *Daed.*" He backed into the rocker, sat down, and put his face in his hands, then looked back up. "I'm sorry."

"There will be talk, Saul. I'm sure of it.

But you won't be here to hear of it, and your *bruders* are stronger than you think." *Daed* reached into his back pocket and pulled out an envelope that Saul recognized right away. "You will be working at your new job in Pittsburgh. With Miriam, after you're married, of course. If that's what you two want, that is."

Saul's heart leaped in his chest. "What?"

"Why didn't you tell me about this?" His father lifted the envelope, then put it in his lap and hung his head. "Never mind. I know why. You're a *gut* boy, Saul. You knew I wasn't able to properly tend to James and Ruben."

"I don't understand." Saul shook his head, trying to piece together what was going on.

"Saul . . ." *Daed* sighed. "I don't want you to leave our community, but in a strange way, I feel you deserve to pursue this dream. You've earned it. But I pray that you will take your faith with you as you and Miriam begin your life in Pittsburgh. It will not be easy for you to make this change. And marriage requires much work, even in the best of times."

Daed reached into an envelope that was on the couch beside him. "Here is the property that I promised you, the deed. Jake Petersheim has always wanted that tract.

I'm guessin' he would buy it from you, and that will give you and Miriam some money to help you begin your life."

Saul stood up from the rocker again and paced for a moment. Then he faced his *daed,* unable to believe what his father was saying. "*Daed,* if you're leaving, that's even more reason why I can't leave." He shook his head, frustrated by all of this. "I can't leave Ruben and James. They aren't old enough. What are you thinking?"

His father stood up, approached him slowly, and put a hand on his shoulder. "I leave in two weeks for Chicago, to a place Noah suggested. You will leave for your new job that same week. James and Ruben will be staying with Rebecca and her family."

"What?"

"Rebecca spoke to Bishop Ebersol, and we can't be angry with her, Saul. She is not part of the problem but part of the solution. Bishop Ebersol said Rebecca cried when she told him of her visit to our *haus.*" *Daed* hung his head and kept his eyes on the floor. "I feel shame for my behavior, but you and your *bruders* should not have to live like this." He looked up. "Rebecca said that her family will help with our farm while I am away, and Ruben and James will take their meals there and spend the nights there."

This was happening too fast for Saul. "But you said that you would be at my wedding. I don't understand how —" He shook his head.

"To leave our world, *sohn,* you won't be baptized, and you won't be married in the Amish faith . . . Are these things you are willing to give up to live your dream?"

Saul thought about marrying Miriam, leaving for Pittsburgh in the next couple of weeks, and living out his dream. And without hesitation he said, *"Ya, Daed."*

"I will pray that you take your faith with you wherever you go."

"And I will pray that you return soon." Saul embraced his father for the first time in years. "I love you, *Daed.*"

"I love you too, Saul." His father squeezed tighter. "I hope you can forgive me for the life I've led over the past years."

"I forgave you a long time ago. You're the best father anyone could have."

He held his father, and they both cried, then agreed it was time that they go together to talk to Ruben and James.

Rebecca took the pot from the stove and pounded across the kitchen floor. She kicked the screen open, marched down the steps, and tossed the rhubarb soup in the yard. The chickens sniffed briefly at the red mush, then turned up their beaks and toddled away.

"Even the birds won't eat that stuff." Aaron chuckled as he led one of the horses to the barn.

"It's not funny, Aaron."

"Why don't you just ask Saul how to make the soup? You must be doing something wrong."

"Because I have been cooking for over twice as long as that boy. I should be able to figure out how to make that recipe." Rebecca pushed back loose strands of hair blowing in her face. She was heading back to the kitchen when she heard a car pulling in, so she turned and put her hand above her forehead to block the sun. Aaron came across the yard and joined her. They waited until two heads came into view within the car.

"Is that . . . ?" Aaron strained to see. "It is. It's Abner and Janet."

"What? Shelby's mother isn't due here until next Friday." Rebecca twisted her neck to the right until she could see Miriam and Shelby on their knees in the garden. "Why are they here early?" She turned back toward the car and frowned, then spoke in a whisper to Aaron. "And I thought they were divorced. Why are they here together?"

Aaron shrugged.

As the car doors shut, Miriam and Shelby joined them in the front yard. Rebecca waited for Shelby to run into her parents' arms since she hadn't seen them in nearly three months, but Shelby walked tentatively toward them.

Abner threw his arms around his daughter, who looked like a limp doll before she slowly hugged her father. "Shelby, we've missed you."

Janet waved to Rebecca, Aaron, and Miriam, then moved toward Shelby. She waited until Abner released his daughter, then Janet hugged her. Shelby pulled out of the embrace right away.

"What are you doing here? You're not supposed to be here until Friday. That's almost a week away." Shelby stared back and forth between her parents, her expression tight with strain. "And what are you *both* doing here?"

Her parents didn't answer her, but both eased around and greeted Rebecca, Aaron, and Miriam. Ben, Elam, and John walked toward them from the chicken coops they were cleaning.

"What handsome boys," Janet said as Rebecca introduced her sons. "And, Miriam, what a lovely young woman you are. We haven't seen you since you were four years old."

"Mom, Dad . . ." Shelby approached her parents. "What are you doing here? Together? Plus, I'm not scheduled to go home until Friday. We just had the barn raising, and . . ." Shelby waved her hand toward the barn.

Janet reached for Shelby's hand. "Honey, we're both your parents, and we both missed you." She took a deep breath and seemed to force a smile. "Besides, your father and I are on friendly terms."

"Since when?" Shelby let go of her mother's hand.

"Sweetheart, we thought you'd be thrilled that we came early." Abner reached out to Shelby as he ignored her question, but she backed up.

"It's not time yet." Shelby stuffed her hands in the pockets of her blue jeans, then bit her lip. This wasn't the response Rebecca would have expected.

Janet pushed a shoulder-length strand of blond hair behind her ear, then pulled dark sunglasses down on her nose. "Honey, how long will it take you to pack? We tried to call, but of course your cell phone is dead, and we kept getting an answering machine for the number here."

"Why didn't you leave a message?" Shelby edged closer to Rebecca, and Rebecca could hear the desperation in her voice. "I'm not ready to go."

"Sweetheart, you've been here so long. We figured you'd had enough of . . ." Abner trailed off, then smiled. "I'm sure your hosts are ready to say good-bye to their house-guest."

"Not at all," Rebecca said, lifting her chin. "We'll miss Shelby very much." Rebecca's voice cracked as she spoke, and she realized how much she truly would miss Shelby.

"Maybe everyone can spend the night?" Miriam walked to Shelby and put an arm around her, and it touched Rebecca at how close the girls had become. She didn't know what kind of trouble Shelby had gotten into before her arrival here, but she had turned out to be a positive influence on Miriam.

"Of course you're all welcome to stay." Rebecca smiled at Janet.

Janet glanced at her watch. "We need to get back to the Harrisburg airport soon so Shelby can catch a flight home. Shelby's Aunt Charlotte, my sister, will be picking

Shelby up at the airport when her flight gets in."

"What?" Shelby looked as confused as Rebecca felt.

Janet turned to Shelby. "Shelby, your father is catching another flight out of Harrisburg for a business trip, and I . . . well, I am leaving for another flight from Harrisburg to meet a — a friend." Janet pulled her eyes from Shelby's for a moment, then looked back up at her. "This was a way for your father and me to get to see you before we each leave, and you enjoy staying with Aunt Charlotte. Right?" Janet smiled. "Or Aunt Charlotte can drive you home, but I know you're not crazy about staying by yourself."

Rebecca stifled a gasp. "You're picking her up just to leave her again?" Right away she knew the remark was snide and uncalled for. It was not her business. But when she felt Shelby clutch her hand in hers, she didn't regret having said it. It was clear to Rebecca that Shelby's parents only came to pick her up because that's what fit into their schedules. *How can they do this?*

Shelby glared at her mother, then turned to Rebecca. "Please, Rebecca. Please let me stay here." Shelby wiped a tear from her cheek. "I'll never be any trouble, I'll be baptized here and live here forever, until I have a home of my own right here in this community. Please, Rebecca." Shelby threw herself into Rebecca's arms. Rebecca was unsure what to do or say.

"That is the most ridiculous thing I've ever heard!" Janet walked toward them, but Shelby did not pull from the embrace with Rebecca. "Are you saying you want to be Amish?"

Rebecca eased Shelby away and whispered, "*Ya*, Shelby. Is that what you're saying?"

Shelby wiped away a tear and faced Rebecca. "When I came here, Rebecca, I was a mess. But Miriam helped me to find my way back to God." She glanced at Miriam and Aaron, then looked back at Rebecca. "All of you did. And Miriam explained to me what a Daughter of the Promise is, someone who takes a spiritual journey where she finds out what faith, hope, and love really mean. I've done that, Rebecca. Please don't send me away."

Rebecca saw Janet throw her hands in the air before she started talking to Abner, but Rebecca grabbed each of Shelby's arms. "You dear, sweet girl. Finding your way to the Lord is a wonderful thing, no?" She smiled, and Shelby smiled back. "But you don't have to be Amish to be a Daughter of the Promise, Shelby. You can take your faith anywhere with you."

Shelby hung her head. "I understand. I'm sure you're ready for me to go."

Rebecca's heart was breaking. She wasn't sure what to do. *Help me to say and do the right thing, Lord.* "No, Shelby. I am not ready for you to go at all." She swallowed hard as she watched a smile tip the corner of Shelby's mouth.

"Honey, we should have contacted you before coming." Janet pushed her sunglasses up on her head. "I can see that you've become attached to Rebecca and all of them, but —"

"It's more than that, Mom." Shelby faced her mother, glancing at her father also. "I love it here. I love the fellowship, the honesty, the way families take care of each other. I love worshipping God in a way that I never have before. There's a peacefulness here that I've never felt before."

Rebecca felt the need to speak up, no matter how much she would love for Shelby to stay in the community. "Shelby . . ." She spoke softly. "You are welcome to stay here, but I want you to know that the peacefulness you speak of can also be found anywhere. The Lord is everywhere."

"Can I really stay?" Shelby turned to Aaron, who nodded with a smile on his face.

"Uh, this is ridiculous, Shelby." Janet thrust her hands on her hips. "You can't stay here."

"Why not, Mother? All you're going to do is send me home, then leave again. That's the way it has been my entire life. When I did something you didn't like, you sent me away." Shelby paused, blinking back tears.

"Shelby, that's not true, and —"

"Mom! Even when I didn't do anything bad, you and Daddy always had somewhere for me to go — summer camps or visits with relatives while you traveled. And it's no different now, even though you're divorced. You're just going in different directions."

"Shelby, we thought you enjoyed those things, and —"

"Mom, I'm happy here. I want to stay here. I can't be a hundred percent sure that I will become Amish, but I want to learn more about it and make that decision on my own."

"Absolutely not," Abner said strongly. "We need to go."

Shelby stood taller. "Dad, Mom . . . I love you both very much. But I'm not going."

Rebecca took a deep breath. "Aaron, Miriam, why don't we let Shelby talk with her parents."

Aaron and Miriam followed Rebecca into the house, and after Aaron went upstairs, Rebecca turned to Miriam. "I don't think I've ever been more proud of you than I was a few minutes ago. You've made a huge difference in Shelby's life."

Miriam smiled, but it wasn't the smile of times past, the smile that Rebecca so longed to see.

"Danki, Mamm."

Rebecca sat down on the couch and patted the spot beside her. She waited until Miriam sat down. "Now . . . we have less than a week to plan a wedding. It won't be an Amish wedding, most likely somewhere in town, but we will still need to have something memorable for you."

Miriam stared at her like she'd lost her marbles. "What are you talking about? Saul and I will be baptized in October, then married here in November."

Rebecca shook her head, then smiled. "No. I don't think so. There's been a change in plans."

19

Miriam tried to wrap her mind around everything. It was all happening so fast. Shelby was staying, and Miriam was leaving, moving to Pittsburgh with the love of her life. Miriam knew she should be the happiest girl on the planet. She was marrying Saul tomorrow at one o'clock. It would be a small private ceremony in a Christian church in town, the church that their friend Barbie Beiler attended. Barbie had helped make the arrangements. And the Fishers would get a new start. Her mother had explained the help Zeb would be receiving, which opened the door for Saul to have a chance at his dream.

Miriam sat down on her bed and glanced around the only bedroom she'd ever had. After a few moments, she put her face in her hands, and the tears came on full force. Once they started, she couldn't get them to stop. She couldn't believe that her mother had worked with the bishop and Saul's father to arrange all of this so that Miriam could go with Saul to Pittsburgh. It was the most unselfish thing a parent could do, and Miriam knew the cost for her parents. They'd never wanted any of their children to leave the community. But *Mamm* told Miriam that she knew the Lord would guide her steps no matter where she went, and that she wouldn't hold her back if she wanted to go with Saul to Pittsburgh.

She wanted to be with Saul, but leaving her community terrified her. It was exciting in the beginning, and Saul's face always lit up at the mention of it. But now she was going to be married — something exciting but frightening on its own — and moving to a new place, leaving the only home she'd known.

"What's the matter, *mei maedel?*"

Miriam lifted her head and quickly swiped at her eyes. *"Mamm."* It was all she could say, then the tears started again. Her mother sat down beside her and pulled her into a hug. Miriam felt like she was five years old, and certainly not old enough to be getting married and venturing out on her own. "I'm scared, *Mamm.*"

Her mother held her, rocking back and forth the way she'd done when Miriam was a child. "I know, Miriam. A lot is happening for you all at once." *Mamm* eased her away. "But you don't have to do anything you don't want to do."

Sniffling, she said, "I know. And I want to be with Saul."

"These are decisions only you can make, *mei dochder.*"

Miriam reached for a tissue on her nightstand, then blew hard. "Saul said we can stay here and raise a family, that we don't have to go to Pittsburgh."

"And what did you say?"

"That I really want to go to Pittsburgh."

"Do you?"

Miriam thought long and hard about the new adventures they would be sharing together as husband and wife. "*Ya.* I do. I'm just scared."

"But it's also not too late to change your mind."

"I want to start a new life with Saul, and I'm excited about going to a new place." She stared into her mother's sympathetic eyes. "Will you come to visit us?"

Mamm smiled. "Pittsburgh is not that far." She paused, winked. "I think we can travel to the city to see our only *dochder.*"

Miriam tried to smile, but another tear found its way down her cheek.

"Let me ask you something, Miriam." *Mamm* cupped Miriam's cheek. "Do you feel led to go on this new venture?"

"I'm so scared, *Mamm.* But not only do I love Saul with all my heart, I do feel led to go in this new direction. I really do think Saul would stay here if I really wanted him to, but I want to share his dream, and I feel like there is something there for me too." She took a deep breath. "I don't know what, though."

"Trust the Lord, Miriam. Follow your heart."

Miriam knew her next comment would be juvenile, but she couldn't marry Saul tomorrow and leave without asking. "I'm not being replaced, am I?"

Mamm smiled warmly. "You don't really believe that, do you?"

Miriam sighed. "No. I guess not. And I am glad that Shelby is staying. Do you think she'll join the church?"

"I don't know." Again she cupped Miriam's cheek. "But either way, *mei maedel,* you are not being replaced. A mother can love all kinds of folks, but there is no love like the love she feels for her *kinner.*" She kissed Miriam on the cheek. "Take my love with you, Miriam, and know that I am always here for you."

"*Danki* for what you did, *Mamm.* Noah told Saul that his father could have died if he didn't get some help with his illness." She lowered her head, then looked up again. "And Saul and I wouldn't have been able to go to Pittsburgh if you hadn't offered to help with Ruben and James."

Mamm chuckled lightly. "We will have a houseful of new folks, and, Miriam, all of them put together will not replace you. But I walk in here and see you crying like this, and it makes me wonder if I did the right thing. Are you sure this is what you want? I don't want you to leave, Miriam, but I want you to follow your path, the one you feel led to follow."

"I'm sure. I'm just scared."

"I know. Me too." She kissed Miriam on the forehead. "Peace and blessings be with you always, my sweet Miriam."

Then *Mamm* swiped at her own tears and wrapped her arms around Miriam.

If there had been any doubts for Miriam, she couldn't remember them as she stared into Saul's eyes the next day in front of both their families. Shelby stood at Miriam's side as her bridesmaid, and both Ruben and James stood for Saul.

She and Saul were wearing *Englisch*

clothes for the first time in their lives. Miriam had chosen a knee-length white dress from a dress shop in Paradise, and Saul was wearing a pair of tan slacks and a white button-up shirt. He'd never looked more handsome. Instead of Bishop Ebersol marrying them, it was a pastor from an unfamiliar church. It was nothing like the Amish wedding ceremony she'd dreamed of her entire life, but when Saul professed his love for her in front of everyone and with a tear in his eye, Miriam knew she was exactly where she was supposed to be. She couldn't seem to shake the feeling that her new life was opening up possibilities that she couldn't yet foresee, but for now, she just wanted to bask in the love of her new husband.

Both her parents cried, along with Shelby, during the short ceremony, but Miriam never hesitated, and she didn't have any more doubts. As she'd told Shelby months ago, you can take your faith anywhere in the world, and Miriam knew her faith in the Lord Jesus would go with her to her new home. Miriam couldn't believe that she was now Mrs. Saul Fisher.

Mamm insisted on making the traditional wedding dinner back at their house after the ceremony: turkey roast with all the fixings. Miriam was glad to have that tradition as a memory of her special day. This afternoon she and Saul would leave Paradise and head for Pittsburgh. Saul had rented them a small furnished apartment near his job.

"I love you so much, Miriam." Saul pulled her around the side of her house, out of sight, then kissed her in a way that made Miriam feel like his wife. She couldn't wait to start their life together.

"I love you too, Saul. With all my heart."

"I know you're scared, Miriam. But I'm going to make you happy for the rest of your life." He kissed her again, his lips lingering, and Miriam thought she would lift off the ground. Afterward he pulled her into a hug, and Miriam buried her head in his chest, closing her eyes.

"I'm not scared." And she wasn't.

Saul held Miriam tight, then they slowly made their way back to the front yard. Saul saw his father standing with Aaron and Rebecca, laughing and smiling, and it warmed Saul's heart. He felt confident that his father would get the help he needed and that Ruben and James would be tended to by Rebecca and Aaron. He hadn't had a chance to talk to Rebecca alone, so he needed to take the opportunity right away.

"Rebecca, can I talk to you for a minute?" Saul asked as he and Miriam approached the group. "Be back shortly," he said to Miriam with a wink. Rebecca followed him to an iron bench near the garden where they both sat down.

"I want to thank you for everything you're doing, Rebecca. It was hard for me in the beginning to understand . . ." He avoided her eyes for a moment, then looked back at her. "Anyway, *danki.*"

Rebecca patted his leg. "I hope you will remember the *Deitsch* for when you bring my baby girl back to visit me." She smiled. "I wasn't sure that I did the right thing. But then something arrived in the mail yesterday." Rebecca reached inside the pocket of her apron and pulled out an envelope. "It was addressed to Ms. Raber, so I opened it, but it was clearly meant for Miriam. I haven't shown it to her yet." She pushed the envelope in Saul's direction. "But clearly our Miriam has dreams of her own."

Saul opened the envelope and pulled out a letter.

Dear Ms. Raber,

It would be a pleasure to have you work at the Watkins Christian School for Children with Special Needs. While we normally hire teachers and counselors with experience and/or a degree, we were so moved by the letter you sent us that we would like to offer you an entry-level position within our organization, and we would be happy to have you as a member of our team. We look forward to hearing from you.

Peace in the Lord's name,
Francis Parker, Director

"Wow." Saul stared at the letter, pleased that Miriam would be pursuing her dream too. "Can I be the one to tell her?"

"Of course. You're her husband." Rebecca smiled, then stood up. When Saul stood up, she hugged him, then kissed him on the cheek. "You're a *gut* man, Saul Fisher. I trust you to take care of my baby."

"I will."

Rebecca turned to walk away, but Saul called after her.

"*Ya?*"

Saul grinned, then folded his arms across his chest. "I have a little something for you, Rebecca."

"What's that?" She raised a brow.

Saul tipped his head to one side. "Miriam sure does want to make sure that you, Aaron, and the boys come to visit us. If I give you this, you have to promise to visit us in Pittsburgh."

Rebecca narrowed her eyes and lifted her chin. "All right, Saul. I'll play along. We'll come visit. Now what do you have for me?"

Saul reached into his pocket and then handed Rebecca a folded piece of paper. "Don't be mad," he whispered. Then he winked at her.

"What?" Rebecca unfolded the piece of paper, and Saul hurriedly walked off, cringing but laughing at the same time.

"I knew it! Saul Fisher, you get back here! I knew you didn't give me all the ingredients for that rhubarb mint soup. I knew it!"

Saul took off running — to go find his wife and share some news with her.

Shelby waved to Miriam and Saul as the car pulled away with them in it. They were going to spend their honeymoon night at Beiler's Bed-and-Breakfast in Paradise, then they were off to Pittsburgh in the morning. Shelby glanced at Rebecca, who was waving frantically following a long good-bye. Ben, Elam, and John were running behind the car waving, and Aaron had his hand over his mouth, as if trying to keep from showing his emotions. They watched the car turn the corner.

After a few minutes, everyone headed toward the house, but Shelby wanted to spend a few minutes by herself. Life had been a whirlwind of events the past week, but she'd never questioned her decision to stay with Rebecca and Aaron. Her parents had eventually realized that she was not going back with them. Shelby hoped they would both be happy, but she had a new life here, though she was going to try to communicate more with her parents, at Rebecca's urging more than anything.

She leaned against the fence, still wearing the plain green dress she'd worn for Miriam's wedding. It wasn't an Amish dress, but it also wasn't anything that Shelby would have chosen prior to arriving here. It was knee-length and conservative, and Shelby found herself to be more comfortable in the dress than something she might have chosen a few months ago.

Rebecca said that she would teach Shelby about the *Ordnung,* which she'd learned was the understood behavior by which the Amish were expected to live. Most of the rules the Amish knew by heart. Shelby wondered if she would be able to learn them all. Saul's father was leaving in a few days for Chicago, and Ruben and James would be moving in too. Shelby had asked Rebecca if she felt like she was running a house for wayward teens. Rebecca had merely laughed and said, "The more the merrier."

Saul had told Miriam that Ruben and James were glad that their father was going somewhere to help him get well, and Miriam's brothers, particularly Ben, had been going over to their house, spending time with them in an effort to make the move easier for them.

This was a new beginning for Shelby, in a place she'd grown to love, in a family that treated each other with kindness and respect. She leaned her head back, closed her eyes, and let the sun warm her cheeks. It was hot. Not as hot as Texas, but there was no doubt it was August.

She was excited about the prospect of becoming a true member of this wonderful community. Rebecca said they would be going to Sisters' Day next week where she would introduce Shelby to other young women her age. And Shelby had offered to take over the garden since Miriam was gone, since usually the women in the household took care of the garden and the yard while the men and boys took care of the fields and other outside chores.

Her newfound relationship with God provided her with a peacefulness she'd never had before, and when she'd tried to explain her feelings to Miriam, her cousin had said simply, "You're a Daughter of the Promise now."

Shelby smiled. "Thank You, Lord. Thank You for this new beginning. I pray for Your blessing and that I've made the right choice."

She slowly opened her eyes, breathed in the smell of freshly cut hay, then pulled her hair into a ponytail with the band she had on her wrist. Someday she hoped to have it pulled tight underneath a prayer covering. Movement on the driveway caught her attention. She anxiously watched the tall man coming toward her.

"Hello, stranger."

Shelby smiled. "Hello, Jesse."

"I hear you are going to be staying around." He tipped his hat back with his thumb, then shot her a slow, easy smile.

"I am."

Jesse's smile broadened. "I'm glad to hear that." Then he offered her his elbow. "How about going on a walk with me?"

Shelby looped her arm in his. "I'd like that."

She closed her eyes and smiled as she walked down the path she knew God had

set before her.
Thank You.

EPILOGUE

Miriam sprinted around their small apartment, double-checking that everything was spotless. Saul had learned to cook all kinds of new dishes at his new job, but he'd chosen to make a simple pot roast for Miriam's family. As it turned out, her new husband wasn't as fond of baking, which was Miriam's specialty, so she'd prepared a pineapple cake for dinner.

She smoothed the wrinkles from her long blue jean skirt, something she'd bought on sale specifically for this occasion. And she'd chosen a conservative blue blouse to wear. Out of respect for her family, she decided against the blue-jean pants she'd become accustomed to. It had taken her some time to slowly convert her clothing in a way that blended in with the *Englisch,* but today she wanted to find a happy medium between her old life and her new one.

"Everything looks great," Saul said as he

threw his arms around her waist when she whisked by him in the tiny den. "And so do you."

She fell into his arms, kissed him on the lips, then playfully pushed him away. "They'll be here soon. I want to make sure everything is perfect."

Miriam hadn't seen her family in three months. Pittsburgh was a four-hour drive from Paradise, and Miriam and Saul hadn't been able to make the trip to their hometown because of their job schedules. Miriam's family had to plan around working in the fields and their other commitments. Today they'd hired a driver to make the trip after their morning chores were done. Miriam wished she had extra bedrooms to offer her family, but right now she and Saul just had their one-bedroom apartment. Miriam was thrilled that they were coming, even if it would only be for a couple of hours. They were expecting her mother, father, brothers, and Shelby. The next visit would be from Saul's father and brothers. Zeb was back home and doing well after his treatment. Ruben and James had moved back in with him. Miriam felt like her life had been a continuation of one blessed event after the other.

Miriam couldn't still the butterflies in her

stomach. She'd written to her family every detail of their lives in Pittsburgh — except for one.

"They're here," she squealed when the doorbell rang. Saul followed her to the door, and she threw herself into each of their arms. "I've missed you so much!" Then she stepped back and smiled at Shelby. "You look beautiful. I'm so sorry I missed your baptism."

"*Danki*."

Shelby had written to ask Miriam if she could wear her clothes, and Miriam was honored to have her do so. In one of Miriam's dark-blue dresses and black aprons, Shelby looked like she'd been Amish all her life. Her hair was neatly tucked underneath one of Miriam's *kapps*. *Mamm* had written to say that Shelby was a good student, and that she'd picked up on the *Ordnung* quickly. Shelby had written to Miriam about a completely different subject matter. Seems she was spending lots of time with Jesse, and Miriam was glad to hear that.

The afternoon seemed to fly by as Miriam and Saul told her family about their jobs, their plans for a bigger apartment soon, and the church they were attending a few blocks away. But Miriam could hardly contain herself any longer.

"We have some news to share." Miriam unconsciously touched her stomach, and her mother's hands flew to her mouth as her eyes rounded.

"Are you . . . ?" *Mamm* stood and walked toward her.

"Ya." Miriam knew she would never completely give up her native dialect. "We are in a family way."

Miriam wasn't sure she'd ever seen her mother jump up and down until this moment. Her father blinked a few times, and Miriam thought he might shed a tear. It was a glorious moment, and Miriam realized that her relationship with family — and God — would be intact as long as she carried her faith with her the way she'd been taught her entire life.

Following congratulations, then dinner and dessert, *Mamm* said the driver would be back for them shortly.

"It all went too fast," Miriam said as she hugged her father, then Shelby and her brothers. She stayed in her mother's arms the longest. "I miss you, *Mamm*."

"I miss you too, *mei maedel,*" she whispered, then eased Miriam away. "But if you think you will raise a *kinner* without *mammi* being a big part of his or her life, you are wrong. We will have to make arrangements to visit even more." *Mamm* kissed her on the cheek. "I have something for you." *Mamm* reached into her plain black purse that she'd carried for years. She handed Miriam a silver-plated letter opener that looked just like the one that had been stolen. Miriam turned it over and gasped when she saw the inscription — *May all your letters be received with an abundance of love.*

"*Mamm!* Your letter opener! Where did you get it?" Miriam handled it with care, knowing how much it meant to her mother.

Mamm reached into her purse again and dug around for a moment, then she handed Miriam a folded piece of paper. "This came in the mail." *Mamm's* eyes watered up as she spoke.

Miriam unfolded the letter and read silently.

Dear Mrs. Raber,

I have no good excuse for what I did, except that I was desperate to take my three-year-old daughter and get away from my husband, Bruce. He was an abusive man, and I'm sorry that he pushed me to do something so horrible. I picked up my daughter from my mother's house, then fled with her. I used the money I took from you to make a fresh start. I'm not sure why I took your letter opener, except that I was scared Bruce would try to harm me. I'm enclosing $10 and returning your letter opener. I saw the inscription on the back. I will pay you back every dime, no matter how long it takes. Please forgive me. I pray God forgives me.

Sincerely,
Rhoda Thompson

"Oh, *Mamm,*" Miriam said softly as she handed the letter back to her mother. "Did you write her back?"

Mamm looked down for a moment, smiling, then her eyes met Miriam's. "*Ya.* I did."

Miriam started to ask her mother what the letter to Rhoda said, but she already knew in her heart that *Mamm* either sent her more money or told her not to worry about the debt. That was the way her mother was. She pulled her mother into another hug.

"Write me often, *mei* beautiful *maedel.*"

"I will, *Mamm.* I promise." Miriam thought about how events had unfolded, in a way she never would have thought possible for all of them. She said a silent prayer for Rhoda and her daughter.

They were almost out the door when her

mother snapped her fingers. "*Ach,* Saul. I almost forgot something that I have for you." She handed Saul a piece of paper from her apron pocket. "Miriam tells me that you are unable to duplicate my famous stromboli." *Mamm* smiled, then raised her shoulders and dropped them slowly. "So here's the recipe for you."

Saul read through the recipe, looked up at *Mamm,* then grinned. "So . . . Rebecca . . . is everything in this recipe?" He folded his arms across his chest.

Mamm tapped her finger to her chin. "Hmm . . . I *think* I remembered everything." She winked at him on the way out the door.

Miriam just laughed as her husband took to reading the recipe again as the door shut. She glanced down at her bare feet, wiggled her toes, then focused on the same ankle bracelet she'd worn that day at the creek. *We've come a long way.*

"I'll figure this recipe out," he said, smiling.

Miriam pulled him into a hug, then kissed him. "I love you, Saul Fisher."

"I love you too, Miriam Fisher."

Miriam closed her eyes and thanked God for the peacefulness she'd carried with her from Lancaster County.

ACKNOWLEDGMENTS

With each book that I write, it seems that there are more and more people who deserve a big thank-you. Please forgive me if I forgot anyone. I know there is no way I could share my stories without an abundance of love from family and friends, particularly my husband, Patrick. You're the best, baby!

To my wonderful sons — Eric and Cory — I dedicate this book to both of you, each so amazing in your own individual ways. Choose wisely in life, try to follow God's plan, and always know how very much I love you both.

To my family at Thomas Nelson, you guys and gals continue to bless me with your encouragement, hard work, and kindness. It's more than a job to all of you, and so often you go above and beyond even my highest expectations of what a top-rated publisher should do. I'm so blessed to have you on my team! (BIG hugs to my editor, Natalie Hanemann — love you!)

Barbie Beiler, are you getting tired of being mentioned in every single book . . . lol? Seriously, I couldn't do this without you. Peace and love to you always, my friend.

Big thanks to my Old Order Amish friends in Pennsylvania and Colorado for helping me to keep each book authentic — and for sharing your recipes with me. Peace and blessings to all of you.

To my mother, Pat Isley, for always being on hand to answer the smallest grammatical question on a regular basis. More importantly, for your encouragement, love, and constant support. I love you very much, Mother.

And everyone should be so fortunate to have a mother-in-law who cooks for them. To the best mother-in-law in the world — Pat Mackey — sending much love and thanks your way!

Janet Murphy, I've thought about the way things played out and how you came to work for me. This is a union truly blessed by God. Not only are you a fabulous assistant and publicity coordinator, but I'm also so fortunate to have you as my friend. I hope we make this entire journey together.

To my agent, Mary Sue Seymour — what

a great year we've had! In addition to guiding my career, we've had some wonderful times together. I see more shoe shopping and trips to P.F. Chang's in our future!

Jenny Baumgartner, some authors dread their line edits, but with you, I know that you will make it as painless as possible, and your great suggestions always make the book so much better in the end. Love and blessings to you and your family. I can't wait to meet you in person someday, hopefully soon!

Not a day goes by that I don't recognize God's hand on my writing. It is only because of Him that I am able to pull together the screaming voices in my head and organize them into a story that I hope both entertains and draws people closer to Him. *Thank You.*

READING GROUP GUIDE

1. Throughout the story, Miriam is sure that she wants to be Saul's *fraa,* but when it finally comes time for her to marry him and leave, she cries on her mother's shoulder. What are some of the emotions Miriam feels as she enters this new phase in her life?

2. Rebecca has two strong reasons for not wanting Miriam to date Saul. What are they, and do you think Rebecca's concerns are valid? Or should she have trusted Miriam to make good decisions and not interfered?

3. Shelby is depressed, void of hope, and doesn't have much faith in the beginning of the story. What are some turning points for her? What and who inspire her to look within herself to seek God?

4. What are some of the things that Shelby loves about life among the Amish? What does she have a hard time adjusting to? What about you? What could you not live without within an Old Order Amish district?

5. Saul is afraid for members of the community to find out about his father's drinking, fearing his family will be shamed. Do you know of someone who kept a family secret that was perhaps not in the best interest of everyone involved? What was the outcome?

6. What would have happened if Rebecca hadn't stepped in to help Zeb? How could things have possibly played out differently?

7. At first, Aaron tells Rebecca that they must let Miriam make her own decisions, but his attitude changes when he finds out that Saul wants to leave the district and take Miriam with him. At what point does Aaron confess his true feelings about Miriam leaving?

8. More and more Amish families are giving up their phone shanties. Most of them have phones in the barn or even cell

phones. What are your thoughts about the Amish embracing some forms of modern technology, but not others — such as electricity and automobiles?

9. Shelby uses her diary as a way to voice her private thoughts, but she stops writing in the journal after she begins to reconnect with God. Have you ever kept a journal, and if so, was it in addition to or in lieu of communion with God? Or neither one?

10. Forgiveness is a theme that runs throughout the book, and several characters must forgive either themselves or others. What are some examples of this?

11. By the end of the book, Shelby and Jesse have formed a friendship. Shelby is now a member of the Amish community, but Jesse mentions earlier on that he has a curiosity about the outside world and what it would be like to leave the district. Do you think he was just saying that because he thought Shelby would be leaving their community, or do you think Jesse might leave? Or is it normal for him to be curious and casually ponder the idea?

12. Saul is driven to live in the outside world and be a chef in a fancy restaurant. Besides his love of food and cooking, how does this external desire reveal what is truly inside of Saul? Is he a caregiver by nature? Does he enjoy pleasing others?

Overnight Blueberry French Toast

12 thick slices of bread, cut into 1″ cubes
1 8-oz. pkg. cream cheese, cut in 1/2″ cubes
1 1/2 cups blueberries (fresh, frozen, or
  canned)
12 eggs
3 cups maple syrup
2 cups milk

Place half the bread cubes in a buttered 9″ × 13″ baking pan. Distribute all the cream cheese on top. Add remaining bread cubes and blueberries. Set aside. In a bowl, beat the eggs, syrup, and milk; pour evenly in the pan. Cover and refrigerate overnight. Then cover with foil and bake at 350° for 30 minutes. Remove foil and bake another 20 to 30 minutes (longer if necessary) until golden brown. Serve immediately.

Cheddar Meat Loaf

3 eggs
1/2 cup milk
1 cup shredded cheddar cheese
1/2 cup quick oats
1/2 cup onions, chopped
1 tsp. salt
1 dash black pepper
1 lb. ground beef

Sauce
2/3 cup ketchup
1/2 cup light brown sugar, packed
1 1/2 tsp. yellow mustard

In a mixing bowl, beat eggs and milk. Stir in cheese, oats, onions, salt, and pepper. Add beef and mix thoroughly. Place in a pan. Mix ketchup, brown sugar, and mustard; pour over meat. Bake uncovered at 350° for 45 minutes.

Stromboli

Dough
1 pkg. active dry yeast
1 cup warm water
1 tsp. sugar
2 Tbsp. vegetable oil
2 1/2 cups bread flour

Filling

1 lb. cheese, diced
1/2 lb. ham, diced
1/2 lb. salami, diced
2 Tbsp. spaghetti sauce (or cream of mushroom soup)
1 medium onion, diced (optional)

Topping

1 tsp. seasoned salt
1 Tbsp. butter, melted
1 16-oz. jar spaghetti or pizza sauce

In a large bowl, mix all the dough ingredients. Wait 5 minutes, then divide dough into six equal parts. Roll each into a circle. Each stuffed stromboli will have a top and bottom circle of dough. On three of the circles, place 1/3 of the cheese and meat in the center, making sure to leave an empty edge all around, then add the onion and sauce. Cover each with a plain dough circle. Pinch edges to seal tight. Sprinkle tops with seasoned salt and bake at 350° for 20 minutes. Brush each with butter, top with sauce, and serve.

AUTHOR TO AUTHOR

The Thomas Nelson Fiction team invited our authors to interview any other Thomas Nelson Fiction author in an unplugged Q&A session. They could ask any questions about any topic they wanted to know more about. What we love most about these conversations is that they reveal just as much about the ones asking the questions as they do the authors who are responding. So sit back and enjoy the discussion. Maybe you'll even be intrigued enough to pick up one of Golden's novels and discover a new favorite writer in the process.

BETH WISEMAN: Hi, Golden. First of all, I'd like to tell you how much I enjoyed *In the Shadow of the Sun King.* As someone who knows very little about seventeenth-century France, I found the details to be fascinating, plus it was just a wonderful story. Can you tell us how you came to write your Darkness to Light series?

GOLDEN KEYES PARSONS: The series is based on my family genealogy set in seventeenth-century France. They were French Huguenots (Protestants) who were being persecuted for their faith by the Catholic government of Louis XIV and had to flee their homeland.

I had no knowledge of my strong heritage of faith until I ran across a published genealogy of the Clavell family packed away in a box. The family history had gotten buried through the years and forgotten. My mother never spoke of it, so I'm assuming that she didn't know either.

BETH: How closely do your books follow your family's history?

GOLDEN: Very loosely. I didn't have access to many concrete facts, so I used bits and pieces of our family's story to flesh out the fictional story line.

For example, in the first book, *In the Shadow of the Sun King*, the time frame is fifty years earlier than when my ancestors fled France, but my editor thought we should incorporate the very colorful character of Louis XIV. However, my family did live in southern France around Grenoble. And they did flee to Switzerland. A Francois Clavell actually was sentenced to the galleys. And so on.

The second book, *A Prisoner of Versailles,* probably follows the story of the literal Clavell family the least. However, King Louis really did send spies into Switzerland to bring Huguenots back into France. He did have a sweetheart from his youth, who people say was his true love, but he was not permitted to marry her. So like all historical novels, the thread of factual history runs through them.

The concluding book in the series, *Where Hearts Are Free,* tells the story of the Clavell family in this country, settling in Central Pennsylvania in the Schuylkill Valley, which they did. The property is still farmland, and there are pictures on my website of those farms. My ancestor, whose name was Louisa, not Madeleine, truly had to sell her sons to redemptioners to pay for their passage over. And her husband was washed overboard with all their money, so she arrived in this country a widow, and then had to sell her children as indentured slaves. I cannot imagine what a strong, courageous woman she must have been.

BETH: What's next for you as far as writing?

GOLDEN: I have a book set during the Civil War in Texas coming out in the fall of 2011 to coincide with the 150th anniversary of the beginning of the Civil War. I loved doing the research on this one. I learned so much about our state that I didn't know. The title is *His Steadfast Love,* and it deals with torn loyalties of a young woman between her Southern family and her sweetheart, who is a Union officer.

BETH: How does your faith play a part in what you write?

GOLDEN: My faith is what and who I am. At no point in my books did I ever stop and say, "Guess it's time to add a little faith message here." In fact, there were a couple of times that I had to go back and tone it down a bit from sounding too preachy. I love to write about the realities of life and then show how God redeems those situations.

BETH: As authors, we know that there is no "typical" day, but how do you prefer to outline your day, given a choice? Do you prefer to write in the mornings or in the evenings? How many words do you push for?

GOLDEN: My brain works better in the mornings as far as writing content goes. Then I work on editing and marketing in the afternoons. A historical runs 90,000 to 100,000, words, so I try to do a chapter a week. My chapters usually run around 3,000 words. Sometimes I make it and sometimes I don't, but if I keep that schedule, I'm pretty much on track. When I get closer to deadline, sometimes I'm writing 2,000 or more words a day.

BETH: If you weren't writing in this time period, what other type of novel would you be interested in writing?

GOLDEN: I love all historical. I used to think I would only want to do European historicals, but since writing in the colonial period in America and now the Civil War book, I'm kind of changing my mind. I've enjoyed them all. I've written some biblical fiction. I'd like to do a time travel novel.

BETH: What is the most important concept that you hope readers walk away with after reading one of your books?

GOLDEN: That God is faithful and will always make a way for us, if we trust Him.

BETH: I'm looking forward to reading the rest of the books in this series. Where can readers find out more about you?

GOLDEN: At my website: www.goldenkeyes parsons.com. Thanks, Beth. I enjoyed the interview.

ABOUT THE AUTHOR

Beth Wiseman has a deep affection for the Amish and their simpler way of living. She is the author of many bestsellers, including the Daughters of the Promise series and the new Land of Canaan series. She and her family live in Texas.

The employees of Thorndike Press hope you have enjoyed this Large Print book. All our Thorndike, Wheeler, and Kennebec Large Print titles are designed for easy reading, and all our books are made to last. Other Thorndike Press Large Print books are available at your library, through selected bookstores, or directly from us.

For information about titles, please call:
  (800) 223-1244

or visit our Web site at:
  http://gale.cengage.com/thorndike

To share your comments, please write:
  Publisher
  Thorndike Press
  10 Water St., Suite 310
  Waterville, ME 04901